WOLFMAN IS BACK

A BRAD COULTER NOVEL

DWAYNE CLAYDEN

Enjoy!

ALSO BY DWAYNE CLAYDEN

The Brad Coulter Series

CRISIS POINT
OUTLAW MC
WOLFMAN IS BACK

Coming Soon

SPEARGRASS - OPIOID

Short Story

HELL HATH NO FURY
AB Negative. An Anthology of Alberta Crime

Publisher's Note: This is a work of fiction. Names, characters, places, and incidents are a product of the author's imagination. Locales and public names are sometimes used for atmospheric purposes. Any resemblance to actual people, living or dead, or to businesses, companies, events, institutions, or locales is completely coincidental.

Published in Canada

Cover Graphic by Travis Miles, Pro Book Covers

Editing by Taija Morgan

Proofing by Jonas Saul and Colleen Peters

Formatting by Dwayne Clayden

Wolfman is Back/ Dwayne Clayden—1st print ed.

ISBN: 978-1-7752564-6-5 (pbk), 978-1-7752564-7-2 (e-book)

❀ Created with Vellum

To My Grandparents.

Della and Jack Clayden
Anne and Ernest Moore

They were so important to me growing up.
I miss them every day.

CHAPTER ONE

MID MAY

Monday Evening

JETER WOLFE TAPPED A CIGARETTE OUT OF THE PACKAGE AND LIT IT from the embers of the previous one. He dropped the dying butt out the car window where it joined a growing pile. The tip grew bright red with each breath. He twisted in the seat, trying to get comfortable. Even with the seat completely back, his knees touched the steering wheel and his head rubbed the roof. At six-foot-five and more than two-hundred and fifty pounds, he was cramped in most vehicles. The next car he stole needed to be bigger—much bigger.

He scratched his beard. He'd let it grow the entire two years he was imprisoned. The dark beard and long hair reinforced the nickname his biker buddies had given him—Wolfman.

A few more visits and he'd know her routine—whom she lives with, where she goes, whom she meets, the vehicles she drives, and the routes she takes. He had to know when she was home alone. He would need enough uninterrupted time.

Her house was on the corner of a crescent. He parked down the street with a clear view of the front of the house and yard. If someone was looking, and curious, they would see him and might wonder why he was parked there. He'd have to park in different places at different times of the day. Changing vehicles after each visit would be a good idea.

Most cops, lawyers, judges, and politicians kept their names and addresses out of the phonebook. But two years ago, his former club, the Gypsy Jokers, had collected the addresses for all the cops, politicians, media, judges, and lawyers who were trying to shut the Jokers down. They'd used a few of the addresses harassing cops, a journalist, and a judge. This address was seared into his brain. He knew one day he would come here.

He checked the duffel bag on the passenger seat. The contents were from army surplus. Everything he needed—one-stop shopping. Binoculars, hunting knife, duct tape, rope, triangular bandages, several pairs of gloves and a pistol. Earlier, he thought about stashing this stuff. No sense having it in the car in case he was stopped by the cops. Then he realized if he was stopped by the cops, having his duffel bag of goodies would be the least of his problems. The gun under his seat would take care of the cops. He smiled at that thought.

A new BMW drove past him and continued straight into her driveway. He tossed the cigarette butt out the window and grabbed the binoculars. The driver's door opened and Jenni Blighe's shapely legs swung out—all nylon up to mid-thigh. Her navy skirt slid farther up as she slipped out. Wolfe held his breath, then the air escaped in a blast. He'd spent over a year in jail waiting to see her again. She was a lot hotter in person than his fantasies. Funny how a memory fades. She walked around the back of the car and herded her kids up the sidewalk and into the house. His eyes were glued to her ass—the ass he'd watched in court for weeks. It seemed like so long ago.

He'd sat in the prisoner's docket for close to a month while she presented the crown's case against him. She'd started out dressed conservatively, dark above-the-knee skirt, colored blouse and jacket with comfortable shoes. Halfway through the trial it changed. She wore fashionable skirts, showing more leg, white blouses, shoes with heels, and often took the jacket off, especially as the afternoon grew warmer. Later he found out Blighe and her husband had divorced. Maybe that accounted for the change of clothing.

He scanned the street, memorizing the location of each house. He worked out escape routes by car and on foot. At some point he'd need to go to the back of the house to figure out his escape options there.

After about five minutes the front door opened and she came outside with her two kids. No longer fixated on her ass, his eyes roamed over her body. She wore shorts and a tight T-shirt. When the sun beamed at just the right angle, he clearly saw the outline of her breasts. It was like she was doing it for him, and he soaked up every moment.

The kids raced ahead of her to a park at the end of the street where he lost sight of them. Wolfe was tempted to walk past the park. Seeing her up close would be a thrill, and also stupid. Bad enough he was in a residential area and sitting in this car, occasionally using binoculars—let alone taking his unforgettable bulk out into the open. He'd waited two years. He could be patient and wait for the right opportunity. Half an hour later they came back into view. Again, the kids raced ahead of her and into the house. She was in no hurry, walking slowly, like she was a model at a fashion show, her wondrous curves on display and her blond hair shimmering.

His heart raced and pressure intensified in his groin. Soon. It would have to be soon.

He'd waited long enough.

CHAPTER TWO

Tuesday Morning

DETECTIVE BRAD COULTER YAWNED AS HE DROVE TO WORK. HE'D missed the action on the street during his one-year leave from work. His life had been normal—almost. Before the leave, when he was on the street, it seemed that no matter where he was, shit found him. Maybe he'd kicked the jinx. Maybe fighting crime would be less adrenaline filled. Maybe.

He parked and stepped into Gerry's Convenience Store.

"Morning, Brad."

Brad grunted and glanced at the newspaper. The headline read: Budget Cuts to Blame for Prison Escape.

Gerry chuckled. "And the top of the morning to you, too."

"Why are you so cheery in the morning?" Brad poured an extra-large coffee. "I don't function until I get caffeinated."

"Try getting up at 5 A.M. to be here by six."

"No thanks. Seven is still too early for me. I like night shifts."

"First day back?"

"I checked in yesterday. Got my new badge and a portable radio. Maybe today I'll get my own car."

"How long were you off?"

"Almost a year. The studying is done, and I've written the bar exam. Now I wait for the results."

"You're not going to practice law?"

"Nope. I'm itching to get back on the street."

"I'm going to miss seeing you every morning on your way to study."

"Don't worry, Gerry, I'm hooked on your coffee. You'll still have to put up with me." Brad glanced out the window. His eyebrows raised.

Gerry followed Brad's gaze. "You see something?"

"Looks like an argument at the gas station."

"Panhandlers hang around there. Probably hitting someone up for change and they refused."

"I'm not so sure." Brad's gaze never left the window as he tossed a quarter on the counter. "See you tomorrow."

Brad stood outside the store, scrutinizing the action across the street. A Chrysler Cordoba was parked at the gas pumps. One guy, dressed in a suit, stood at the open driver's door, shaking his head. He said, "Leave me alone."

A hefty guy shoved the driver against the car. He punched the driver in the face twice, then threw him on the ground. His partner, a skinny guy, kicked the driver repeatedly in the ribs.

Brad started toward the assault. "Hey, what the—"

The big guy glanced at Brad and said, "Let's go." He slid into the driver's seat. His partner sprinted around the front of the car and jumped into the passenger's seat.

The driver rolled away from the car.

The engine roared, tires squealed, and the car raced across Parkdale Boulevard, cutting off traffic, and headed east.

Brad tossed his coffee into a trash bin and slid into his car. He backed away and sped after the carjackers. The car's owner was leaning against a gas pump. He looked okay.

Brad grabbed his portable radio. "Detective Coulter to dispatch. I am in pursuit of a brown Chrysler Cordoba."

"Roger, Coulter," dispatch replied. "Uh, why are you in pursuit?"

"I'm pursuing carjackers."

"We don't have a call for that."

"Well, you will. Get a cruiser and paramedics to the gas station, 3400 block of Parkdale Boulevard."

"Roger."

"I'm eastbound on Parkdale Boulevard. Do you have backup rolling?"

"They're on the way."

Brad's Firebird caught up to the Cordoba as it veered left onto Kensington Road. At Fourteenth Street they turned left and at the next intersection turned left again onto Fifth Avenue. When they reached Crowchild Trail they turned right, heading north.

Brad kept pace, telling dispatch and responding cops his direction of travel.

At Twentieth Avenue the carjackers made a hard left through rush-hour traffic, colliding with several cars on the way across, trailing fenders, bumpers, and other vehicle parts. The car coasted into the McMahon Football Stadium parking lot, rubber sailing off shredded tires and sparks flying from the rims.

Brad weaved his way through the accidents to the south-side parking lot. By the time he reached the disabled car, the two occupants were out and running. Brad grabbed his portable radio, jumped out of his Firebird, and pursued. "Dispatch, I'm in foot pursuit of the suspects. They're heading into the stadium from the south side. Have backup come in from the north."

The suspects raced across the parking lot to a gate secured with a heavy chain. They managed to squeeze through an opening and onto the football field. Brad ran after them, also squeezing through the opening. The two suspects were sprinting down the football field.

Brad smiled. For five years he'd played university football on this field. Chasing someone here was second nature. Funny how old instincts came back.

At the south forty-yard line, the hefty suspect stopped, gasping for air. On the way by, Brad connected with a serious forearm smash to the man's head. Glancing back, he watched the unconscious suspect do a faceplant at the thirty-yard line.

The skinny suspect slowed near the fifty-yard line. Brad increased speed and tackled him hard to the turf. Brad rolled the suspect onto his stomach, yanking back his arm.. Brad slapped the handcuffs on tight. He dragged the suspect y his foot to the thirty-yard line where his partner lay staring up at the sky with a confused expression and gasping for air. *I love this job.* He'd take this over a suit and courtroom any day.

Brad didn't have a second set of handcuffs, so he stood over them. "Don't you shitheads move."

Sergeant Jerry Briscoe and four uniformed officers entered the stadium by the north gate. The uniformed cops sprinted to Brad. Briscoe sauntered way behind.

Brad asked the officers to handcuff the second suspect and take them downtown. As the cops left with their arrests, Briscoe finally caught up.

After Brad's partner Curtis Young was killed four years ago, Brad had been partnered with Briscoe. To say Briscoe was rough around the edges was an understatement. But he was a good cop and a good man and had helped Brad through the months after Young's death. Along the way they'd become friends.

Briscoe wandered over to Brad. "You're not officially back to work yet, so thank you, Joe Citizen." Briscoe paused and took a few deep breaths. "Now run along and leave this to the pros."

"You sound a little out of breath," Brad said.

"You couldn't have let them run to the end zone?"

"The walk too much for you?"

"Not the way I like to start my day," Briscoe said.

"An easy jog for me."

"Well, aren't you fricken' special. Rookies are supposed to do all the running."

Brad smirked. "Really, you're still referring to me as your rookie?"

"You were and will always be my rookie."

"That's Detective Rookie to you, Sergeant."

"You spent a lot of years running on this field," Briscoe said. "Must be like old times."

Brad smiled. "It did bring back some memories."

"So, tell me why you were chasing these pukes."

Brad told him about the assault, carjacking, and chase.

Chuckling, Briscoe said, "How does this shit find you?"

The suspects were in separate interview rooms, side by side. Brad stood in a large viewing room and watched the suspects through one-way mirrors. After they were arrested, they were transported in separate cruisers. They'd had no contact with the other. The big guy had put his head on the table and looked like he was sleeping. He wasn't. That was one of the ways career crooks acted. They thought if they were calm they'd get out. The fact Brad caught them red-handed was kind of incriminating.

His smaller partner was the opposite. He nervously glanced around the room and jumped at every noise.

Brad turned to the sound of a door opening. A tall guy with slicked-back graying hair stepped in and extended his hand.

"Detective Ed Walsh, Robbery."

Brad took the hand. "Serg ... *Detective* Brad Coulter."

"Coulter? The TSU guy?"

"That's me."

"A detective now. Good for you. What unit?"

"That's a little fuzzy. Today's my first day. I'm working with Detective Tommy Devlin."

Walsh shook his head. "Shit, your first day. You haven't even started work and you collar these two. Not a bad way to start. You might have set the bar a little high, though."

"I'm a shit magnet. Trouble finds me."

Walsh laughed. "Well, Detective, shall we interview these pukes?"

"You bet."

"Let's see what the big guy has to say. His name is Phil. Lots of priors for theft, car theft, and minor assaults. We've been after these two for months. They're generalists—carjacking, robbery, burglary. We think they're good for at least twenty cases."

Phil made a big production about waking up when Brad and Walsh entered.

Walsh took a seat across from Phil. Brad leaned against a wall.

"How long was I asleep?" Phil rubbed his eyes. "Why am I here?"

"That's funny, Phil," Walsh said. "I'm Detective Walsh. You've already met Detective Coulter."

"Yah, he's the guy who gave me this headache. He hit me with something."

"You must have a head injury," Brad said. "You were running and tripped on the thirty-yard line."

"That's bullshit. Whatever you think I did, I didn't. I'm innocent."

"You assault a driver, steal his car, cause several traffic accidents—all witnessed by the detective," Walsh said. "Then you run into the football stadium with the cop in pursuit. The last thing you are is innocent."

"You can't prove shit." Phil glared at Walsh, then turned to Brad. "I want him charged for assaulting me. It was police brutality. I ain't done nothin'."

Phil leaned back in his chair and put his arms across his chest. "I got nothin' to say."

Walsh stood and walked to the door. Brad followed him to the hall.

"That's it?" Brad asked. "What's your strategy?"

"That was just the warmup," Walsh said. "I needed to see what his position was. Now we talk to his partner, Glenn. Once I hear what Glenn has to say I play them against each other."

"But these guys know that's what you're going to do."

Walsh nodded. "You bet they do. We plant a seed in one room, another seed in the other room. Then give them time to think, to wonder what the other guy is saying. The saying, 'honor among thieves' is false. You'll see. The only question is who breaks first."

They entered the second interview room. "Glenn, I'm Detective Walsh." He slapped a folder onto the table and sat. "I think you've met Detective Coulter."

Glenn's eyes moved between the detectives.

Walsh took a seat across from Phil. Brad stood by the door.

Walsh opened the folder and flipped through the pages. He shook his head a couple of times.

"What?" Glenn asked.

"Oh, my." Walsh closed the file and shook his head again.

"What the—" Glenn stared at the folder. "What's in there? What's going on?"

"Well, Glenn, you've been a very bad boy in your short twenty-five years. Already two stretches in prison. This will be strike three. These crimes will put you back there for a long time. Especially when you're the leader."

"What? Who said that? Did Phil say that? I ain't no leader."

Walsh shook his head. "That's not the way I heard it. You're the brains and Phil is the brawn."

"I don't know nothin' about no brawn. I was just hitchhiking. I don't know Phil. Next thing I know he's beating that driver and we're running from the cops."

"Just hitchhiking," Walsh said.

"Yeah, heading to British Columbia."

"Detective Coulter, did you hear that? Hitchhiking? Glenn must think we're stupid. How does that make you feel?" Walsh pounded the table with a fist. Glenn twitched. "That's the oldest excuse there is. *I was just hitchhiking.* Do you think this is my first interrogation?" Walsh opened the file and pulled out a piece of paper with handwriting on it. He passed it to Brad, who nodded and handed it back. "Phil has a whole different story." Walsh put the paper back in the file folder.

Glenn held his head in his hands. He groaned and shook his head. Finally, he looked up. "I ain't taking the fall for this. Give me paper and I'll write it down. That asshole was beating up queers and guys picking up hookers on the stroll. He said they'd never call the cops. Sometimes the guys with the hookers were rich, and we got a lot of money. Then he had the idea that if we took their wallets, we could go to their houses next and clean them out, too."

"Start at the beginning and write it all down." Walsh slid paper and a pen to Glenn. "When you're done, I'll talk with Phil."

Brad and Walsh stood in the hall.

"That was quick," Brad said. He had seen a lot of interrogations, but Walsh made it look easy.

"Most of these guys aren't that smart. Some keep their mouth shut and demand a lawyer. Others, like these two, can't wait to turn on each other. Glenn crumbled faster than most. By the end of the day I'd bet we clear twenty or more cases. Let's see what Phil says now."

Walsh sat in front of Phil while Brad stayed by the door. "Well, we talked to Glenn and he says this was all your idea. He was just hitchhiking and didn't have anything to do with this." Walsh pulled out the same piece of paper and waved it in front of Phil. "It's all right here." He slid the paper into the file folder. "So, based on Glenn's information, we cut him loose."

"What?" Phil yelled. "That little shit was involved in every one of them."

"Every one of them?" Walsh asked.

"Yeah, yeah, it was all his idea. He was out of money and looking for an easy way to get some cash. He said he knew a guy who would buy stolen cars. I'm telling you, man, it was all his idea. He said between rousting guys on the stroll and boosting cars, we'd make a ton of money."

Walsh leaned close to Phil. "Well, we let Glenn go." Walsh tapped the file folder. "It's all here in his statement. He claims he didn't have anything to do with this and it was all your idea. The carjacking and all the other things. You got anything else to say?"

"Are you crazy?" Glenn said. "The carjacking was his idea and all the other stuff, too. He's the one who said the home invasions would be easy. He knew where to fence stuff. There's lots of cash. He's the one who said that robbing Johns on the hooker stroll would be easy cash."

"All right," Walsh said. "We'll see if we can catch your buddy before he's released." Walsh got up to leave the room. "If what you say is true, I'm gonna need you to put that down in writing. You willing to do that?" Walsh tossed paper and a pen to Glenn. "Start writing, and it better be the truth. If you put lies into a sworn statement, I promise you, the judge will be angry."

"Yeah, yeah. Damn right. That lying motherfucker."

They left Glenn to write his statement.

"Who's the leader?" Brad asked.

"Doesn't matter," Walsh said. "We've got enough to charge them both and hold them until I figure out everything they've done. The crown prosecutor has the final say. But I'd be surprised if they see the real world in fewer than fifteen years."

"I should get to my new job," Brad said. "I'm already late. Nice working with you."

"You too, Coulter. Good luck."

He *had* missed the adrenaline rush. It was good to be back.

CHAPTER THREE

Brad took the stairs to the second floor and entered the detective bureau. The big room hadn't changed in twenty years —or more. The ceiling was smoke-stained, the carpet worn down to the underlay, and the desks second-world-war surplus. The desks faced each other two by two in pods of four. Detectives occupied half of them. Brad glanced around the room. Years of cigarette smoke, coffee and sweat permeated everything. This morning, the freshly brewed coffee was the strongest. Since he'd tossed his away, he followed the aroma and poured a cup.

Four years ago, he'd met with Detective O'Shea in this room after an armed robbery of a Brinks armored car. Brad had fought with one suspect, who got away. When he walked into the detective office that night, he was in awe. Street cops weren't allowed in the sacred detective office. Walking in now as a detective was quite different. Back then, he thought it was all secret stuff including passwords and handshakes. O'Shea had died when a guy who was high from sniffing glue shot him in a standoff that lasted hours. Five other cops were injured. The suspect had escaped from the collapsed garage and was brought down in a hail of police bullets. The whole thing was a shit-show from the beginning, but it had initiated important changes.

Brad shook off the memories and absorbed the atmosphere. He was a detective now and belonged here. He just needed to learn the secret handshake and password.

He snaked his way to the back of the room where he found an office the size of a storage room. Detective Tommy Devlin sat at a desk. Brad and Devlin had worked together over the last four years, first in the Tactical Support Unit and then two years ago fighting outlaw bikers. Devlin's real passion was under-cover, hanging out in the shadows and taking down drug dealers.

"'Bout frickin' time." Devlin dropped a pen and looked up. "Grab a seat. Your first day back and already you're causing shit."

"I prefer to think of it as good police work. I already have two arrests. How about you?"

"I don't know how you do it, but shit finds you. I hear they ran."

Brad smirked. "Yeah, that was the best part."

"Lots of guys bet you wouldn't be back. I wasn't sure, either." Devlin leaned back in his chair. "Tell me about your year off, Mr. Counselor, sir."

Shrugging, Brad said, "Deputy Chief Archer talked with me about my career and where I thought it was going. I told him TSU was great. He said I needed to aim higher and that I should consider writing the bar exams. I made the mistake of telling

Maggie what Archer said. She agreed and then told her dad, Judge Gray. He was all over the idea and smoothed the path for me. A year ago, Archer gave me a leave of absence. I studied fourteen to eighteen hours a day. I'd take a break jogging with Lobo, then back to studying."

"That doesn't sound like fun."

"Not at all. The last law course I took was eight years ago so I had a lot of refreshing to do before I could even start prepping for the exams."

"All studying and no fun."

"Lots of studying. But the last couple of months were with Vaughn Matson, the chief crown prosecutor. That was interesting. A few times I thought I could be a prosecutor and maybe I should stay. But I missed the action so now I'm back."

"Matson and Judge Gray couldn't convince you to stay?"

Brad shook his head. "They tried. Maggie and her dad ganged up on me every family dinner. Matson made sure I was working on the challenging cases. None of it worked."

"So, I'm working with a card-carrying lawyer, huh," Devlin said.

"Not yet. I wrote the bar exams, but I don't know if I passed. The letter should come in a few weeks."

"How's Maggie? She still loving being a paramedic?"

"Yup. She loves it. Although I think she's become more cynical."

"That happens to most of us," Devlin said. "If you don't become cynical you must not be paying attention."

Brad leaned forward. "Tell me about this team."

"Okay." Devlin held out his hand. "The team consists of"— he lowered one finger—"you"—he lowered a second finger —"and me. Not much of a team—you and me. After all the shit with the bikers two years ago, I proposed a special unit to focus on high-risk offenders. It took a while to get through all the red tape, but now we're up and running."

"Just the two of us?"

"Yup, for now," Devlin nodded.

"How does this work?"

"We get cases from detectives—scumbags they think are good for serious stuff—and we track them. Or prosecutors let us know when high-risk offenders like sexual predators have been released from jail. We keep tabs on them, follow them from wherever they're living to work, then back home. We try to catch them violating their release conditions like staying away from schools and playgrounds. We'll gather information on the Hells Angels. You can reacquaint yourself with our friend, Jeremy Pickens."

"I really hate that guy," Brad said. "What a prick. He played us like a fiddle and hitched his star to the Hells Angels."

"He's still president and they're getting stronger," Devlin said. "The Angels control all prostitution, drug trade, and extorsions in the city."

"I'd love to take him down."

"You might get your chance. That will be our back-burner case—the one we work on when things are quiet."

Brad rolled his eyes. "You think things will ever be quiet for us?"

"Probably not. We even have an official name. We're the Serious High-Risk Offender Program, or SHOP."

"SHOP?" Brad laughed. "That's the best you could think of?"

"*Tracking scumbags* was already taken." Devlin slid a pager and charger across the table. "We're on call all the time. Our hours vary depending on what we're working on. Probably more evening and night shifts than day shifts, unless we're in court. Maggie gonna be okay with this?"

"We talked," Brad said. "She'd be happier if I was flying a desk, but she also knows that would drive me crazy, and then I'd drive her crazy. Besides, it's not like she works nine to five. She did have a few choice words for you, though."

"A paramedic with a potty mouth, I like that. How's living together?"

"Like any couple, I guess," Brad said. "We have good days and bad days."

"You two ever gonna get married?"

"She's mentioned it."

Devlin grinned. "Who's the holdback? You?"

"Yeah, I guess. It's the job, it's—"

"She understands the job," Devlin said. "After four years I don't think much surprises her."

"As much as I try to leave work at work, you know shit follows me."

"There's that—"

Devlin's phone rang. He snatched it up on the second ring, listened for about a minute, then hung up. "Your first case."

"What is it?"

"You'll be interested," Devlin said. "Two days ago, Jeter Wolfe escaped prison. The Wolfman's back. We need a plan."

Twenty minutes later, Brad leaned against the wall in the briefing room, watching the street cops come in for the afternoon shift briefing. The briefing room had chairs for about fifteen cops and standing room for another ten. The rookies and younger cops sat anxiously in the front rows. The veterans jock-eyed for space against the back wall. A couple of older cops, the ones always late for briefing, rushed into the room and, seeing no space against the wall, grudgingly took chairs in the back rows.

Brad nodded to Briscoe, who grinned from the back row. Normally, this briefing would be his to give. He was taking full advantage now that Brad and Devlin would be in charge. The room filled beyond capacity. Some cops going off shift had stopped by. The rumor mill was working overtime with the news that Wolfe had escaped. Except it wasn't a rumor, it was the horrible truth. The temperature in the room rose quickly. Brad sniffed the air—a few guys must have forgotten to shower before work.

The room buzzed with a dozen conversations. Some whis-pers, groups laughing, and a few loud talkers trying to drown everyone out.

Devlin strode to the front of the room. A few cops stopped talking, but most continued. "Hey, time to get started."

No luck—the noise continued.

"Hey, maggots," Devlin yelled. "Shut the fuck up!"

The room instantly quieted.

"That's better. We've got important shit to cover. First, if you have been wondering why the city has been so peaceful over the last year, it's because Sergeant—excuse me, *Detective* Coulter was attaining higher education. He's now a lawyer."

Brad bowed.

There was a chorus of boos, insults, and lawyer jokes.

"Okay, save that crap for later. Oh, if you find yourself working with Coulter, I suggest you wear a vest and a helmet—

he tends to attract shit. He's been beaten several times, shot several times, and bombed. More than any other cop—hell, more than all of us combined. Other than that, he's swell."

Devlin glanced at his notes. "Most of you already know this stuff, but for our keener front-row rookies, a little crime history. Two years ago, the Gypsy Jokers and Satan's Soldiers biker gangs fought for control of prostitution and the drug trade. Coulter, as sergeant in the Tactical Support Unit, and me, in narcotics, were right in the middle of that shit, fighting both gangs. We lost an officer and many others were injured. Ultimately, both bike gangs lost and the Hells Angels moved in. As a city, we traded one problem for an even bigger one."

Devlin clicked the remote for the slide projector and an image of Wolfe from his biker days filled the screen. Wolfe wore his Gypsy Jokers vest and was standing by a Harley Davidson motorcycle.

"Jeter Wolfe was the Gypsy Jokers' Sergeant at Arms. He did all their messy stuff—assaults, rapes, and murders. Two years ago, he had been near death from a beating he took from the Hells Angels and was not expected to live. But he did. He was found guilty of three murders, and the kidnapping and repeated rapes of two sixteen-year-olds. During the trial, he threatened the crown prosecutor Jenni Blighe, and the girls he'd assaulted. Wolfe said that when he got out, he'd come for them."

Devlin clicked the remote and Wolfe's mugshot filled the screen. "A few days ago, Jeter Wolfe, a thirty-four-year-old Caucasian male, escaped from Edmonton Max."

Brad stared at the face of the vicious and sadistic killer he hoped he'd never see again. Certainly not outside of prison. His pulse increased and his jaw clenched as the hatred returned.

The next photo showed Wolfe in the prison gym. "As you

can see, Wolfe is huge. A year ago, the prison guards tried to hold him down so they could shear his hair and beard. Wolfe put three of them in hospital. After that, they left him alone. He hasn't cut his hair or beard for more than two years. His nickname, Wolfman, is fitting. The prison guards said Wolfe didn't miss a workout—every minute of his exercise time went to weights. How many of you can make that claim?" Devlin flexed a bicep and glanced around the room.

"At first, Edmonton Max and the provincial government downplayed the escape because of recent budget cuts to prisons. The night Wolfe escaped they were short- staffed. So, they dragged their feet on releasing information about the escape. Probably hoped they'd catch Wolfe quickly and no one would be the wiser. But then a cellmate of Wolfe's made a deal with the crown prosecutor in Edmonton. He said Wolfe obsessed over crown prosecutor Jenni Blighe and was pretty specific on what he'd do to her after he escaped. That's when the Edmonton cops got a brainwave and notified us. Coulter, you got anything to add?"

Brad stepped to the front of the room. "We think Wolfe killed at least six people during the biker war. We could only prove three murders. Of course, none of the bikers talked. Wolfe is violent, manipulative, and too smart to be easily caught. Wolfe should be considered armed and extremely dangerous. Don't try to take him alone. In fact, don't try to take him with fewer than about six guys, two dogs, a tank, and the Tactical Support Unit. He'll do anything, I mean anything, to stay out of prison. When the Jokers and Soldiers fell apart and came under the Hells Angels, most bikers distanced themselves from Wolfe. He's had very few visitors in prison. He has a few contacts in Calgary, so it's possible he'll reach out to them."

"It would be crazy for Wolfe to go the Hells Angels' Clubhouse," Briscoe said. "He knows that's the first place we'd search."

"You're right," Brad said. "But we need to cover every possibility. Devlin has a team from Guns and Gangs watching the Hells Angels' Clubhouse. We're going to up the pressure on them tonight."

CHAPTER FOUR

Tuesday Evening

JETER WOLFE FELT GOOD. THE FREEDOM WAS EXHILARATING, AND HE was horny—he needed to take care of that. After almost a year in remand awaiting trial, then a year in that hell hole in Edmonton, he was free, and he wasn't going to waste a moment. Escaping prison hadn't been hard—he kicked himself for not figuring it out sooner. He'd gained the trust of the prison guards —model prisoner, they'd said. Well, except for the beard fiasco. The key was getting a job in the laundry. After finding the weakest of the delivery guys, the rest was easy. A threat or two to the delivery guy and a visit from one of Wolfe's former cellmates to the delivery guy's cute wife and all was set. The biggest challenge was concealing his bulk in the laundry bin. The little runt had almost given it away struggling with the heavy bin. The lazy guards at the gate didn't even get out of their chairs to check the truck.

The car came from the University of Alberta student parking. A beater, to be sure, but it was covered with dust. The owner wouldn't miss it anytime soon. The cash came from a couple of his cellmates who were out on parole. Not a lot of cash—he'd need to find another source. So, he came to Calgary. His old pal Jeremy Pickens, president of the Calgary Hells Angels, might part with some money.

Wolfe drove to the new clubhouse in Ogden. As he turned the corner, he saw the police vehicles—everywhere. The street had a red-and-blue glow. He slowed. His eyes drifted to two guys dressed in casual clothes walking his way—a tall guy with broad shoulders and a shorter, stocky guy. *Coulter and Devlin.* The cops that hunted and destroyed his club and put him away for fifteen years. He fought the urge to drive the car into them.

Another day, another time. He eased his foot down on the gas and despite his inner rage, he calmly turned at the next street corner heading north, just like a law-abiding citizen. A few blocks farther he merged into traffic and headed east.

The farther he drove the more the rage burned. He pounded the steering wheel. He thought of turning around and heading to her house. Not now, not today, not when he was angry. That had to be done carefully. It had to fulfill the fantasy he created. She would have to wait. Not too long, but not tonight.

He cruised the hooker stroll on Seventeenth Avenue. Despite the cool night, the hookers were numerous. Several glanced in his direction and a couple flashed their boobs—nice, but not what he wanted. Then at the corner of Seventeenth and Thirty-Third, he saw her—young, slender, with long blond hair. She stood back from the others, like she was scared. He pulled up to the curb. The closest three hookers ambled to the passenger window. He reached across and rolled down the window.

One leaned into the car, her heavy breasts resting on the window ledge. "What'll you have, doll?" She was chewing gum and blowing bubbles. "You're a big man. I'll bet everything else is big. You got something in mind?"

Wolfe reached across and roughly pawed her breasts, then slapped her face. "Not you, cow. Her." He pointed to the young blonde.

"She's a baby. She won't be able to handle a real man like you. I know what you need and you won't be disappointed."

"No. Her."

"Fine. See you later when you find out she can't get you off." She turned to the girl. "He wants you."

The girl trudged to the car.

Wolfe opened the door. "Get in."

The girl looked back. The older hooker nodded toward the car. "Get in. Get the cash first."

———

Brad and Devlin stood outside the Hells Angels' Clubhouse in the southeast. Two years ago, the Angels had renovated the Satan's Soldiers' former clubhouse. They'd increased its size to accommodate all the members. The most significant change was the fortifications. An eight-foot concrete wall surrounded the building. A massive iron gate was the only way in, and it was guarded 24/7. The stink from the meat-packing plant nearby saturated the air. An odor Brad remembered too well.

With the area secured, K9 and the Tactical Support Unit searched the clubhouse and gathered the bikers. They escorted the bikers outside to uniformed cops, who searched the bikers again and shoved them into cruisers or wagons.

Brad recognized one of the handcuffed bikers. He tapped Devlin on the shoulder, and they headed toward the biker.

"Slim Pickens. Well, isn't this a surprise. Just like old times."

"What do you think you're doing, Coulter. This is bullshit. You don't have any right to raid our clubhouse."

"After you screwed us last time, you think you get special treatment? Well you are absolutely right. How are you enjoying the special treatment so far?"

"You're funnier now than you were before. What the hell is this about?"

"Your buddy, Jeter Wolfe, escaped from prison."

"He was in prison in Edmonton. Why the hell are you looking here?"

"We figure he's not going to stay in Edmonton very long," Brad said. "There's nothing there for him. He'll head here, and when he does, what will he do? Look up his old buddies. Don't you think?"

"Wolfe and I were never buddies," Pickens said. "He's crazy. All you had to do was ask, Coulter. I would've told you if I'd seen him. If he came here, I'd kill him myself."

"That's bullshit and you know it. You screwed us over two years ago—that's going to follow you. We're not gonna take a chance this time. So, talk. When was the last time you saw Wolfe?"

"I haven't seen him or talked to him for a year or more," Pickens said. "I visited him a couple of times the first year he was in jail. He knew stuff about our old club, the Gypsy Jokers, that I didn't know. He wouldn't tell me anything, so I stopped going. I think the head injury from the beating affected him. All he talks about is sex, torture, and revenge. He'd describe in detail his fantasies about what he'd do to that prosecutor Jenni

Blighe, Annie, and that lady cop. It was vile stuff. One thing for sure, he was definitely set on revenge. Oh, yeah, Coulter. He wants to cut off your nuts and feed them to you or your paramedic chick."

"I'll take pleasure sending him to the great biker gang in Hell," Brad said. "I get it. During his trial he threatened lots of people. That's why he was locked away for fifteen years."

"You two better take this seriously," Pickens said. "I'm telling you, he's worse than ever. If he's out on the street, you guys better be worried. Nobody who was involved in his trial is safe, especially not the women."

"Call us the second you see Wolfe or he contacts you," Brad said. "If you don't, and I find out you've been holding back on us, get used to having all these cops here."

"I don't want him anywhere near my club or me. He's bad news for everybody. If I see him, I'll let you know."

Brad glared at Pickens. Two years ago, he had played them. A lot of people got hurt in Picken's push for control of the biker gangs in Calgary. In the end, Pickens became the president of the Hells Angels. For the last year and a half, biker gangs had kept a low profile. But Brad wasn't under the illusion that they had stopped the criminal activities. There were drugs on the streets, prostitution, and extortion. Pickens was the mastermind.

Brad pulled out his handcuff key, turned Pickens around, and took off the handcuffs.

"Letting you go is probably the stupidest thing I've done in a while. But I don't have anything to charge you with. Just remember our deal."

Pickens rubbed his wrists as he walked away.

Brad and Devlin headed back to their car.

"You really think that asshole will let us know if he hears from Wolfe?" Devlin asked.

"I don't believe him for a second," Brad said. "He's a lying prick—always was and always will be. We'll keep guys on this place. We should put a tail on Pickens. If Wolfman is in Calgary, he'll contact Pickens."

"I'll ask, but we're already using a bunch of cops on this. I don't think I'm gonna be able to get any more."

"Pickens is right about one thing," Brad said. "Wolfe is a sexual predator. If he has sex on his mind, he won't wait long."

CHAPTER FIVE

Tuesday Evening

MAGGIE GRAY PULLED THE AMBULANCE OUT OF STATION 12 AND drove toward downtown. Her rookie partner, Rick Fola, gingerly held a coffee cup.

"No bumps," he said. "I don't want to wear this coffee."

"We could get coffee when we get to Station 1," Maggie said.

"This coffee is likely the only nourishment I'm going to get for hours," Fola said. "If dispatch is moving us downtown, we can expect a busy night."

"Maybe the firefighters at Station 1 will let us in on dinner."

"Fat chance of that," Fola said.

"They like me, though." Maggie turned off Memorial Drive and headed down Fifth Avenue. "I'll vouch for you."

He snorted. "When did that happen? They made your life hell when you first got there."

"You'd be surprised what banana bread and cookies will do."

Fola laughed. "How's Brad's new job?"

"He had a busy day."

"What unit is he in?"

"The Serious High-Risk Offender Program. They call it SHOP."

"That's not the catchiest name I've heard."

"Brad thinks it should be MFOTL."

"Okay, I'll bite. What does that mean?"

"Motherfuckers on the Loose."

"Not too catchy, but fits better. Was he excited about getting back on the street?"

"I think it was a bit of a struggle going in to work today. Then, on the way to work he ends up in a car chase." Maggie told Fola the details. "So, he had two arrests before his shift started."

"That's crazy."

Maggie shook her head. "Not unusual for him. He could be on a deserted island and I swear somehow crime would find him."

Three beeps sounded from the radio. "Medic 12."

"Medic 12, go."

"What's your location?"

"First Street and Tenth Avenue southwest."

"Respond to the sixth floor, 626 Twelfth Avenue Southwest. Meet fire on the scene. One patient with burns."

Fola grabbed the mic. "Roger, dispatch, 12 responding."

"That call came in ten minutes ago." Maggie activated the lights and siren.

She parked behind a line of fire trucks. They got out of the ambulance, piled their kits on the stretcher and rolled it to the apartment building. They lifted the stretcher over a few hoses crossing the sidewalk and snaking into the building.

A firefighter met them at the door. "I'll take you up to the sixth floor."

They followed the firefighter into the elevator. When the elevator doors opened on the sixth floor, the smell of burned chemical was strong. Firefighters were setting up exhaust fans in the hallway and at the apartment door.

They were led past the firefighters, into the apartment, and through the living room. Maggie saw a beautiful ebony baby grand piano in one corner. The apartment was immaculately furnished. She didn't see any fire damage in this room.

"Where was the fire?" Maggie asked.

"The bedroom," the firefighter said. "She was smoking in bed and fell asleep. The cigarette ignited the sheets and bedspread. She woke up, saw the fire, and tried to put it out herself."

"What did she use?"

"She had a glass of water by the bed. Then she hit it with a pillow. The pillow caught fire, too. Finally, she got it out, but burned her hands pretty bad."

They entered the bedroom. The smell of burned plastic and flesh was overwhelming. Maggie walked over to a woman in her mid-fifties who was wearing a dressing gown and sitting in a chair. Her face was screwed up in pain, tears rolling down her cheeks.

"My name is Maggie, this is Rick. We're paramedics. What's your name?"

"Rose."

"Rose, where does it hurt?"

"My hands."

"Let me look at your hands."

Rose held out her trembling hands. Her wrists were red, with big blisters near her hands. Her fingers were black and charred with what looked to be skin hanging off in strips.

"On a scale of 1-10, with 10 being the worst pain you've ever had, how would you rate it?" Maggie asked.

"Nine," Rose said. "Maybe a ten."

"We'll be able to help you with the pain." Maggie looked closer—it didn't look like skin. It was brittle and covered her hands.

"What's that?" Fola asked.

"Plastic," Maggie said. "The pillow had a plastic cover. When it caught fire, the plastic melted onto her hands." The plastic had cooled and now both hands looked like they were webbed with plastic connecting the fingers.

"Fola, start an IV, normal saline," Maggie said. "I'll give oxygen and get the morphine ready."

"Sure can," Fola said.

Once the IV was in place, Maggie administered 5.0 mg of morphine. "Rose. This will help your pain. If this doesn't work, I can give you more morphine."

Fola slipped on surgical gloves and gently placed sterile gauze bandages over the hands.

Firefighters helped Fola lift Rose to the stretcher, then maneuvered the stretcher out of the apartment and into the elevator. Maggie gathered their kits and equipment and joined them. On the main level, firefighters rolled the stretcher to the ambulance.

Brad ran out of Bowness Park heading for home. Lobo, his German shepherd, ran at his side. Four years ago, Brad's partner Curtis Young was training Lobo for K9. When Curtis was killed in the line of duty and Brad was wounded, Brad adopted Lobo. Now he was Brad's companion on jogs and had been vital in Brad's healing from the death of his partner.

They slowed to a walk for the last block. Brad loved everything about his house. Built in the mid-1920s, the two-story stood out from the newer homes on the block. Surrounded by tall pines and overlooking Bowness Park, it was everything he could hope for.

A car pulled up to the curb in front of them. Maggie slid out and grabbed her gym bag from the back seat. Lobo raced ahead and ran circles around Maggie. Brad walked over and kissed Maggie.

"Yuck." She stepped back. "You're soaked and you stink."

"Thank you, dear. I missed you, too. It was a long run. Both of us needed it."

Lobo raced ahead onto the porch and waited at the front door.

Inside, Lobo sped through the dining room to the kitchen. Maggie stuffed her kit into the entrance closet, then headed for the kitchen. Lobo stood over his food bowl and barked twice.

"Yeah, yeah," Brad said. "After I get some water." He grabbed a glass off the counter, filled it with water, and drank thirstily. He filled the glass a second time, then fed Lobo. "How was your night?"

"Quiet for the most part. We had one disturbing call." She recounted the call of the lady with the burned hands.

"That's awful," Brad said. "Will she be able to play again?"

Maggie shrugged. "I don't know. I hope so."

They sat at the old oak kitchen table while Lobo gobbled his food.

"How's your rookie working out?" Brad leaned back in his chair and sipped more water.

"He's doing fine. Like most, he's book smart and street dumb. But he's keen to learn. He's still a little uncomfortable working with me. Not sure if it's because I'm a woman, I'm a woman bossing him around, or just the usual nerves when you first hit the street."

"I know the feeling," Brad said. "When I finished recruit classes and started my first shift, I realized I didn't know shit. The second night, my partner got in a fight with a couple of druggies. I didn't know if I was supposed to help him or let him pound on them. He was doing great, they didn't stand a chance and in less than a minute, he had them on the ground. He looked up. I was frozen to the spot. He said, 'I could use a second set of handcuffs.' I felt like an idiot. Within a few weeks I was the one getting in scraps."

"It was the same for me. Remember when I came to police HQ for the suspect having a seizure?"

Brad smiled. "How could I forget."

"My partners had chewed me out for not taking control of scenes," Maggie said. "I was determined to show them I could do it. But you were there and quite a distraction."

"That worked out, I think."

"You think!"

"Four years later, you're here."

"True," Maggie said. "Tell me about your new job."

Brad told her about working with Devlin and what he'd be doing. "My first case is tracking down Jeter Wolfe."

"He's escaped?"

"Yup, from maximum security," Brad said. "They think he got out in a laundry cart."

"How did he fit?" Maggie asked.

"He must have taken up the whole cart," Brad said. "I'd hate to be the guy pushing the cart. Anyway, he's out."

"He was in jail in Edmonton," Maggie said. "Will he come here?"

"During the trial, he threatened everyone responsible for his conviction. We're certain he's heading here. He may already be here."

"You've kinda jumped right back into the action. Just like old times."

"Once we get Wolfe, it will settle down," Brad said.

"Do you believe that?"

Brad grinned. "No."

Maggie stood and kissed Brad. "I worked all night. I'm going to bed. What time do you need to be at work?"

"I should shower, and then head into work."

Maggie smiled. "No way! I was going to take a shower, too. I'll race you."

CHAPTER SIX

Wednesday Morning

BRAD HAD BEEN AT THE OFFICE, MAKING A LIST OF PLACES WOLFE might hide and people he'd contact, when he got the call. A body at a rundown hotel in the southeast could mean a lot of things. Overdose, suicide, or murder. He didn't want to get ahead of the facts, but a death in the area they thought Wolfe was hiding seemed like a bit of a coincidence.

When Brad arrived at the scene, Devlin and another guy, with the distinct look of a cop, were standing outside the motel room.

"This is Don Griffin—homicide," Devlin said, nodding at the guy. He motioned toward Brad. "Brad Coulter."

Griffin extended his hand. "Coulter."

Brad took the hand. Griffin had a firm grip. Brad sized up Griffin. They stood eye to eye and had the same build. Griffin's eyes, almost gray, were always moving, as if expecting some threat to appear suddenly. He had the look of someone who had seen it all and had become numb.

"What do we know?" Brad asked.

"Dead hooker—young, blonde, abused, and beaten," Griffin said.

Brad nodded. "Who found her?"

"Cleaning lady," Griffin said. "This one was her last room for the day. She opened the door, used a wooden chock to prop it open, grabbed a basket of cleaning supplies, then entered the room. Scared the shit out of her. She was hysterical. EMS took her to the hospital."

"I don't suppose there're any cameras here." Brad glanced around.

Griffin laughed. "Are you kidding? Lucky there're light-bulbs. The room was bugged though. It's crawling with them. You should tuck your pant legs into your socks."

"That's good, real good," Brad said, cringing. "Do we have anything to work with?"

"The manager says a big guy checked in late last night," Griffin said. "Wanted the end room and paid cash. He left about two hours later driving an old, dark, four-door sedan. Maybe a Pontiac Parisienne. When the cleaning lady found the body before noon, he put two and two together—and let me tell you, that wasn't easy for him."

"Did you show the manager Wolfe's photo?" Brad asked.

Devlin nodded. "It was Wolfe."

"Jeez," Brad said. "Can I take a look?"

"Sure," Griffin said.

Brad followed Griffin and Devlin to the crime scene. They

stopped at the doorway. Griffin stepped back, allowing Brad access. It took his eyes a few seconds to adjust from the sunny outdoors to the dimly lit room. It was a typical low-end motel room that could be rented by the hour—small, with barely enough space for a bed. It smelled of cigarette smoke, sweat, and a musty, old-room scent. Then there was the odor of shit. He turned his head and took a deep breath of outside air. As bad as death scenes were, bowels releases added additional foulness to the air.

A single bulb in the middle of the ceiling did little to light the room. The victim was naked, face down at the end of the bed. Her upper body on the bed, her knees touching the floor. Her head turned to the left beyond the normal range. Her arms were secured behind her back with wide gray tape. There was a strip of tape over her mouth. Her eyes bulged out of their sockets. From this angle, she looked a bit like Annie, the girl Wolfe had repeatedly raped two years ago.

Just out of jail and Wolfe was starting where he left off. Damn. Brad stepped outside and joined Griffin and Devlin. Devlin puffed on a cigarette.

"How the hell does he escape from maximum security?" Brad asked. "This is bullshit."

Griffin nodded. "I'll stay with Ident. Nothing here for you two."

"Sure," Devlin said.

"I've been working on a list of places Wolfe might hide and people he'd contact," Brad said. "We can work on that today."

Sergeant Sturgeon from Ident came to the door. "Hey, Coulter, congratulations on moving to the dark side, the detective bureau." He pointed at the room. "It's going to take most of the day to process this scene. I'll catch up to you guys tomorrow morning. Your office?"

Brad couldn't shake off the feeling that this was only the beginning.

CHAPTER SEVEN

Thursday Morning

BRAD HAD GRABBED A SMALL MEETING ROOM TO WORK IN. HE leaned back in a chair, drank coffee, and stared at the wall where he'd put everything he could think of about Wolfe.

Wolfe had come west with Felix Keaton, a big wig in the Hamilton Bandidos Motorcycle Club who took over as president of the Gypsy Jokers. Wolfe did all of Keaton's dirty work—torture and murder. Wolfe's perversion with young teens was well documented. In Hamilton, charges were laid but didn't go to court. The victims didn't show. That was until Brad and Devlin put him away two years ago with Annie's testimony.

Pickens was the only one left from the Gypsy Jokers' leadership that Wolfe had associated with, and Pickens already told Brad he'd have nothing to do with Wolfe. Not that Brad believed the lying pile of shit.

The list of people Wolfe would seek out was very small. The

places he could hide, staggering. Wolfe wasn't stupid. Still, if Wolfe wanted to blend in, the southeast was the place.

Devlin entered, grabbed a chair, and glanced at the wall. "Not a lot of possible contacts—that's it?"

"What about his cellmates?" Brad asked. "One already talked. Maybe others are willing to make a deal. Especially those released in the last six months."

"I'll work on that," Devlin said.

Brad sighed. "How does a guy that big, that ugly, and that mean stay hidden?"

"You know how it is. No one is going to rat out Wolfman. I stopped into the drug unit on my way here. They've been all over the southeast. They got a few leads, but either Wolfman had never been there, or he was gone. They'll keep pounding the pavement."

"What's his play? When he escaped, I was sure he'd go after Jenni Blighe."

"We were late getting her protection because we were notified late," Devlin said. "He might have gone there earlier."

Brad nodded. "Sure, but if he did, why didn't he attack? Not that I want him to, but if she was his target, he had a few days right after he escaped to get her."

"What does she think about the protection?" Devlin asked.

"At first she said she didn't need protection. But I think she was glad we pushed it. Wolfe really shook her up with his threats at his trial."

"Has her protection reported anything suspicious?"

Brad shook his head. "Nada. They're outside her house when she's home and they follow her to work and back or whenever she goes out."

"What about Annie?" Devlin asked.

"She's secure," Brad said.

"How do you—"

Brad shook his head. "Need to know. But trust me, she is good. I guess we should hit the streets tonight."

The door opened. Sturgeon and Griffin strode in and grabbed chairs.

"Missed you at the autopsy, Coulter," Sturgeon said.

"I got tied up on stuff here."

Sturgeon laughed. "You've hated autopsies since you were in recruit training. I heard you upchucked your breakfast before they'd made the first cut."

"It's the mix of biological and chemical smells I can't take. You're saying you enjoy autopsies?"

"You will too, *when* I solve your case."

"You've got something big?"

Sturgeon shook his head. "No, but if I did—"

"Jerk."

"What do you have? Anything?" Devlin asked.

"Not much you don't already know," Sturgeon said. "Cause of death was a broken neck. That's not as easy to do as they show on TV."

"But that wouldn't be an issue for Wolfe," Brad said.

"That's true," Sturgeon replied. "She'd been violently raped several times. The medical examiner thinks she was dead when the anal rape occurred. We're going to have to wait for testing on the sperm. She had cigarette burns and bite marks over her thighs and breasts."

"That's Wolfe," Brad said. "It's consistent with what he did to Annie and Sissy."

"The room was covered in fingerprints, and miscellaneous body fluids," Sturgeon said. "I don't think the room had been cleaned this century. We'll do our best on the prints, but don't hold your breath."

"So, nothing that points conclusively to Wolfe," Brad said.

"Looks that way." Sturgeon stood. "I'll keep working on it. I'll let you know if I find anything."

"Right, thanks," Brad said.

After Sturgeon left, they were quiet. Each man was deep in thought.

When Brad was playing university football and he looked back for a pass, he would sometimes get a sudden feeling of doom or a sense of darkness a split second before he was blind-sided. He was getting that same feeling of impending doom now.

Wolfe might not be coming after Blighe and Annie. Maybe he knew they'd be protected. Instead, he's going after other women the cops couldn't predict. If he didn't have a pattern, he'd be near impossible to catch. *My gut tells me that Wolfe is more vindictive than careful.*

Devlin broke the silence. "I don't think there's much we can do during the day. We should hit the streets at about 8 P.M. I'll go out with the narcotics guys and roust the dealers. Find out if they've seen or heard Wolfe is around."

"I'll take the bars and pubs," Griffin said. "Wolf's typical hangouts."

"Alone?" Brad asked.

"You worried about me?" Griffin blew Brad a kiss. "And we've just met."

"That's not what I meant," Brad said. "As tough as we all are, we wouldn't stand a chance against Wolfe."

"I would if I shot him," Griffin said.

Devlin chuckled. "I'm okay with that."

"Come on guys," Brad urged. "Trust me. Don't go near him alone. Not even with a partner. If you spot him, call in everything we've got. Understoodd?"

Griffin crossed his arms, but nodded. "Roger that."

"What are you going to do?" Devlin asked.

"I'm going to check on the protection of Annie and Jenni Blighe," Brad said.

Griffin stood. "Let's meet here tomorrow morning. If I don't shoot Wolfe tonight."

CHAPTER EIGHT

Thursday Afternoon

BRAD LEANED AGAINST HIS CAR AND SCRUTINIZED THE neighborhood. The older homes screamed husband, wife, and two to four kids. Houses in good repair, lawns cut, and large, mature trees providing shade. There were bikes and toys left unattended. Most of these people left their doors open and had never experienced theft. On this side of the street, several apartment complexes interrupted the tranquil neighborhood. Not that they were noisy or an eyesore, they just stood out in contrast to the bungalows. The street was quiet with little traffic, except at the end of the day when workers came home, or students were finished classes. Brad chose this building for Annie. Twenty-four-hour security and the latest in security locks. It was close to Mount Royal College, in Briscoe's district, and less than fifteen minutes from Brad's house.

Brad hadn't been waiting long when Briscoe arrived and strolled over.

"Nice day," Brad said.

"A nice day is when I'm at home with the boys," Briscoe said. "This is just another frickin' workday."

"Aren't you a ray of sunshine. Do you need a hug?"

"Don't know what you're so happy about with Wolfe on the loose. You can't hide it from me—you're worried."

"Of course I'm worried." Brad straightened. "He's already struck once. He'll do it again if we don't find him."

Briscoe nodded toward the apartment building. "There's no way he can find Annie here. You and I are the only ones who know."

"And the security detail," Brad said.

"You hired them. If you don't trust them, that's on you."

"No. They're good. Let's check things out." Brad headed up the sidewalk. At the door they were met by a security guard. He recognized Brad and Briscoe.

"Good afternoon. What brings you two out?"

"Just checking in," Brad said. "Have you seen anything suspicious?"

The guard shook his head. "Nope. This is a very quiet neighborhood."

"Good." Brad reached into his jacket pocket and pulled out a photo. "Have you seen this guy around here?"

The guard took the photo. "Nope, haven't seen him. He's big."

"He is," Briscoe said. "If you see him, call 911 right away."

The guard handed the photo back. "Who is he?"

"The meanest SOB you'll ever meet." Brad held the man's gaze. "Call us. Don't do anything on your own if you see him."

"Sure."

"We're going up to the apartment," Brad said.

"She's not here."

"I know," Brad said.

They got off the elevator and headed to her apartment. Once inside, he checked that the windows were locked. He checked the doorframe to see if anyone had tried to force it open, but it was in pristine condition.

Briscoe wandered over to his side. "Looks good to me."

Brad nodded. "How often do you have cops driving by?"

"They try to come here every hour. That's not always possible when it's busy."

"Do they have Wolfe's photo?"

"You bet," Briscoe said. "Briefed them myself."

"Did you tell them who's here?"

"Come on, really?" Briscoe shook his head. "I ain't that stupid. They think it's a big wig politician. I told them Wolfe has been making threats. They're good with that."

"Sorry. I didn't mean anything. Just thinking out loud."

"You were just spouting off. There was no thinking involved."

Brad smiled. "Thanks for everything you do. I need to check on Blighe and her detail. Can you talk to Annie's detail when she comes home from college?"

"You bet." Briscoe rested his hand on Brad's shoulder. "It'll be okay."

"I wish I believed that."

CHAPTER NINE

Friday Morning

THE NIGHT BEFORE, WOLFE HAD DUMPED THE CAR IN AN underground parking lot downtown. Then he began looking for a replacement. He found a newer Chevrolet Impala. It would fit better in her neighborhood. He planned to change cars every day in case someone reported him to the cops. They'd be a day late looking for a car he'd already dumped.

Wolfe drove from a shithole of a motel toward the northwest. It was funny the things you missed in jail. For him, it was hotdogs. He stopped at a 7-Eleven in her neighborhood and bought two hot dogs and a large coffee. He drove a few blocks and parked down the street from her house. He munched the hotdogs, enjoying every bite. As much as he liked the dogs, he liked the thought of time with Blighe better. Even half an hour. But he wanted more time, much more time. He'd had plenty of time in jail to work out his plan, his fantasy, and he'd need hours with her. Just thinking about it caused a stirring in his groin.

Her car was parked outside, in front of the attached garage.

Maybe in the warmer weather she didn't bother putting the car in the garage. He'd file that away in case he needed it later.

The front door opened and the kids raced to the car. She came out, locked the door, and walked to the car. She wore a loose, untucked blouse and jeans. *That's different.* Maybe Fridays were casual days at work. That's not to say the tight jeans over her butt weren't worth watching. She got the kids settled in the back seat and walked around to the driver's side. She backed the car out of the driveway. He saw her for a brief moment as she drove past.

Wolfe started the car, about to follow her, but a gray Crown Victoria pulled away from the curb and followed. As they passed him, they didn't look in his direction.

I'll be damned! A protection detail. He decided he'd stay. He off shut the car, grabbed the coffee, and walked toward her house. He looked up and down the street. There wasn't a soul in sight. When he got to her driveway, he looked around again, then walked up to the front door. He tried the handle —sure enough, locked. He peered into the house through the front door window. The glass was beveled and distorted his view, but it looked like a closet to the right, room with French doors to the left, and a hallway leading to the back of the house.

He stepped off the porch and made his way around the front of the garage heading to the backyard. The path at the side of the house sloped downward. At the back, the lower level opened to a lawn with a swing set. The sliding doors looked like they'd be easy to open, if needed. He peered through the glass and saw a room filled with kids' toys. To the right was a set of stairs leading up to a deck. He climbed the stairs. A large window faced the backyard. He could see through to the front door. In front of him was a room with a sofa and stuffed chairs. To the left was the kitchen. In between was a staircase leading upstairs. He smiled—the bedrooms.

His mind wandered to the fantasy. He could see her climbing the stairs, ass swaying. A flash of light came from the front door, jolting him back to reality. Looking through to the front door, he saw her stepping into the house and closing the door. *What the hell?* She wasn't supposed to be back until five at the earliest. Her back was to him. She locked the door, turned, and looked toward the deck. His heart raced and he felt a twinge of panic.

He bolted across the deck, down the stairs, and tucked himself tight against the house. The door opened and footsteps crossed the deck.

She must have seen him.

He imagined her looking to the backyard. She walked to the far side of the deck, then back until she was standing above him. She stood there for what seemed like minutes. In fact, it was only a few seconds, then her footsteps retreated and the door closed.

He exhaled loudly—he'd been holding his breath. He sprinted across the yard and vaulted the four-foot fence. He didn't slow or look back but kept running and jumping fences until he was at least a half-dozen houses away. He inched up the side of a house. The gray Crown Victoria was parked in front. She was talking to the cops, her arms flying around, then she pointed into the house. They rushed in. Wolfe walked down the sidewalk to his car, resisting the urge to run.

In his car, he chastised himself. What the hell had he been thinking, checking out the house? He'd thought she was going to work. Maybe she didn't work on Fridays. She took the kids to school and her protection followed. Then she came home—alone in the house. He'd have to get into the house when she dropped off the kids and her protection was with her. Perfect.

CHAPTER TEN

Friday Morning

BRAD STOPPED AT GERRY'S FOR A COFFEE THEN DROVE NORTH. Rather than use city cops to protect Annie, Brad had hired a private security firm that protected oil executives when they traveled to places like the Middle East. They were expensive, but worth it. What's the point of having money and not spending it?

His investments were doing great. His financial advisor, Danny, was a classmate from university. Over several years of economics classes, they'd designed an investing strategy that had worked well for over five years. They started investing close to the bottom of the 1973-74 stock market crash. There were plenty of deals to be made. The challenge was knowing which stocks would rebound the quickest. They'd had a few duds, but overall, they were doing fantastic. Danny managed the portfolios now. Brad figured his kids and his grandkids would be able to get good educations without having to work. If the stocks kept going like they were, even his great-grandkids would be set.

Jenni Blighe had a protection detail provided by the police service. These teams were trained by the RCMP and assisted when the prime minister or other dignitaries were in the city. He turned onto the street that led to Blighe's house, driving slowly, checking out the homes on each side—a middle-class neighborhood with houses less than ten years old with well-manicured lawns. Overall, a nice location. Blighe's house was situated on a corner with a pie-shaped yard—narrow front yard with a larger backyard. In front, a short driveway and attached garage.

A gray Crown Victoria farther down the road caught his eye. Brad drove past and glanced at the occupants. He was surprised to see two men, suits and white shirts, in the car. Jeez, a blind man would know they were cops. Brad drove to a cross street, swung a U-turn and parked behind them. Before Brad opened the car door, the two cops were on their way toward him. Brad rolled down his window.

One cop stopped at the front of the Firebird, the other walked to his window. "Can I see some ID?"

Brad passed his badge wallet out the window.

The cop opened the wallet, glanced at the badge and passed it back. "Can I help you, Detective?"

"Thought I'd drive by and check the protection on Blighe."

"We've got that covered, sir. What's your interest?"

"I'm on the team hunting for Jeter Wolfe. Anything suspicious around here?"

"Nothing until this morning."

"What happened?"

"Blighe drove her kids to school. We followed her to the

school and back. No incident. She unlocked the front door and stepped inside. Almost immediately she came back out and yelled that there was someone on her deck. We ran in but didn't see anyone on the deck or in the backyards to either side. We think she saw her reflection in the back window. The sun was in the right position."

"Did you check the house?"

"Of course," the cop snapped.

"Why didn't you check the house before she went in?"

"Look, Detective, this is what we do, protection. I won't tell you how to do your job, you don't tell me how to do mine."

Brad held his hands in front of him. "I didn't mean any offense, just asking. I have another question."

"What?"

"Why are you guys in an obvious cop car and suits?"

"Our boss thinks it's best to show Wolfe we're here. Then it's less likely he'll attack. If that's everything, we need to get back to our job. Maybe you want to do yours and arrest Wolfe." He turned heel and walked back to his car.

Brad shook his head. *Assholes.* Two cops parked out front. That's it. No one watching the backside of the house. *Shit.* If Wolfe were here, he'd have figured out the backside was vulnerable. He'd need to talk to Devlin about this.

They sat around the table. Brad sipped a Coke. Devlin, chair leaning against the wall, napped. Griffin was marking locations on a map that he thought were likely places Wolfe would try to hide out. Some he'd already crossed out from his searches earlier in the day.

The door opened. Briscoe walked in and took a seat. He looked around the room. "I'm guessing by the looks around the table you've hit a wall."

"Yup," Brad said. "Trying to find Wolfe during the day is useless. The bars are empty, the drug dealers are sleeping, the hookers are sleeping, and the bikers are at work. Well, those who have a job. Do you have something for us?"

Briscoe shook his head. "I talked to the guys watching Annie yesterday and again today. They haven't seen anything suspicious. Except for a couple of guys who are interested in her."

Brad sat up. "What? Who? Did you run their names? Where do they live?"

"Relax," Briscoe said. "You act like her dad. Everything's cool. And yes, I did check them out. Clean as a whistle. Regular boy scouts. You might want to figure out how you're going to handle it if she goes on a date. Her protection detail fits in among the students and instructors. On a date, not so much."

"Any guy lays a hand on her and he's dead," Brad said.

"I think guys who worry about their daughters on dates were the guys on the prowl in their teens," Briscoe said. "The young lady's father had reason to be worried."

Brad looked up. "Screw you."

The others laughed.

"Do you guys have anything?" Briscoe asked.

Brad told them about the obvious protection of Blighe.

"That's one way to do it," Devlin said. "Not the way I'd do it. It does nothing to help us catch him. All that'll do is make Wolfe focus on a random target, like he already has. Or the cops will get executed in their car and never see it coming."

"Should we get some undercover guys there, just in case?"

Devlin shook his head. "We don't have the resources and

we're not at the point where the chief will write a blank check for overtime."

"So, we wait until Wolfe strikes again?" Brad said.

"We're gonna have to be lucky to catch Wolfe," Griffin said. "He's not going to make it easy. He's likely been sitting in a cell for years perfecting a plan and fantasizing about the women."

"Shit," Briscoe said. "There must be something else we can do?"

"We've got every street cop looking for him," Devlin said. "We've got every undercover cop and detective checking bars, motels, and shelters."

"We're doing all the right things, the by-the-book things," Brad said. "My gut tells me it won't be enough. Wolfe's been quiet for too long."

"What do you think he's gonna do?" Briscoe asked.

"I don't know. But it's gonna be nasty."

CHAPTER ELEVEN

Friday Night

NEAR MIDNIGHT, WOLFE PARKED THE PONTIAC NEXT TO A STAND OF trees by the MacDonald Bridge. It was an excellent place to meet. No streetlights and the bridge was seldom used. The overcast sky, threatening rain, obscured the moon and stars.

He'd found the Pontiac in the underground parking of an upscale apartment complex downtown. He unlocked the door in seconds with a coat hanger and hotwired it moments later. There were dozens of underground parking lots in the area. A ready supply of cars whenever he needed a change of ride. He left the beater in a corner parking spot.

Three days since the hooker. Five days on the run. Wolfe was out of cash and out of options. He knew it was risky contacting Slim Pickens. Two years ago, they were members of the Gypsy Jokers' Motorcycle Club. There'd been a war with the Satan's Soldiers for control of the drug and prostitution trade. Pickens was the treasurer, Wolfe the Sergeant at Arms. Pickens, a man he had fought with side by side in the biggest biker war in Canada. The man who had turned against them all and not only stayed out of jail, but became the president of the Calgary chapter of the Hells Angels. Pickens was a traitor and Wolfe would love to kill him, but Wolfe was desperate. Wolfe was begging.

A dark Lincoln Town Car stopped in front of him. The driver and passenger got out and stood by the front fenders. Wolfe grinned. These two gorillas had been hanging around Pickens for years. Made them feel important, he guessed. Wolfe waved and walked toward them. As he reached the Lincoln, the passenger pounced and slammed Wolfe over the hood of the Lincoln. The driver drove a kidney punch into his side. Waves of pain raced to his brain.

"What the f—" he managed before a second punch lit up the other kidney. Strong arms secured him while hands quickly and proficiently searched, finding his hunting knife and tossing it away. They spun him around, the men holding his arms tight.

The back door of the sedan opened and a man in a dark suit approached.

Wolfe gasped. "Slim."

"You stupid ass." The toe of a hundred-dollar shoe nailed Wolfe in the nuts.

He doubled over and dropped to the gravel. He gasped for breath. "Slim … what … why?"

"It's Jeremy now. Jeremy Pickens. I'm a businessman. I don't associate with the likes of you. You got my clubhouse raided cuz the cops thought you'd come here. I thought, no, Wolfman isn't that stupid. Then you call me on the phone."

Pickens nodded. A bodyguard's boot smashed into Wolfe's ribs.

"I will say it once only. Stay away from me and my business. Don't call. Don't come near me or the clubhouse. Don't talk about me. You're dead to me, you rotten piece of shit. The cops are swarming this city looking for you. If I see you again, or find out where you are, I'll send the boys after you. They'll cut your balls off and rip out your tongue. Then they'll kill you."

Pickens leaned down and patted Wolfe on the cheek. "Is that clear?"

Wolfe's eyes blazed, but he nodded.

"Good. Now, I am not without some mercy." Pickens nodded to his driver, who pulled a thick envelope out of his pocket and handed it to Wolfe. "A one-time payment for you to disappear. Go back east. Go to the States. If you stay, next time I see you, you're dead."

Wolfe lay on the ground for several minutes trying to catch his breath, his arms clutched over his bruised ribs. Pain still rocketed up his back from his kidneys and his nuts were on fire. As the pain lessened, his anger raged. He'd see Pickens again and it would end differently. He'd get Pickens alone. It would be a slow, painful death. He'd keep Pickens alive for days. Maybe longer. Wolfe imagined the days of torture. Oh, yeah. It would be sweet.

He rolled onto his knees, gasping for breath. When the pain subsided, he crawled in the gravel searching for his hunting knife. Then he stood and staggered toward his car.

He felt the heat rise up his neck. His arteries pulsed in his temples. He was pissed at his situation. *Legitimate businessman, my ass.* Pickens could wear all the fancy clothes he wanted. He could look like a hotshot with a fancy car, drivers and body-guards, but he was still a punk.

Wolfe opened the envelope. Thousands of dollars—maybe five thousand—enough to get him away from this stupid city. Not yet. Not before he had her. Every detail had been planned over two years. He would not be denied. Still not the right time. But the urge was there.

First, he needed a place to crash for the night. The cops would be checking all hotels, motels, and shelters, so they were out. The Stampede grounds were close. He'd find a place to park for the night. In the morning he'd figure out his next move.

It was still dark early Saturday morning when he heard the vehicle. He was stiff from the cramped sleep in the car. He sat up and glanced around, trying to remember where he was. An old truck rumbled past and stopped at the last barn. The truck door opened then closed. The lights inside and outside the barn came on. A chick wearing a plaid shirt, jeans, and cowboy boots walked out of the barn and back to the truck. What mattered were the blonde pigtails. She lowered the tailgate, lifted a bag onto her shoulder and walked into the barn. She made several trips. As she picked up another bag, he slipped out of the car.

CHAPTER TWELVE

Saturday Morning

Sergeant Briscoe was counting down the minutes until he was off shift at 0700 hours. The last hour was the hardest. Then the call came in: "Body by the river."

He arrived at the same time as the first cruiser and led them down the steep bank to the river where they found a person, upper body tangled in some bushes and legs floating in the river. At first, he thought it was a guy—plaid shirt, jeans bunched up around an ankle, and cowboy boots. A cowboy who got too drunk with the boys and came down here to pee. Then he saw the tangled blonde hair, a pink bracelet, and a small school pinky ring. Female.

Briscoe called to the cops, "Help me pull her out of the river and onto the jogging path."

They gently set her down. Her shirt was open and her bra

had been cut off. She wasn't wearing panties. Her jeans clung to one ankle.

Briscoe knelt beside the girl and felt for a pulse. "She's alive!" He lifted his radio. "Dispatch, 401. We've got an unconscious female. Tell EMS to put the gas to it!"

"Roger, 401. EMS should be there in thirty seconds."

Briscoe pulled off his duty coat and laid it over her.

He pointed to one of his cops. "Give me your jacket." He turned to another cop. Go up the bank and wait for EMS, tell them to bring lots of blankets, then hustle them down here. The rest of you, keep everyone, especially the press, away."

Maggie Gray was the first paramedic down to the river and saw Briscoe. Over the years they'd become friends and had been first responders on some of the most gruesome crimes in the city. She was a hardened veteran now.

"Hello, Briscoe," she said. "What do we have?"

"Hey, Mags. A jogger called about an unconscious person by the river. We found her tangled in the bushes, legs in the river, and we pulled her out. I got a pulse and she's breathing."

Maggie nodded. "Fola, drop the blankets here and run back to the ambulance. Get the spineboard and straps. Leave the stretcher up there but bring some cops back with you to help carry her up the bank to the ambulance."

"New guy?" Briscoe asked.

"Yup. I have my own rookie now. Rick Fola. Good kid."

Briscoe glanced over at her. "He looks older than you."

"Probably." Maggie laid a blanket on the ground. Briscoe

helped Maggie roll the girl onto the blanket, then Maggie wrapped blankets tight. "She might have been raped."

"Yeah, that's what I figured." Briscoe keyed his portable radio. "Dispatch, we've got an unconscious possible rape victim. Notify sex crimes and you should give homicide a heads up, this may become their case. She don't look too good."

"Roger, 401," came the response.

"What kind of animal would do this?" Maggie asked, more to herself than Briscoe.

"We're embroiled in an ongoing manhunt for an escaped prisoner," Briscoe said. "It's likely he's responsible for this."

"Wolfe?"

Briscoe's eyebrows raised. "Sounds like you have been chit-chatting with your roommate."

"Brad mentioned it the other morning. He and Devlin are leading the search for Wolfe. He didn't say much, but he was worried something like this might happen."

Briscoe sighed. "We all need to be worried."

There was yelling from above. A man with cameras slung around his neck raced down the embankment with cops close behind. As he reached the river, he raised a camera as a constable tackled him. They rolled into the river. The cameraman came up sputtering. "You idiot! You ruined my cameras. I'll sue your ass."

As the cameraman crawled out of the water, Briscoe extended a hand. The cameraman grabbed Briscoe's hand and climbed onto the riverbank. Briscoe swung the cameraman's arm behind his back and slapped on one handcuff, then the other. "You're under arrest for contaminating my crime scene, asshole." Briscoe pushed him toward the dry constable. "Take him downtown. Book him and seize his cameras."

Fola was back with the spineboard and more cops. They slid the spineboard under the victim, strapped her in, and wrapped her in more blankets. With the help of the officers, they carried the girl up the riverbank to the ambulance.

As Fola climbed into the driver's seat and Maggie into the back, she said to Fola, "Let's get going and make some noise. Let the Holy Cross Hospital know we'll be there in about three minutes with a critical rape victim." She waved to Briscoe and slammed the ambulance door as they sped off, sirens wailing.

Brad found Maggie in the emergency department coffee room. He took a seat across from her. She stopped writing her report and set her clipboard on a chair.

"How's the girl?" he asked.

"She's still unconscious," Maggie said. "There's no doubt she was raped, but I don't know why she's unconscious. It could have been from a number of things. The emergency physician is assessing her now. Then he'll send her for X-rays and analyze her blood. Until the results are back it's hard to say what her prognosis will be. Do you know her name?"

"Briscoe tracked down the foreman of the barns and got her name," Brad said. "Billy-Lou Hanlon. She works at the Stampede barns in the morning, then goes to school. She's training to be a barrel racer. The work in the morning pays for her lessons and the cost of owning a horse."

"Jeez, that's the shits," Maggie said.

Brad closed his eyes. His chin dropped to his chest. An overpowering sadness weighed down on him. Wolfe on the loose made him sick. Two years ago, when Wolfe was near death and tied to a post, Brad wished they'd left him to die. Now a teen was dead and another clinging to life. He vowed he wouldn't make that mistake again. Wolfe needed to die. He lifted his head and leaned back in his chair.

"Where's Briscoe?" Maggie asked.

"He went to pick up her parents and bring them here. He said her truck is missing. We've put out an APB. Briscoe thinks Wolfe took it. They found an abandoned car near the barns. He's pretty sure it's Wolfe's. This is messed up. How do I find this animal before he gets to his next victim? How does a man that size hide?"

"You'll figure it out," Maggie said.

"Not sitting here, I won't." He stood and kissed Maggie on her forehead. "Are you heading home?"

"As soon as I finish this report we'll drive to the station and then home for sleep. When will you be home?"

Brad shook his head. "I have no clue. I'll check on Billy-Lou later." He walked to the door, stopped and turned to Maggie. "With Wolfe on the loose, you need to be very careful at work. Don't take any chances. Call for police backup if anything seems suspicious."

"I can take care of myself," Maggie said. "But yes, I'll be extra careful."

Brad nodded as he left the coffee room. He walked through the emergency department heading toward his truck.

"Hello, Detective Coulter," a voice called. "Welcome back."

He stopped and turned. "Hello, Tina."

"That's Detective Davidson to you." She hugged him.

Brad stepped back. "I heard you'd made detective. Sex Crimes. Congratulations—I think."

"Thanks," Tina said. "I'd like to interview the girl. Is

66

she awake?"

Brad shook his head. "She's unconscious. Her name is Billy-Lou Hanlon."

"Okay," Tina said. "I'll check back later."

"Let me know what she says."

"You bet. I'm working on something that might help us track down Wolfe. The FBI has a new team that investigates rapists and serial killers. It's pretty new, but I've read their research and course material. The idea is that you gather as much information as you can on the cases and look for patterns or linkages. You compare what you have on your suspect with that of other, similar suspects. I'll collect everything we have on Wolfe, age of victims, nationality, lifestyle, and the details of the attacks, and put together an analysis. It might assist us in finding him."

"Good luck with that," Brad said. "We already know he likes young, blonde teens. We know he's a sexual deviant. What you're doing might work if we didn't know who the assailant was, but we know it's Wolfe. I'm not sure there's much you can add."

"You'd be surprised what information I can dig up."

"Okay, so if it is Wolfe, and I know it is, why'd he kill the prostitute?" Brad asked. "He abused Annie two years ago over weeks. The bite marks and cigarette burns are consistent with his MO. But it was about sex, domination, not torture, not murder. He kept Annie and Sissy alive."

"A man changes in jail," Davidson said. "Two years without a woman may have resulted in explosive pent-up need. Perhaps once that need is met, he will fall back into old patterns. The serious head injury two years ago didn't help. He's had time to fantasize about what he'd do when he got out. We thought it wouldn't happen until he'd served at least fifteen years of his life sentence. This will go one of two ways—either this satisfied his need for sex and violence, or this was practice for his real target."

"These attacks are random," Brad said. "One a hooker and the other a hardworking kid."

"You're right. I'm sure he went looking for the hooker, young and blonde. Billy-Lou might have been all about opportunity, but they both have a lot of similarities—they look like Annie."

"Annie's his target?" Brad asked.

Davidson shrugged. "No way to tell for sure, but she might be. He also made descriptive threats to the crown prosecutor. She's older, but attractive, blond, and slim."

"That description fits a lot of ladies, including you."

"I suppose," Davidson said. "Either he's after Annie and Blighe, and he'll strike soon, or these two attacks gave him a taste of domination and torture, and he'll escalate. Any young blonde would be a potential target. No matter which direction he goes, it's going to get worse."

"Worse than this?" Brad asked.

"Much worse. The United States has some very sadistic rapists. We haven't seen that here. Although Wolfe would be right up there with the worst in the US."

A black Suburban parked beside them. Sam Steele and Charlie Zerr, dressed in tactical gear, climbed out and walked toward Brad. Steele and Brad had worked on the Tactical Support Unit for almost five years. They'd become friends and stayed friends even when Brad was promoted to sergeant in TSU. He hadn't seen much of his friend this last year while studying law.

After returning from Vietnam in 1975, Zerr had joined the police in 1976. His training as an Army Ranger with the United

States Army got him fast-tracked into TSU. While Steele saw the humorous side of everything, Zerr was more serious with a dark sense of humor.

"Are you following me?"

"Maggie hired us to keep an eye on you," Steele said.

"And she's not paying us enough," Zerr added.

Davidson stepped closer to Zerr, holding out her hand. "I don't think we've met. I'm Tina Davidson."

"Charlie Zerr. I've heard about you."

"From who?"

"Brad."

"All good things, I'm sure." She glanced at Brad.

"Nothing but the best," Brad said.

Davidson glanced at Zerr's left hand. "No ring, but then most cops don't wear a ring. Are you single?"

"Yes, ma'am."

"We should stay in touch." Tina turned back to Brad. "And you? Still single?"

"Not if Maggie has her way," Steele said. "Wedding bells are in his future."

"I see," Tina said with a chill.

"Do you think we can get back on target," Brad said. "If Wolfe got off on this, what'll he do next?"

"As I said, he might be okay for a day or two, or weeks. He'll relive this over and over until it takes hold of him. Then he'll go hunting."

"Hunting?" Steele asked.

"Unfortunately, that's the right word—he has a type. This girl is sixteen or seventeen. So was the prostitute and so is Annie. When he gets the urge again, that's the type he'll look for."

CHAPTER THIRTEEN

Sunday Morning

BRAD AND MAGGIE WERE ENJOYING AN EARLY-MORNING JOG through Bowness Park. Lobo plodded beside them, whimpering occasionally. He wanted to run free. They'd run in silence on the first loop around the park, each lost in their own thoughts.

"What're you thinking?" Maggie asked.

"There you go, using your paramedic superpower again."

"It's not that hard. As you were running you pursed your lips, chewed your lips, crinkled your nose, and you have a pissed-off look on your face."

Brad laughed. "That sounds more like a focal seizure. See, you teach me stuff and I remember."

"So, what's up?"

"I don't know how we're going to catch Wolfe. His two attacks were random—nothing at all to link them. He's consistent in what he does so we know he's responsible for the attacks.

As far as I can tell, he's doing this alone and doesn't have any friends he can count on."

"What about the Hells Angels?"

"He'd be crazy to contact them. Pickens and Wolfe never got along. Saying they hated each other is mild. Wolfe would need to be very desperate before he contacted Pickens. He'd kill Wolfe if he contacted the HA."

Lobo raced ahead, dove into the river, and lay in the shallows, cooling off. Brad and Maggie sat on a rock.

"Are you glad you took this new job?"

"Sure, it's great. I didn't think I'd ever see Wolfe again, let alone be hunting him. I figured it would be other shitrats."

"You and Devlin know Wolfe best. You two are the right guys for this."

"Not that it's helping us right now. I don't want to think about this anymore today. How's your rookie?"

Maggie leaned back on the rock and watched Lobo. "Still needs more experience to get used to the reality of the work. It's not pretty on the streets, the things you see. I don't know how much he gets that yet."

"I remember a rookie paramedic a few years ago. She was pretty naïve about life on the street. She turned out okay."

Maggie punched Brad on the arm. "Turned out okay!"

"Ouch. Lobo, help!" Lobo lifted his head, then dropped it back in the water.

Maggie laughed. "He still loves me the most."

"Never been a doubt about that."

"He doesn't dive for rocks anymore?"

"Once we started doing attack training, I guess diving for rocks was boring. But Lobo gets pretty wound up when he's attacking Sam."

"What does Sam think of this?" Maggie asked.

"He says he hates it, but he doesn't mean that. It's his way of burning off stress and instead of jogging to keep in shape, Lobo gives him a good workout."

Maggie stood and stretched. "Should we head back?"

"Lobo, time to go home."

He stood, stretched, and shook. Maggie was the closest and took most of the water.

They kept a slow pace on the way home. Lobo caught the scent of something, probably a squirrel, and zig-zagged in front of them, nose to the ground, but failed to locate his quarry.

"So, Tina Davidson is on the case with you."

"What?" Brad turned to Maggie.

"Yesterday right after you left the coffee room, I headed to the trauma room to get some more patient information. You and Tina were having a pretty intense conversation."

"Yeah, sure. She's in sex crimes now and she's assigned to the case. She was just asking what I knew."

"You two were pretty close together. I saw Tina giving you the puppy dog eyes, 'Oh Brad.'"

"What, no, that's not it at all. Well, maybe she still thinks she has a chance, but, no way—"

Maggie laughed. "You don't need to get defensive."

"I'm not, it's just—"

Maggie shook her head. "I stopped worrying about Tina years ago. But it's fun to watch you squirm. Race you home." Maggie took off in a full sprint, Lobo at her side.

CHAPTER FOURTEEN

Monday Morning

BRAD AND GRIFFIN WERE IN THE MEETING ROOM HAVING COFFEE
when the door opened. Deputy Chief Archer walked in, Devlin
and Davidson close behind.

Brad jumped out of his chair.

"Relax." Archer took a chair. "I'd hoped that we'd have early
success in apprehending Wolfe. That didn't work out. Starting
right now you four are leading the hunt for Wolfe. Drop everything else. I know you've been doing that informally, but today
it's official. Figure out what you need—manpower, equipment,
warrants, whatever—and I'll make it happen. But you four need
to stop this son of a bitch. One more assault or death and we'll
have a full-scale panic on our hands. We keep this team confi-
dential. No fancy code names."

"Too bad," Devlin said. "I was kinda hoping for Rabid Wolf
Patrol."

Archer glared at Devlin. "What progress have you made?"

They looked at each other around the table. No one wanted to start the conversation. Brad set his coffee cup on the table and leaned forward. "We don't have much. Any place we thought Wolfe would go, or anyone we thought he'd reach out to, is a dead end."

"You're sure he's responsible for the assaults?"

"Positive," Brad said. "I think he came to Calgary immediately after escaping in Edmonton. He made a lot of threats at his trial. I think he plans to carry out these threats. So far, his victims have been random. At some point he'll go after one of his targets."

"I've talked with the RCMP. They're going to put some of their guys on this as well."

"Well, there goes our secrecy," Brad said.

Archer grinned. "As sure as we are that Wolfe is still here, I'd be negligent if I didn't let the RCMP know. Hell, he could be in Yorkton, Saskatchewan, by now."

"I don't think so," Brad said.

"Why not?"

"First, who'd go to Yorkton? Second, Wolfe doesn't run, he's too high on himself. He's having fun and not going anywhere. It's a game to him. He'll keep killing until he makes good on his threats or we stop him."

"Who do you have under protection?"

"We've got a police team with the crown prosecutor Jenni Blighe. I've got a private security team with Annie and she's in a secure complex."

Archer nodded and steepled his fingers under his chin. "Who else did Wolfe threaten?"

Brad glanced around the table. The others were perfectly

happy that Brad had taken the lead. They had no intention of taking it away from him.

"Davidson."

Archer glanced across the table at Davidson. "Maybe you shouldn't be on this team."

"There's no way you're taking me off this," she said. "Brad's not the only one who was involved in the biker war two years ago. I saw Wolfe up close, and I saw what he did to Annie and Sissy. I want his ass back in prison. Please, Chief, I can help. Outside this building I'm with a partner or someone from this room."

"I'd feel better if you had a protection detail."

"Not now. Not yet. That would slow me down. You said we needed to catch Wolfe quick. I can't be burdened with bodyguards."

Archer looked around the room. There was silence for almost a minute. "Okay. None of you work alone. Never. If you don't have a partner, you don't go out on the street. Understood?"

They all nodded.

"I can ask some of my old team on TSU if they're willing to do some extra work," Brad said. "I'm sure they'll jump at the chance for overtime, and a piece of Wolfe."

"Okay, I can live with that, for now," Archer said. "You need to resolve this, soon."

"What about going public?" Davidson asked. "Let the public know about Wolfe. We might get tips that way."

Archer stood and put on his coat. "We can't go to the media. Not yet. We've managed to keep Wolfe's name out of the press so far. But that won't last. You need to capture him fast. Once his name goes public, we won't be able to get ahead of the panic. And it'll make Wolfe extra careful."

Brad had two choices for a partner that night. Sam Steele and Charlie Zerr were the guys Brad had counted on many times. They both had military experience and were calm under pressure. Either one of them would be perfect. Brad called Steele first. He couldn't get away. His wife, Emma, didn't like regular night shifts, let alone volunteering for extra work—and certainly not with Brad. He talked Charlie Zerr into working with him. Brad drove to Zerr's house.

Zerr met him at the end of the driveway. "Are you kidding? We're going to talk to hookers in a new Firebird?"

"What's wrong with that?" Brad asked. "They'll think we're high rollers."

"Sweet baby Jesus. That's not the high-end stroll."

"I'll let you drive."

"As much as I'd like to drive, I'll leave that to you."

"Why?"

"You still look too much like a cop," Zerr said.

"And you don't?"

"At least the hookers won't see you first." Zerr rolled up the sleeve on his right arm. "Army Ranger tattoo. It's part of our cover story."

"What's that?"

"We're US military training with the Canadians at Suffield."

Brad drove toward the southeast. They talked about TSU and the increase in marijuana grow-ops. Brad talked about his new job. They drove in silence for a few minutes.

"Boss. I've got something to ask you."

"Sounds serious. " Brad snatched a glance his way. "Ask me anything."

"It's about dating."

"You're having trouble getting dates?"

"That's not it. You and Maggie both work crazy shifts but you stay together. How do you do that?"

Brad shrugged. "It's not easy. We dated for a few months about four years ago, but she broke it off. There were a few reasons, but it wasn't about shift work. With me a cop, and her a paramedic, what we see can be disturbing. We can relate to each other's bad call and can listen. But I don't want to bring it home to Maggie. She has just as many—no, she sees more bad crap than we do. That's the biggest thing—keeping that stuff at work. Don't let shift work get in the way. When you both have time off, make it count."

Zerr nodded. "That makes sense."

"Are you dating a shift worker? A nurse?"

"Yeah, I'm dating. It's early in the relationship but shift work does get in the way."

Brad glanced at Zerr's big grin. *Well, I'll be.* Tough, cynical Army Ranger was smitten.

Twenty minutes later they were cruising Seventeenth Avenue.

It was a warm spring night and they drove with the windows down and the eight-track blaring *The Wall* by Pink Floyd followed by *Against the Wind* by Bob Seger and the Silver Bullet Band.

They drove a couple of miles down Seventeenth Avenue and then back, pinpointing the hookers. They tended to stay in groups close to buildings. They'd also selected locations where cars could easily park.

The first few hookers were suspicious. When Zerr showed Wolfe's, picture they stepped away from the car and told Zerr to "fuck off." It took a while to get their routine right. The ladies seemed okay with Zerr, but gave Brad suspicious looks. They stopped at a liquor store and bought a case of beer. They emptied half of them in the parking lot and tossed them throughout the car. Then they each popped one. That seemed to put the ladies at ease. But for the next hour they struck out. Brad wondered if he'd lost his appeal. He couldn't even pick up a hooker. Ahead, a group of ladies stood against a building laughing and having a smoke. Brad pulled to the curb and Zerr leaned out the window, beer in hand, and waved. "Hey, you visions of beauty, who'd like to party?"

Two hookers looked up and down the avenue, then approached the car. One was older, with large breasts that threatened to pop out of her low-cut T-shirt. The other hooker was younger, early twenties, but already had the look of someone who'd had a hard life. They crowded close to the window. "What are you boys looking for? You gonna share a girl or are you interested in two. We could all party, if you know what I mean."

"You guys cops?" the other hooker asked. "You look like cops."

Zerr laughed and showed them his arm. "See this here." He pulled his T-shirt up to his shoulder and pointed at a tattoo. "That one's from the United States of America Army Rangers."

"You're bullshitting me," the second hooker said. "If you're a Ranger, why're you here?"

"We're training with the Canadian army at Suffield Base. I'm Sam. He's Tommy."

Brad stifled a laugh and looked straight ahead. He didn't think Devlin and Steele would think this was funny.

Zerr leaned close to the older hooker. "We got till six tomorrow morning to have fun, then back to the base."

"Call me Cher." She nodded over her shoulder. "The baby is Barbie. What do you mean by fun?"

"We've got a motel room for the night, what are you offering?"

"Two of us all night for a hundred dollars. Whatever you want."

"Deal." Zerr got out of the car and gave her fifty dollars. "You get the rest later." The hookers slid into the back seat.

"Kinda cramped here," Cher said.

Zerr climbed in and Brad pulled away from the curb. A couple of blocks up he turned right and then into a dark school parking lot.

"What the hell?" Cher pounded on Zerr's seat. "There ain't motels anywhere near here."

Brad stopped close to the school and shut off the car. They turned in their seats to face the hookers.

Cher stopped pounding on the seat and instead beat her fist against Zerr's head. "Let us out, assholes. We're gonna report you to the cops."

Zerr grabbed her wrists. "Do you think the cops will care?"

"Let me go!" Cher shouted.

Barbie was pressed tight to the side of the car, tears flowing down her face. "I don't want to die like Gail. Did you kill her?"

"What are you talking about?" Zerr asked.

"Last week, Gail drove off with a guy," Cher said. "We never saw her again. Heard she was killed."

Brad turned on the interior light and showed his badge. "We're cops. We want to know about your friend."

"We've got nothing to say," Cher said. "Now open the goddamned door."

"Not gonna happen," Brad said. "You have a choice. Talk to us about Gail or go to jail for soliciting two cops."

"You approached us," Cher yelled.

Brad smiled. "That's not the way we'll write the report. Who do you think the courts will believe?"

"If we talk to you, you promise to let us go."

"Absolutely," Brad said. "Gail have a last name?"

Barbie sniffled. "Tell them."

"Fine," Cher said. "But you'd better let us go. Her name's Gail Wilson. Last Tuesday we were working the same spot you found us. A car pulls up and I head to the car. At first I thought he'd take me. He was hands all over me. But then he slaps me and points to Gail. I didn't like this guy. He was big with wild hair and a full beard. There was something off about him. Anyway, Gail got in the car and they drove away. I never saw her again. She was just a baby."

"Have you seen this guy since?"

Cher shook her head.

Brad pulled Wolfe's picture out of his pocket and showed it to her. "Is this the guy?"

Cher's hand flew to her mouth. "Oh my God. That's him!"

CHAPTER FIFTEEN

Tuesday Late Afternoon

BRAD'S HOUSE WAS PERFECT FOR TRAINING LOBO. BRAD WALKED around the house hiding small baggies. When he was satisfied with the location of each baggie, he opened the kitchen door. Lobo raced inside, barking.

"Lobo, sit."

Lobo stopped just inside the door, tail wagging, body vibrating, and panting. Brad waved an open plastic bag under Lobo's nose and said, "Lobo, seek."

Lobo bounded to his feet, spun in circles, then sniffed under the kitchen table, jumped onto the chairs, and then headed to the pantry. He waited. Brad opened the door. Lobo leaped in, nose low to the ground, he sniffed for a second or two, then put his front paws on a shelf and sat back on his haunches.

Brad reached to the spot where Lobo had been sniffing and

pulled out one of the baggies. "Good boy, good boy. Look for more. Seek."

Lobo ran into the dining room and sniffed around the table and chairs. He moved into the corner, sniffed at the China cabinet for a second or two, then padded to the floor vents. He sniffed at one, two, then three floor vents. At the third vent he sat.

Brad reached into the vent and pulled out another baggy, stuffed it in his pocket, and rubbed Lobo's head and ears. "Good boy, good boy."

Lobo found four bags upstairs, and three more in the living room. He pulled at the cushions of the couch and sat. Brad grabbed two more baggies. The front door opened. Lobo jumped and raced to the door. Maggie stepped in. Lobo ran around her excitedly, jumping up and down.

Brad walked over to Maggie and kissed her. "Something smells good."

Maggie handed him the flat box. "Your favorite: pizza."

"That's great." Brad walked to the kitchen, set the pizza on the counter, reached into the cupboard, and pulled down two plates. "Tonight's your last night shift. Maybe you can help me train Lobo."

"I'm not letting him chase me and chew on my arm like he does with Steele."

"No, not doing attacks, he's getting pretty good at finding things. The last couple of weeks I've been hiding his toys, my shirts, and shoes. He has no trouble finding them. So today I upped his game, I hid bags of marijuana."

"Where the heck did you get weed?"

"I borrowed some from work. I'll put it back tomorrow."

"Lobo better find all your stashes."

Brad grinned. "He will."

"I'm starved," Maggie said. "Let's eat."

Brad carried the pizza, plates, and napkins to the dining room. Maggie set two glasses of milk on the table. Each reached for a slice of pizza and began eating.

"You got home pretty late last night. Did you get anywhere?"

"Got a name for our vic. Zerr and I found two hookers who saw our murder victim, Gail Wilson, get into a car with Wolfe. She hung with these two hookers. They kinda looked after her."

"Not well enough," Maggie said.

"I can't imagine what that life is like."

"Not living. Just surviving."

Brad nodded. "Now we know for sure it was Wolfe and that he was in the southeast, at least he was a week ago."

"I'm surprised the hookers would talk to you."

"They talked to Zerr. He played the military card and they bought it."

"He must have a way with the ladies."

"Now that you mention it, he was pretty smooth talking to them."

"Maybe he's back there tonight."

"Oh, don't think so. He's got his eye on someone else."

"Who?"

"I don't know."

"Did you ask?"

Brad shook his head as he chewed. "He didn't volunteer and I didn't ask. He'll tell me when he's ready. I got the feeling he hasn't dated a lot."

"That surprises me. He's a good looking guy."

"Really?" Brad glared at Maggie.

"I'm not blind. I was wrong. He's not good looking, he's gorgeous."

"If I said that about a lady—"

"I'd kill you. Right there, on the spot."

"That's what I thought."

"It's your fault."

"How's that?"

"You taught me to shoot and gave me a gun."

Brad nodded. "That I did."

"Do you have any leads on Wolfe?"

"Tina's sure Wolfe is on a rape and killing spree. These rapes are random, but they fit his type. When a woman fits his type, he'll attack. Right now, he's satisfying his perversions, and practicing for the real target or targets. We think Blighe is his target. He threatened her at his trial. Now that he's out, he's going to seek revenge on those who put him in jail."

"Is Annie in danger?"

"Maybe."

"You need to protect her. Hide her away somewhere."

"I've already got a team with her 24/7. She doesn't know that. They'll keep her safe."

"You haven't told her?"

"No sense scaring her. Anyway, I've got it covered. She'll be safe."

Maggie glared at Brad. "Are you serious? Wolfman already killed one girl and hospitalized another, and you say he's sure to kill again." Maggie's eyes went wide. "Oh my God. You're using her as bait!"

"No. Not at all. You know I'd cover all the bases. She's been safe for two years."

"What do you mean by that?"

Brad closed his eyes. *I said too much.*

"What aren't you saying? No secrets, remember."

"Okay. I've been taking care of Annie for two years," Brad confessed.

Maggie's brow furrowed. "What?"

"I'm covering her expenses—housing, groceries, tuition, books, that sort of stuff."

"Are you kidding me. Why didn't you tell me?"

"I didn't say anything because I worried this would happen. That Wolfman would get out, or other bikers would come looking for her. She's in a secure apartment complex with security. It's in Briscoe's district so he keeps an eye on things."

"You told Briscoe and not me."

"The fewer who knew the better."

"I wouldn't tell anyone."

"No, but you'd want to see her, to know she's okay—to do Auntie Maggie stuff. I couldn't risk that."

"She comes for dinner several times a month and you didn't think to include me."

"She's well protected. Since Wolfe got out, I've hired guys from a private personal protection company. They're ex-cops or ex-military. They do protection for politicians and CEOs of major corporations. Wolfe doesn't stand a chance. If he shows up, he'd be taken down by a half-dozen guys before he gets within ten feet. This way she can still go to college, and not worry."

"Are you sure she's safe?"

"She's safer than the prime minister—trust me."

"Wolfe terrifies me. He's everything vile. I hope you capture him soon."

"We have a half-dozen operations looking for Wolfe. This is only one of them."

"I'm still worried." Maggie wiped her mouth with a napkin and pushed away from the table. "I need to shower before work."

"I can help." Brad jumped out of his chair.

CHAPTER SIXTEEN

Tuesday Evening

BRAD AND LOBO WALKED TO BOWNESS PARK WHERE THEY MET Steele. The plan was for Steele to wander through the trees in the park, zig-zagging, backtracking, and crossing his path. This would be the big test for Lobo.

Brad gave Steele a fifteen-minute head start. Brad sat on a park bench with Lobo at his side. His tail swept back and forth.

It's funny how you can see clearly looking back but can screw things up in the moment. In his mind it was obvious that Annie's location was kept secret. He'd convinced himself it was best for Annie. Tomorrow he'd get Annie and have her stay with them.

Brad stood and Lobo bounced to his feet, whimpering. Brad held Steele's T-shirt in front of Lobo, who sniffed several times, then set off on Steele's track. Lobo was focused. He ignored a rabbit that crossed their path. A squirrel chirped at him as he walked past—no reaction. In the playground, kids screamed and shouted—Lobo didn't care.

Steele had set a good trail. For the next half hour Lobo followed Steele's scent. Finally, they came to a park bench beside the river where Steele was waiting.

"Holy shit!" Steele said. "That's awesome. I didn't figure there was any way he'd track me. He's got this nailed."

"Yup, that was great. This means we can to go back and work on attacks."

"Find yourself another victim. Find some keen young cop to get chewed like a raw steak."

"Maybe I should," Brad said. "It sounds like this is too tough for you, muffin."

"Screw you."

"Does it help if I say I have cold beer."

"That's more like it."

They sat on the back deck, feet on the railing, drinking beer. Lobo lay at Brad's feet, asleep.

"I love this view," Steele said.

"I never get tired of it," Brad said. "It's a safe place away from the world we work in."

"I may move in with you."

"I'm not sure Emma would like that."

"Oh, don't bet on that. Some days she'd be happy if I was somewhere else."

"So, the shine is off the marriage. What did that take—four years for her to get tired of you?"

Sam laughed. "You're a fine one to talk. When are you going to make an honest woman out of Maggie?"

"How're things at TSU?" Brad asked.

"You are so predictable. You tease the crap out of all of us, but when it comes your direction, you deflect."

"What are you talking about?"

"You're deflecting," Sam said.

Brad shook his head. "Not so. How's TSU?"

"And there's the change of subject."

"Just answer my question."

"It's not bad," Sam said. "With Knight as our sergeant things are a little—I mean, *a lot*—stricter, more military. Different from you."

"A change is good," Brad said. "Sometimes you have to change the coach."

"We didn't need a change. We were coming together nicely as a team. Then you screwed us over to be a bottom-feeding, scum-sucking lawyer."

"That's hurtful." Brad clutched his chest. "Lawyers occasionally have feelings, too."

"Not the ones I've dealt with," Sam said.

"How're things with Emma? She must be keeping you on a short leash, not letting you out to play last night."

"She doesn't make a big deal when I'm called out or late getting home. Except when she finds out I went drinking with Zerr after work she gets pissed. She needed me home last night. She wasn't feeling well."

"Is Zerr leading you astray?"

"I blame it on him, but maybe sometimes I suggest the beer."

"I'm not sure you two will ever grow up. I had hope when you married Emma, but—"

"We've got some news."

"What's that?"

"I'm gonna be a dad."

"Well congratulations. That's great. When?"

"Well, I think it was after the Saint Patrick's Day party at Devlin's."

"Not that, you ass. When is Emma due?"

"Oh, that. Mid-December."

"That calls for another beer."

CHAPTER SEVENTEEN

Late Tuesday Night

BRISCOE HADN'T SLEPT MUCH THAT DAY. TOO HOT AND THE IMAGES of the teen by the river came back in technicolor. Like she expected him to have stopped what happened. Like he should have done something. He'd given up on sleep by 1400 hours and went to his garage and loaded cartridges for his revolver. "Hot loads" he called them. A little extra gun powder for a bigger impact. Against regulations, but he didn't give a shit. He lived by the motto *better to be tried by twelve than carried by six*. It had served him well. He supplied about fifty cops with the hot ammo.

By 2000 hours he was dressed and ready for his night shift as the district sergeant. He got an update from the evening district sergeant before he went off shift. So far, quiet. The APB on Billy-Lou's truck had a few calls come in, but they were either the wrong license number or the wrong type of truck. You'd think the cops would read the bulletins given out at briefings.

Briscoe met with the night crews at 2300 hours then hit the streets. The first two hours were quiet. After coffee with a couple of crews he headed out again. He didn't mind night shifts. It gave him time to skulk around on his own. He seemed to be able to find crime most nights. Tonight was proving difficult. He gave up on the downtown core and headed up Fourteenth Street. He drove past Annie's apartment building and checked in with security. Nothing suspicious to report. Bored and grasping at straws, he headed into Glenmore Park.

He backed the van into a stand of trees across from the public washroom. After midnight, the park attracted older men looking for teen boys. At least he could chase the pervs out of the park. Over the next hour or so several cars loaded with teens parked across from Briscoe. He waited until they were out of the car then walked over. He scared the shit out of them when he came out of the shadows. He could be a mean SOB, but this was a big night for the kids. He made them dump out any liquor, toss the bottles in the garbage, and sent them packing. After he chased out the first half-dozen cars, the word must have spread as no cars came for a half hour.

Then a sedan drove in front of Briscoe and parked next to the restroom. Briscoe waited for the kids to get out, then he'd roust them. But it wasn't kids. A big guy slid out of the car, glanced back to where Briscoe hid, then walked into the restroom.

At first he thought he was seeing things. There were other guys as big as Wolfe. Hell, half the bikers were big and ugly. He thought about the BOLO, but it was for a truck. Still, his gut was spinning in circles—he always trusted his gut.

He keyed his mic. "Dispatch, 401. Have units block both entrances to Glenmore Park. No one in or out."

"Roger, 401. What's happening?"

"I'm not sure yet, I'll get back to you."

He radioed records. "I need a check on a license number." He gave the information.

"401, it comes back to a Volkswagen. That plate isn't reported stolen."

"Call the registered owner," Briscoe said. "Have them check to see if the plate is on their vehicle."

"Okay, standby."

Time dragged. Finally records came back. "The owner checked, and his rear license plate is missing."

"Thanks, records." Briscoe changed radio channels. "Dispatch, 401. Connect me to Detective Coulter."

"Roger, 401."

Time dragged again. In real time it was less than thirty seconds—in his head it was minutes.

A sleepy voice said, "Coulter."

"Brad, it's Briscoe. I think Wolfe's in Glenmore Park. I've got cruisers at the entrances."

Brad's voice changed. "Are you sure?"

"I'm in the park in the trees across from the restroom. A big dude, Wolfe's size, is in the restroom. The plates on the car don't match—they're stolen. Yeah, I'm sure."

"Hot damn," Brad said. "I'm on my way."

Briscoe keyed his mic. "Dispatch, get Detective Devlin and TSU responding to the park."

"Roger, 401."

Briscoe waited for backup. He didn't stand a chance against

him alone. Shooting Wolfe came to mind, and if Wolfe gave him a reason —

He tapped the steering wheel. Then pulled binoculars out of his briefcase and focused on the restroom door. The door opened and the man was highlighted by the outside light. Dark eyes surrounded by dark hair and beard peered back. *Wolfe!* He walked to the back of the car, lit a cigarette and sat on the trunk. Briscoe watched and listened to the radio. Both entrances were blocked. Coulter, Devlin, and TSU were all responding. Wolfe lit another cigarette from the butt of the first. It seemed he didn't have a care. He pushed off the trunk and took a few steps toward Briscoe. Whether Wolfe's eyes had adjusted to the darkness or something else spooked him, he tossed the cigarette to the ground and jogged back to the car.

The engine started and the car reversed.

Wolfe knew the cops would be searching for the girl's truck, so he dumped it, then stole a sedan and a license plate from another downtown parking lot. A smaller car would have been less obvious, but there was no way he'd get his bulk into one. He needed a place to lie low and get some sleep. The park would do for tonight. Tomorrow he'd get everything he needed for Friday morning. Maybe a trip back to army surplus, they had good shit.

Wolfe drove into the park and stopped by a restroom. He took care of business, cleaned up and headed back to the car. He loved the warm weather, full moon, dark sky, and tons of stars. He yawned but decided he'd have a smoke, then catch some sleep. He lit the cigarette and sat on the trunk of the car, star gazing. As he looked across the sky, he realized he didn't know the name of a single star. He looked for the north star. He'd heard it was the brightest. They all looked bright. He lit a second smoke and walked away from the car. Maybe he'd see the stars better in the dark. As his eyes adjusted, he saw thousands of stars. Who knew there were that many? He yawned and stomped out the butt. When he looked up he saw a vehicle hidden in the trees. He put both hands on his forehead and squinted—a police van.

Oh shit! His heart raced, his temples throbbed, and his hands twitched. He jogged back to the car. As the engine roared to life, he slid a gun out from under the driver's seat and set it on the seat next to him. He backed out and accelerated toward the exit.

He didn't look back but could feel the cops following him. At the exit, two police cruisers, lights flashing, blocked the exit. A cop stood in front of the cruiser, waving for Wolfe to slow down. He accelerated.

The cop's arms waved frantically, then he dove to the side of the road. The car struck the front end of one cruiser, sending it spinning off the road. The crumpled cruiser came to rest against some trees.

Wolfe continued through Lakeview toward Glenmore Trail, his front bumper dragging and sparks flying.

CHAPTER EIGHTEEN

BRAD RESPONDED WITH LOBO HOWLING FROM THE BACKSEAT. THEY were close to Crowchild Trail when Briscoe came on the radio.

"Wolfe crashed through the roadblock. I'm in pursuit heading north on Crowchild, toward Glenmore Trail."

Brad was approaching the intersection when a car blew the red light. Sparks flew from under the front of the car. A sergeant's van followed close behind, lights flashing and siren sounding.

Brad spun the steering wheel of the Firebird, the rear end swung around, then he accelerated. He keyed the mic. "Briscoe. It's Coulter. I'm behind you."

Two clicks of the mic in acknowledgment.

"Dispatch. 912 and 401 in pursuit of the suspect vehicle," Brad said. "North on Crow from Glenmore."

"Roger, 912."

The car braked hard at Fiftieth and turned east. Briscoe had trouble keeping up in his old van. Brad wanted to take over the lead in the chase but couldn't. It was Briscoe's chase. So, he watched in frustration as the sedan pulled away from Briscoe.

The car swung south on Sixteenth Street and raced south. At Thirty-Eighth Avenue he turned east and then north on Fourteenth Street where the speed exceeded sixty miles an hour in a thirty-mile zone.

Other police cruisers joined in behind. Dispatch directed downtown units to intercept at Seventeenth or Twelfth Avenues.

At Twenty-Sixth Avenue the car braked suddenly and Briscoe slammed into it, the back end of the van lifting off the ground. Brad swerved to avoid the collision, drove onto the sidewalk and back onto the road. He checked his rearview mirror; Lobo seemed okay.

He accelerated. The car, several blocks ahead, crossed Seventeenth just ahead of a cruiser that skidded into the intersection. Brad veered around the cruiser, the back of his car fishtailing. Next time he got close, he'd hit the rear fender and knock the car out of control.

Wolfe was at least five blocks ahead. Brad lost sight of the vehicle as it turned right on Twelfth Avenue.

When Brad turned onto Twelfth, there was no sign of Wolfe. Brad slowed, and coasted down the block, checking each apartment complex parking area for the car.

Dispatch directed cruisers into the area, closing off any escape route.

A siren chirped behind Brad and he stopped.

Devlin walked up to Brad's window. "I've got undercover cars moving through here. We'll find him."

"Yeah, well, I had him."

"We've got the area surrounded. He won't get away."

"What are you wearing?" Brad asked.

"Sweatshirt and pants. They said to get here quick."

Brad shook his head and pointed to the passenger seat. "Get in."

Devlin climbed in beside Brad.

Lobo jumped, paws on the back of the seat, and barked.

"Jesus," Devlin yelled. "He scared the crap out of me."

"I hope you didn't soil your nice grandpa pants."

"Asshole. What the heck is he doing here?"

Brad laughed and scratched Lobo's ears. "He likes to ride with me."

Devlin shook his head.

"I want this to end tonight," Brad said. "I hate that bastard."

They listened to the radio as units moved in tighter. TSU radioed they were in the area. *Sounds like Steele.* Brad cruised the avenues and alleys until they were back at Fourteenth Street.

"Dispatch, 114. We've got him. Eastbound on Tenth from Fourteenth."

Brad swung his car back onto Tenth.

"There, next block." Devlin pointed to a dark vehicle moving in the next block. A dark Suburban, lights on and siren blaring, swung in behind Wolfe.

"Let TSU know we're behind them." Brad hit the gas.

When Wolfe started to turn onto Eighth Street, the Suburban accelerated, striking the back corner of the car.

The car slid sideways through the intersection, through a fence, and came to rest against a telephone pole. The momentum of the TSU truck sent it farther down the block.

As Brad stopped, the driver's door opened and Wolfe lumbered toward the railway tracks.

Brad jumped out of his Firebird and opened the back door. He attached a harness to Lobo, then raced after Wolfe.

Wolfe had a good head start. Brad caught glimpses of him as they ran between the railcars. Brad spotted Wolfe a couple of railcars ahead. He glanced over his shoulder, then disappeared between two boxcars. Brad and Lobo sprinted to the railcar and jumped between the cars to the other side—Wolfe was gone. Brad listened for boots on gravel, but heard nothing. Lobo, nose to the ground, tugged on his leash.

"You got a track, buddy?"

Lobo barked once.

"Okay. Seek." Lobo sniffed the ground a few times, then jogged toward a railcar. He stopped, sniffed the ground, turned in circles, then crawled under the car. Brad called Lobo back and they jumped between two cars.

Once over, Lobo picked up the track and sprinted down the gravel between the tracks, then stopped ten cars ahead and whimpered.

Brad shone his flashlight under the car. The light illuminated a man crawling to the other side.

Crap.

They jumped between the railcars again. Wolfe was four or six cars ahead. *Enough of this shit.* "Lobo, sit." Brad unleashed Lobo and said, "Take him, take him, take him."

Lobo bolted after Wolfe, who looked over his shoulder once, then twice. As Lobo grew close, Wolfman stopped running. His arm swung up, gun in hand.

Oh, shit. Brad aimed his pistol at Wolfe. Before Brad could fire, Lobo leaped, and sank his teeth into the arm holding the gun. Wolfe screamed, and fired a shot harmlessly into the night sky.

Lobo clamped down on Wolfe's arm and swung his head sideways.

Wolfe screamed and wildly threw punches with his other hand. The blows glanced off Lobo's head. Wolfe grabbed Lobo's jaw and tried to pry it open—useless. Lobo sunk his teeth deeper into Wolfe's arm.

Brad took his time getting to Wolfe. "Lobo, drag." He dragged Wolfe toward Brad.

"Get this fucking dog off me!"

"Lobo, shake." He shook his head violently from side to side.

Wolfe screamed louder.

"Lobo. Out." He held tight. "Lobo. Out." Brad grabbed Lobo's collar and pulled him back.

Realizing Lobo wasn't going to let go, Brad grabbed the harness and said, "Out."

He dragged Lobo away from Wolfe.

Lobo backed away, growling, hackles up.

"Jeter Wolfe, you're under arrest. Onto your knees, facing away from me."

Wolfe sank onto his knees. Lobo jumped closer, barking.

Brad stepped behind Wolfe. "Hands on your head."

"I can't. My arms are shredded."

"Do it anyway," Brad ordered.

Wolfe lifted both arms. His right arm dripped blood.

"Lobo. Watch." He ran around and faced Wolfe, growling.

Brad picked up Wolfe's gun and tucked it into his belt.

Wolfe shifted on his knees. Lobo pounced, barking wildly.

"Get that fuckin' dog away from me!"

Brad stepped behind Wolfe, grabbed his uninjured arm and slapped a handcuff on his wrist.

Lobo growled, inches from Wolfe's face.

"Keep that dog away from me, or I'll kill him."

"Yeah, I don't think that's gonna happen, Wolfe. You don't stand a chance against him. Don't move."

Brad pulled the cuffed hand down to Wolfe's back, then jerked the other arm back and cinched the cuff tight.

Wolfe yelled, "You and your dog are dead, Coulter. You hear me, *dead*. I'm gonna make you watch while I carve up your mutt. Then I'll slowly cut you to pieces."

Brad grabbed Wolfe's injured arm and squeezed. Wolfe screamed.

"Get up."

Wolfe stood.

"I'm going to search you. You so much as twitch and Lobo will be all over you. Understand?"

"Fuck you."

"Good. As long as you understand. Lobo. Watch."

Lobo faced Wolfe, snarling, legs coiled, ready to spring.

Brad searched Wolfe, finding a hunting knife, a package of cigarettes, a lighter and a pocket full of bullets.

"Let's go." Brad shoved Wolfe toward Tenth Avenue.

A gunshot echoed from between the railcars.

CHAPTER NINETEEN

Devlin caught up with Steele and Zerr at Wolfe's car. By then, at least a dozen vehicles crowded the intersection, cops running in all directions.

"Where's Brad?" Steele asked.

"He and Lobo took off after Wolfe."

"Call him on the radio," Steele said.

"Can't," Devlin said. "The dumbass left it in the car when he was harnessing his dog."

"No sense searching as a group," Steele said. "Let's split up and each take a track."

"Sounds good," Devlin said, "I'll take two uniforms and go down the first track."

Devlin pulled out his pistol. Steele and Zerr had rifles. They jumped between two railcars and out of sight.

Devlin followed the fence while the uniforms looked under the railcars, trailing Devlin by a half-dozen cars. In the darkness it was hard to make out any shape. He peered down the fence looking for movement. Seeing none, he walked over to the rail-cars. Maybe Wolfe was hiding under a car.

He turned to a noise behind him. From a hole in the fence, three scruffy men with guns walked toward Devlin.

"RCMP, stop right there."

Devlin raised his hands, still holding his pistol, and backed against a boxcar. As he was about to tell them he was a cop, a gunshot pierced the night.

From the darkness, someone yelled, "Gun!"

The closest guy raised his gun to Devlin, finger on the trigger. Devlin stared, transfixed on the gun. To him, the finger moved ever so slowly. *This is it.*

Then a shot was fired. The burly Mountie dropped his gun and slumped to the ground. Devlin was tackled and his gun flew out of his hand.

Then the area was swarmed with men with guns and itchy trigger fingers. Everyone was shouting. In the dark, they all looked alike.

Behind them, Steele and Zerr, stepped out of the darkness, yelling, "Calgary Police Tactical Unit. No one move. Put your guns down." Flashlights attached to their rifles shone over the group. Three other TSU teams came through the fence and surrounded the scruffy group.

"We aren't dropping our guns until you lower yours," one of the other full-bearded men said.

"Calgary Police, drop your guns," Steele said. "Drop your guns now!"

"We're cops ... RCMP. RCMP!"

"We've got eight rifles pointed at you," Steele yelled. "We'll sort this out later. Now on the ground, assholes!"

The leader said, "On the ground, boys."

"Slowly set your guns on the ground."

They complied.

"Place your hands on your heads. Devlin, get over here."

Devlin picked up his gun and walked over to Steele.

"Check the fricken' ID around my neck," the leader yelled.

Zerr stepped forward and pulled out a lanyard. He shone his flashlight at the tag. "Yeah, they're RCMP. Sergeant Stinson."

Stinson stood. "I've got an officer shot. He needs an ambulance."

Steele nodded to a tactical cop who walked over to the shot cop.

"Shot in the left shoulder. I'll dress the wound, but he needs to get to the hospital."

"Dispatch, this is 114," Steele said. "We need EMS to Tenth and Eighth for a gunshot wound. He's conscious and bleeding. But he's walking."

"Roger, 114. We have EMS staged a couple of blocks away. ETA one minute."

"Roger." Steele pointed to two of his team. "Help him to the ambulance."

Devlin stomped over to Stinson. "What the hell are you doing in my city, screwing up my arrest?"

Stinson held his hands out in front of him. "Hey, buddy, calm down." In the dim light Devlin saw a red face and clenched jaw. "You shot *my* guy."

"Fuck you," Devlin said. "It wasn't me."

Stinson pounced on Devlin. Steele pushed between them and held Stinson back.

Stinson glared at Steele. "Probably one of you glory boys got trigger happy."

"Don't push your luck, asshole," Steele said. "If we shot him with a rifle, he'd be missing his shoulder."

Stinson pointed to the two constables that had been with Devlin. "Then them."

"Did either of you shoot this guy?" Devlin asked.

"No, detective," one cop said. "We were a few cars back when we heard the shot. We didn't even get our guns drawn. It wasn't us."

"That's bullshit. I want their guns, now," Stinson demanded. "From all of you."

"Not gonna happen," Devlin said. "I'll make sure they're tested and you get the results. Maybe you should check your own guys. Friendly fire, maybe?"

"You're in deep shit, asshole. You screwed up an RCMP undercover operation. When our superintendent finishes with your chief, you'll be lucky to keep your jobs."

"Yeah, whatever." Devlin sneered. "What big operation do you have going in Calgary?"

"We were about to arrest Jeter Wolfe. We were in pursuit. Jurisdiction doesn't matter. RCMP cover the whole country. That's what the 'C' stands for."

"Not into Calgary, shithead. Not without letting us know. Where's the teamwork?"

"Just following a lead that led us to Wolfe."

"What lead, we didn't know … scanners. You prick. You were listening." Devlin stepped toward Stinson, ready to fight again. "You thought you could swoop in and take the arrest."

Steele pushed between them again.

Brad, with Lobo at his side, walked up to the group, pushing Wolfman. "He's gonna need EMS." Brad glanced at the scruffy guys, then to Devlin. "Who's this?"

"Mounties," Devlin said.

"I order you to turn your prisoner over to us," Stinson demanded.

Brad gave Stinson the once-over. "Who the hell are you?"

"Sergeant Stinson, Serious Crimes, RCMP. Wolfe is wanted on a federal warrant."

"Which we just executed." Brad nodded and grinned. "Well, Sergeant Stinson, I believe *we* got our man."

CHAPTER TWENTY

FOLA TURNED THE AMBULANCE ONTO TENTH AVENUE AND STOPPED. The road was jammed with cruisers parked at all angles.

"That's a lot of cops," Fola said.

"This is what happens when a cop is shot." Maggie saw damage to the front of the district sergeant's van and a damaged car against a telephone pole. Uniformed cops stood around the car. Parked behind the car was a Firebird. Her heart beat faster. "Get the kits."

"Shouldn't we wait for—"

"Get the kits." She didn't have time to argue with the rookie. She jogged toward the car.

Briscoe emerged from the group. "Mags, slow down. Brad's bringing the suspect back. He has bites on his arm."

"Bites?"

"Yeah. I think Brad let Lobo have some fun."

"Lobo?" Maggie shook her head in disbelief. Bad enough Brad risked his life, now he's got Lobo involved. What a pair.

"Dispatch said a cop was shot." Maggie looked around the scene, eyes darting back and forth.

"It's a Mountie. They're bringing him here."

Maggie keyed her portable radio. "Dispatch, send another ambulance to our location. There are two patients."

Fola was at her side with the kits. The second ambulance drove past.

In the dim light she saw Brad walking toward her. Zerr and Steele were on either side of a handcuffed suspect. Lobo circled the man, growling.

When they got closer, she recognized the suspect. *Wolfman.* The hair on her neck stood and her heart pounded. *Thank God, they got him.*

Brad stopped beside Maggie. Steele and Zerr continued to the ambulance with Wolfe.

"I don't want to know what happened … yet," Maggie said. "Just tell me Wolfe's injuries."

"He's not too bad. Dog bites to his right arm."

"Lobo?"

Brad grinned.

They walked to the ambulance.

"Don't get too close to him unless you absolutely have to," Brad said. "Let us know before you do anything near him. No telling what he might do."

Wolfe was sitting on the bumper, hands behind his back. Steele and Zerr stood on either side of Wolfe. Lobo stood in front, growling.

Maggie stepped toward Wolfe. "I'm a paramedic. I'm going to assess you."

"I ain't done nothin'."

"Can you tell me what happened?"

"Fuckin' cops rammed my car," Wolfe said. "Then sent a wild dog after me. He fuckin' shredded my arm."

"Where do you hurt?"

"Where do you think I hurt? My fuckin' arm looks like hamburger."

"Did you lose consciousness?"

"Fuck no."

"Do you take any medications?"

"You offering some?" He leered at Maggie.

She felt a chill up her spine.

"I got a few other places I'd like you to check."

"That's enough, Wolfe," Brad said.

Lobo responded to Brad's voice, barking wildly.

Wolfe glared at Lobo. "Ah the brave cop is protecting the lady paramedic. Oh, now I get it. This is the bitch you were pounding two years ago. I see why you're protecting her. Nice. Real nice. I'd like to see her naked in the daylight."

Before Brad could react, Steele punched Wolfe, snapping his head back. Lobo pounced, knocking Wolfe against the ambulance. Brad pulled Lobo back by his harness.

Wolfe spit blood. "Looks like she's got a couple of cops she's servicing."

Brad pulled Maggie aside. "It's probably a good idea to have Fola look after Wolfe."

Maggie jerked her arm away. "Not a chance. You're coming with us, aren't you?"

"Yeah. Zerr and Steele, too."

"Then I'll be fine." Maggie climbed into the ambulance.

"Load him up," Brad said. "Maggie's gonna need a hand."

Zerr yanked Wolfe to his feet by one arm. Steele grabbed the other.

They shoved Wolfe into the ambulance. He dropped heavily onto the stretcher. Steele stood at the back door, Zerr near the front.

Devlin met Brad at the back of the ambulance. "What a fricken' mess. RCMP *were* listening to us on scanners. They hoped to scoop us."

"Who's shot?"

"A Mountie. Shot in the shoulder. The problem was we had plainclothes cops in there. They had undercover cops. No one with ID. Everyone waving guns."

"There were two shots," Brad said.

Devlin nodded. "I was facing the Mounties when we heard the first shot. I don't know where the first shot came from."

"Wolfe was going to shoot me," Brad said. "Lobo got there just in time and Wolfe's shot fired into the sky."

"That solves the mystery of the first shot," Devlin said.

"What about the second shot?" Brad asked.

"I think one of their guys thought the first shot was from me and fired. I guess it's a problem for Internal Affairs—theirs and ours."

"Wouldn't have been a problem if the Mounties had stayed out of this," Brad said. "I'm taking Steele and Zerr with me to the hospital. I'm not going to let Wolfe give Maggie any crap."

"Right," Devlin said. "I'll finish up here and meet you later at the station."

"Can you get someone to take my Firebird to HQ?" Brad handed a leash to Devlin. "And take care of Lobo for me. He'll need to take care of business and he needs water. He should probably get a rabies shot as well—he was recently chewing on a rabid piece of shit."

Brad jumped into the ambulance. Wolfe lay on the stretcher—a pair of handcuffs on each wrist attached to the stretcher frame. Maggie was cleaning the dog bites with saline and bandaging the wounds, with Steele beside her.

The stretcher frame groaned as Wolfman fought against his restraints. "Bitch."

Zerr leaned over Wolfman and pushed hard on his chest.

"Can you sedate him?" Brad asked.

"Sure," Maggie said, "but he'll be out of it."

"If he gets too groggy, I'll question him in a few hours."

While Maggie drew up the medication, Brad tried to tighten the belt across Wolfe's chest. There was no excess strap to pull.

Maggie injected the drug through Wolfman's jeans into his thigh. "Bitch. I'm gonna kill you."

"Shut up or I do it for you." Zerr slammed Wolfe's shoulder back onto the stretcher.

Wolfman stopped struggling and swearing. He glared at Zerr and in a calm voice said, "I'll take pleasure killing you real slow, tough guy."

"I can't wait to see you try."

CHAPTER TWENTY-ONE

BRAD GUIDED A WOBBLY WOLFMAN TO THE BACK COUNTER AT headquarters. Zerr and Steele stood on either side of Wolfe. The emergency physician had given Wolfe another sedative, cleaned and bandaged, and gave a tetanus shot.

The desk constable looked up at Wolfe. "Well hello, big fella."

"Jeter Wolfe," Brad said. "Warrant for escaping custody, two charges of rape and one of murder. I need an interview room."

The constable smiled at Wolfe. "A lot of cops have been looking for you." He pointed down the hall. "Take number five at the far end."

Brad grabbed Wolfman's arm and shoved him down the hall.

Devlin caught up to them. "Your dog's in my car with the window cracked. He better not crap in there."

"He'd never do that," Brad said. "He does have a thing for leather seats, though—but he's tired, he might sleep."

Devlin followed Brad into the interview room. They handcuffed Wolfman to the table. Steele and Zerr stood outside the interview room. Wolfe was still feeling the effects of the drug and was compliant. Devlin was about to close the door when he was pushed aside.

Brad turned to the commotion. "Why the hell are you here?"

Sergeant Stinson blocked the doorway. "I'm here to get my prisoner."

Brad strode to the door and shook his head. "Are we doing this again?"

"We're taking the prisoner." Stinson took a step forward.

Brad blocked him. "On whose authority?"

"I'm RCMP and I'm ordering you to turn over my prisoner."

"We're charging him with two rapes and a murder," Brad said. "Those charges come before the warrant for escaping from Edmonton Max."

Brad stepped close to Stinson. He had a few pounds on Brad, but Brad towered over him.

"How about I give you a lesson in Canadian law," Brad said. "First, a Canada-wide warrant can be executed by any sworn police officer. Second, he's in Alberta, and I was sworn in under provincial legislation. Third, Wolfe is in Calgary and I'm a Calgary police officer. Fourth, we found him, we chased him, we arrested him, and we'll see this through to court. Fifth, get the hell out of here before I arrest you for interfering with an investigation."

Stinson shoved Brad and he stumbled backward into the table. He couldn't believe Stinson would put his hands on a cop. *Okay, game on.* Brad lunged at Stinson, who suddenly disappeared into the hall. Zerr had Stinson in a chokehold. Steele and Devlin blocked a couple of Stinson's guys from entering the interview room.

A voice boomed, "That's enough."

Deputy Chief Archer pushed into the room and glared at Zerr. "For Christ's sake, let him go."

Zerr released Stinson, who gasped for air. His face bright red, his jaw clenched. "Who the hell are you?"

"Deputy Chief Archer. Why are you in my building?"

"I'm Sergeant Stinson, RCMP, Serious Crimes." He pointed to his guys. "We're here to collect that prisoner and escort him to Edmonton Max."

"Do you have a court order?"

"No, but—"

"Did you arrest him?"

"We were about to when your guys barged in. They shot one of my guys."

"Coulter, did you shoot a Mountie?"

Brad worked hard to suppress a grin. All this was serious but Stinson was comical.

"No, sir."

"Steele, did TSU shoot a Mountie?"

"Negative."

"We're not going to solve this here," Archer said. "Ballistics will determine what gun was used. Until then, you gentlemen can leave this building. Thank you."

Stinson and his team started down the hall, then Stinson stopped. "This isn't over!"

"Zerr, Steele. Escort these men out of the building."

"Our pleasure," Steele said.

Archer turned to Brad. "Let's interview *your* prisoner."

While they were in the hall, Wolfe's medication was wearing off. As Brad, Archer and Devlin walked into the room, Wolfe yelled, "Let me out of here." He stood over the table, his shackled hands limiting movement. He kicked over the chair. "I swear I'll get away. I'll hunt all of you. I'll take your women, while you watch. You'll die slowly in a living hell. I'll get off on every scream!"

"No sense interviewing him," Archer said. "Put him in cells while the crown prosecutor deals with the Mounties."

Brad closed and locked the door.

Archer stood in the hall. "By the way, nice work."

CHAPTER TWENTY-TWO

Devlin's car had not been destroyed by Lobo. When Brad got to the car, Lobo was in a dead sleep.

It was close to 6 A.M. when Brad staggered through the front door of his house, Lobo at his heels. "I hope you had a nice sleep while I was inside HQ."

Lobo stretched and yawned.

"Let's get your breakfast." Lobo raced to the kitchen, knowing he'd get a reward.

Brad filled the bowl with hamburger and rice and set the bowl on the floor. Lobo dove in, slurping loudly.

Brad made coffee and poured a cup. Coffee would make sleep difficult. But Maggie would be home in a couple of hours and she'd want to talk about the night. What the hell. He took the coffee to the living room and sat in his recliner. He set the coffee on the end table, leaned back and closed his eyes.

Brad ran after Wolfe through the darkness and fog. When he was close to Wolfe, he disappeared. Brad ran in the darkness, then saw Wolfe ahead of him. Again, when Brad got close, Wolfe was gone. Brad stopped at an old warehouse. The door was open. Brad drew his gun and stepped inside. He was blinded by bright lights. When his eyes adjusted, he scanned the room. Gail lay on a bed, bleeding onto the floor. Billy-Lou floated in a river. Annie was tied to a bed, screaming. Jenni Blighe in a courtroom, eyes ablaze in terror as she staggered back toward a wall. From the left, he heard Maggie shout, "Brad, Brad—"

He woke suddenly, Maggie hovering above him and Lobo watching him with a curious look.

"Brad. Are you okay?"

He blinked a few times and sat up. "Yeah, I'm okay. Having a crazy dream."

"You work one nightshift and you're out cold," Maggie said. "You're out of practice. You used to love night shifts."

"That was before I was talked into getting back into law. A year off the street changes your habits."

"But you studied into the early hours."

"That was different, it was all brain drain. Last night was high adrenaline and emptying the tank. What time is it?"

"Eight."

"I wasn't asleep that long." He grabbed the coffee and took a gulp. "Dang, it's cold."

"Longer than you think. I'll get you a fresh cup." Maggie took the cup to the kitchen with Lobo close behind.

"I already fed him," Brad shouted. "Mooch."

Brad took another sip of coffee and closed his eyes. barked. The back door opened and shut. Lobo barked continuously— arguing with a squirrel. He hated squirrels.

Maggie came back, handed Brad his cup and sat on the couch. "What a night. How did you get involved in that mess?"

Brad started with the call from dispatch that Briscoe had located Wolfe in Glenmore Park and finished with the confrontation between Archer and Sergeant Stinson at HQ.

"The RCMP hate you guys."

"Yeah, I know. The feeling is mutual."

"No, they *really* hate you. They were beyond furious. Their sergeant could barely talk."

"They're not good about cooperating."

"The Mountie who was shot says you guys did it," Maggie said. "Their sergeant thinks it was TSU. They're going to make a big deal about this."

Brad shrugged and sipped his coffee. "It wasn't us. There were a lot of cops there and most were in plain clothes. It was dark. Tensions were high. Ballistics will determine who fired the shot."

"The RCMP tried to get the bullet but Devlin grabbed it first," Maggie said.

"They were planning their cover-up. They can't accept we out-policed them."

"Didn't Briscoe find Wolfe by accident?" Maggie asked.

"Like I said, good police work." Brad grinned. "You have to be good to be lucky."

"You hold on to that fiction. At least Annie is safe now."

"I'll keep my eye on her until after the trial. If this works out okay, she'll never know she was in danger."

"Tell me about Lobo." Maggie pursed her lips and glared. "How did he just happen to be in your Firebird in the wee hours of the morning?"

Brad shuffled uncomfortably in his chair. "We'd been out

with Steele. I didn't want to leave him at home. I didn't plan to use him, but it's good I did. Wolfe was about to shoot me when Lobo pounced. Wolfe's gun fired into the sky, then Lobo got his first real bite. He was great."

Maggie shook her head. "I hope this isn't a regular thing."

"Probably not, but you know that over the past four years, he could have saved me a few injuries."

"More like dozens of injuries."

"I gotta get ready for court. You going to bed?"

"Not just yet. I have something new, red, and slinky."

Maggie raced up the stairs with Brad close behind.

CHAPTER TWENTY-THREE

SHORTLY BEFORE 9:30 A.M., BRAD RUSHED INTO THE COURTROOM. He found Devlin seated in the first row, behind the prosecutor Jenni Blighe. He slid onto the bench.

"Nice of you to show up," Devlin said.

"I was a little short on sleep last night—well, this morning."

"You had as much time to sleep as I did. Oh, yeah, Maggie got off shift around seven. Now I get why you're short on sleep."

Brad grinned. "Have you talked to Blighe today?"

"Yup. They kept Wolfe sedated overnight. She doesn't know if he has a lawyer. Not much is gonna happen today. This is his first appearance and the court clerk will read the charges."

"Thank you for explaining the law to me," Brad said. "I didn't know any of that."

"I just figured your mind was elsewhere and that you needed a refresher."

"Ass."

"Coulter."

Brad stood and walked over to Blighe. "Good afternoon."

"Good work," Blighe said. "I understand that your dog made the arrest."

"Yes, Lobo did."

"Is he a trained K9?"

"Well, not really. I trained him myself."

She pursed her lips for a moment. "That might be an issue. Not huge, but if Wolfe gets decent counsel they may go after that. Just be ready when we go to the preliminary hearing to answer why you had the dog and what his training is."

"Yes, ma'am."

She smirked. "You're going to 'yes ma'am' me?"

"Just being respectful."

"You know that you could be standing in my place as the prosecutor?"

"I could, but then who would have arrested Wolfe?"

Blighe grinned. "Good point. They'll bring Wolfe out in a few minutes. He was groggy until about seven, then started shouting, so expect an outburst from him when he sees you. He already spewed venom at me."

"Don't worry about me," Brad said. "The sight of Wolfe in chains makes anything he says harmless."

They turned as the back doors opened. Sergeant Stinson and two of his minions stepped in. Stinson glared at Brad, then pointed to seats on the back bench. Stinson's eyes bored into Brad.

Then the court clerk opened the door to the side of the judge's bench. "Order in the court. All rise. Judge Ethan Gray presiding," the court clerk announced.

Brad knew Judge Gray—Maggie's father—well. He'd

pushed Brad for almost three years to write the bar exams. Brad should know soon if he passed.

Judge Gray took his place on the bench. "Be seated."

The back door opened and a mid-forties man with a disheveled look sprinted to the front of the courtroom. "My apologies, Your Honor. I only now had access to my client. Kenny Bridge, representing"—he shuffled through papers he was holding—"Jeter Wolfe."

"Welcome, Mr. Bridge." Judge Gray nodded to the court clerk, who stood.

"Case 8011395, Crown versus Jeter Wolfe."

Two court guards escorted Wolfe into the courtroom.

Brad turned as a door opened and the guards pushed Wolfe to the prisoner's docket. He looked around, first glaring at Blighe, then he spotted Brad. Wolfe's dark eyes blazed with fury. "You motherfucker!" He lunged toward Brad but was restrained by the guards.

"Mr. Bridge," Judge Gray bellowed. "Get control of your client or we will proceed without him."

"Yes, sir, I uh, I'm not sure what to do."

Judge Gray glared at Bridge. "Mr. Wolfe. I will not tolerate outbursts in my courtroom. Now please take a seat and shut up."

The guards shoved Wolfe onto a chair.

"Ms. Blighe," Judge Gray said, "are you ready to proceed?"

"Yes, Your Honor, the crown is ready to proceed with the charges."

"Very well. Madam clerk, please read the charges."

The court clerk read the charges, starting with escaping lawful custody, then theft over times three, first-degree murder, attempted murder, two counts of rape, criminal negligence while operating a vehicle and assault with a deadly weapon.

As each charge was read, Wolfe's grin grew wider.

"Mr. Wolfe," Judge Gray said, "do you understand the charges as read?"

"I understand that Coulter is a pig and a dead man. I understand that the prosecutor is a slut and I will rape her until she's dead."

"That is enough, Mr. Wolfe," Judge Gray said. "Guards, please remove him from my courtroom."

Two more guards raced into the courtroom. Still, the four of them were barely able to push Wolfe through the door. His wild laughing echoed back from the hall.

Once the door closed the judge turned his attention to Bridge. "I understand that you have just met your client. If you continue to represent him, I'd suggest you figure out how to keep him under control. Are you prepared to enter a plea?"

Bridge stood and buttoned his jacket. "No, Your Honor, not at this time. We reserve our plea to a future date."

"Very well, Mr. Bridge. We will reconvene in exactly two weeks at 9:30 A.M. to hear your client's plea. Court adjourned."

"All rise."

They stood as Judge Gray exited.

Blighe turned to them. "Well, that was interesting. I'll make sure he gets an evaluation for fitness for trial before we're back here. I'll start building my case. I'll need to see you two in my office at 9 A.M. tomorrow. Good day, gentlemen."

They watched Blighe leave.

"Is it wrong that I can hardly wait to meet with her tomorrow?" Devlin said.

"As long as it's just about this case you should be okay."

"What, you think she wouldn't go to dinner with me?"

"Not if you were the last male on the planet," Brad said.

"So, maybe?"

CHAPTER TWENTY-FOUR

Wednesday Late Afternoon

BRAD STEPPED THROUGH THE DOORWAY OF THE BOARDROOM. Griffin and Devlin were boxing the files while Tina pulled photos and notes off the walls.

"Let me give you a hand," Brad said.

"An hour late and we're almost done," Griffin said. "But I'll let you buy us beers."

"Can do." Brad leaned back in a chair, his hands behind his head, and put his feet on the table. "I love hard work. I could watch it all day."

"Get your ass over here and take these boxes to records," Tina said with a laugh.

"That's a lot of boxes."

"Better get at it right away," Griffin said. "I'm thirsty for those beers you promised."

"I think I said one beer."

"Negatory, young Sherlock," Griffin said. "It was definitely beers and you're wasting time."

Brad disappeared for a few minutes then returned with a two-wheeled dolly. He loaded five boxes and set off for records.

"He's not as dumb as he looks," Griffin said.

Devlin laughed. "Don't sell him short."

"Brad *is* doing a good job, you know." Tina shrugged. "Wouldn't kill you to tell him once in a while."

"Now he's got you sticking up for him," Griffin asked.

Tina rolled her eyes and flicked a paperclip at him.

"Jeez, Tina," Devlin said. "Coulter's bulletproof. He gives as good as he gets."

Tina nodded. "This was different. It was personal. He was beyond worried Wolfe would get Annie. Wolfe threatened Maggie, too."

Devlin held out his hands. "Hey, he and his dog were awesome."

"Tell him that, not me. And I just said once in a while—not like we want him getting a big head or anything, like you two." She winked.

Tina shoved the last of the photos in a box and headed out the door.

"Aren't you joining us for beers?" Griffin asked.

Tina grinned. "Not today. I've got other plans."

CHAPTER TWENTY-FIVE

Thursday Morning

THE NEXT MORNING BRAD AND DEVLIN WALKED ACROSS THE underground parking and waited for the elevator. Each held an extra-large cup of coffee. Neither looked like they'd slept much. They stepped out of the elevator on the eleventh floor and were blinded by the morning sun blazing through the floor-to-ceiling glass. Brad turned away from the sun and glanced to the south. He still felt a sense of awe when he saw the Calgary Tower. At six hundred and twenty-six feet, it was one of the tallest buildings in the world and the symbol of Calgary. They turned, backs to the sun, and headed down a hall. Brad led the way, weaving past offices, then an open area packed with desks. He stopped outside an office and said, "Good morning."

Blighe looked up from her desk and pointed to chairs around a table. "Take a seat." She slid her office chair over to join them. "I can't tell you how relieved I am that you arrested Wolfe. He made several threats during his trial—very specific details on what he'd do to me. It was months before I got a good night's sleep. When he escaped, the sleepless nights returned. I was paranoid, thinking I was being watched, especially at home."

"He's worse now," Brad said. "The time in jail did something to him. He was always rough with women, but he's changed."

She laced her fingers together. "I know. Yesterday, as soon as Wolfe saw me, he started ranting. Little of it makes sense. He talks of violent sex, revenge, and killing."

"Maybe he found religion in prison," Devlin said.

"Yeah, Satan worship." Brad shook his head.

"He gives me the creeps," Blighe said. "I want him back in a secure facility as soon as possible. Once he pleads to these charges, we'll return him to Edmonton Max."

"That can't happen soon enough," Brad agreed. "Have you heard from the RCMP? I saw Sergeant Stinson and his henchmen in court yesterday."

Blighe rolled her eyes. "Oh, yes. Many times. From the highest levels. I'm not sure what they want. They failed to capture Wolfe—you did. End of story. They have no further role."

"That breaks my heart," Brad said.

Blighe smiled. "I want to start work on Wolfe's preliminary hearing for the murder and rapes."

"We're not anywhere close to having the evidence for a preliminary hearing," Brad said. "We won't get the blood typing results back for at least a week. Ident has a lot of evidence to sort through. Who knows when they'll have fingerprint confirmation. We need to interview Wolfe, but we may never get a statement from him."

Blighe nodded and looked at her notes. She flipped through

several pages, then sat back with her hands in her lap. "There's no good way to say this ... I need to interview Annie."

"No way in hell!" Brad yelled. "Not on your life. There's no way I agree to that."

"I know of your relationship with her, but she's an adult now. She can make her own decision."

"Don't you dare ask her. She's going to college and doing well. She has friends and can finally go out to public places. If she testifies, all that progress disappears. She'll be right back to where she was two years ago. You can't."

"I hear you. One of Wolfe's victims is dead, and the other in a coma. The evidence is circumstantial at best. Annie can testify to similar fact evidence."

"Detective Davidson can corroborate the similar fact evidence," Brad said. "We'll interview Billy-Lou Hanlon as soon as she wakes. I found a hooker who can put Gail Wilson in a car with Wolfe the night Wilson was killed. We've got time to find other evidence. You don't need Annie."

Blighe sighed. "Maybe Billy-Lou will regain consciousness. Maybe you'll find additional evidence. I can't wait for *maybes* to become a reality. You know I need to use the best evidence. Which is better? Annie, a nineteen-year-old college student, or a hooker with a long list of soliciting charges? I'm building the case now and Annie is a key part of it. I'm interviewing her next Tuesday."

"Call the chief prosecutor Vaughn Matson. I want to talk to him. He'll back me."

"I already talked to the chief crown prosecutor," Blighe said. "Matson agrees with me."

CHAPTER TWENTY-SIX

Sunday

Brad and Sam were enjoying a beer on the back deck. Lobo slept at Brad's feet. Then Lobo went from a sound sleep to fully alert and barking. The door to the deck opened and Annie stepped out. Lobo's tail wagged rapidly as he licked Annie's hand.

"I thought you were prepping me for my meeting with the prosecutor. Instead I find two drunks."

"Grab a beer and join us," Brad said.

Annie's hand came out from behind her back, holding a beer. "I already did."

"Are you legal drinking age?" Sam asked.

"Of course—weeks ago." Annie smiled.

"Wait a minute ... I thought you were nineteen then," Brad said.

Annie laughed. "For a hot shot investor, your math sucks."

"You and Maggie often share a bottle of wine."

"True, but I never drove home those nights. Didn't you wonder why I slept over?"

"I thought it was my charm and wit," Brad said. Brad pointed to a chair. "Have a seat."

Once Annie was seated, Lobo curled up at her feet. "What a good boy, Lobo."

"What a traitor," Brad said.

Annie turned the beer in her hands, then peeled the label with a fingernail. "Do I have to meet with the prosecutor Tuesday?"

"I'm afraid you do."

"I don't want to relive what Wolfe did to Sissy and me. It's only since January that I've started to live again—to trust people and go out. Isn't there another way?"

"I understand, Annie, but I don't think there is," Brad said.

"She interviewed me and questioned me in court two years ago. Isn't that enough?"

Brad felt like crap for pushing Annie to do this. He'd seen the demons she'd fought. Too many times she'd sunk so low he and Maggie were worried she'd use drugs to numb the pain. A few times they thought Annie would commit suicide like Sissy. Officially it was deemed an unintentional overdose, but Brad didn't believe that. During those darkest times, they convinced Annie to stay with them. When it was at its worst, they never left her alone. When Maggie was at work, Brad studied from home. On Maggie's days off, she kept a close watch on Annie. Over time Annie had regained self-esteem and confidence and was excelling at college. There was a chance reliving Wolfe's horror would push her back to the darkness.

Brad took a long drink. "Annie, Wolfe attacked two women

131

after he escaped. You know that. One is dead and the other is in a coma. Wolfe did things to you and Sissy that were his trademark. If the prosecutor can show the attacks on you and Sissy had the same MO, then you will be speaking for those two girls who can't."

"I don't get it. Why does it matter? Wolfe doesn't care. He'll never show remorse. He's already serving a life sentence. Send him to rot in jail."

"That's an option," Brad said. "But the parents of those girls need closure and the best way for that to happen is for Wolfe to pay for those crimes. It won't bring Gail back from the dead. Billy-Lou is still in a coma. If she wakes up, she'll have a long road to recovery. Putting Wolfe back in prison and holding him responsible for the crimes he's committed against these young women is the best we can offer those parents."

"I'm scared."

"I'll be there," Brad said.

"I don't think the prosecutor will let you into the interview."

"She won't have a choice. She has to let me in."

"Why?"

Brad smiled. "Because I'm your lawyer."

Brad came back with fresh beers and handed one to Annie and Sam. Maggie and Emma, Sam's wife, followed. They carried glass tumblers with ice and clear liquid. Maggie sat next to Brad and set her drink on the deck.

"Hitting the hard stuff today, Emma?" Brad asked. "I get it. After a shift with Sam, I need to deaden pain, too."

Emma held the glass up. "Just Sprite." She grinned at Maggie.

"She's driving," Sam said quickly. "She knows that if I'm with you I'll drink a dozen beers."

"Why is that on me," Brad said. "I don't twist your arm and force beer down your throat."

"Really," Emma said. "That's what he tells me happens."

Maggie and Sam laughed.

Brad shook his head. "So, what's Zerr up to this weekend?"

Sam and Emma exchanged a glance.

"He's, um, on a date," Sam said.

"About time," Brad said. "Anyone I know?" Brad took a drink of beer.

This time Maggie and Emma exchanged glances.

"Tina Davidson," Sam said.

Brad choked on his beer.

"Don't be sad, dear," Maggie said. "She's moved on. It was bound to happen sooner or later. Will you be okay? Do you need a minute? A tissue? A hug?"

Emma, Annie and Sam burst out laughing.

Brad's head tilted back, staring at the sky. "Oh, Mags, you're hilarious. I'd love to talk about this all day, but how about this —let's not."

"Two years ago, when Tina rescued Sissy and me from the bikers and Jeter Wolfe, I knew she had eyes for Brad," Annie said. "She was nice to me, but she lit up when Brad arrived." Annie looked at Maggie. "But you two belong together."

"Jeez, I can't take any more of this," Sam said. "Someone promised me a steak."

Lobo's head popped up.

CHAPTER TWENTY-SEVEN

Tuesday Morning

ANNIE SAT SILENTLY IN THE PASSENGER SEAT. BRAD LOOKED OVER several times, but she didn't acknowledge him. They drove in silence.

He made a left turn and parked in front of Gerry's store. "Do you want coffee?"

Annie didn't move. "No."

He shrugged and walked into the store. This was the stuff he was bad at. First, trying to figure out what a woman was thinking was a non-starter. Second, from experience he knew that whatever he said would be wrong.

"Morning, Gerry."

"Hey, Detective. Haven't seen you for a few weeks."

Brad poured a cup of coffee. "Lots of late nights. The last thing I needed as I stumbled home at 6 A.M. was a coffee."

"I saw you on TV."

"My five minutes of fame."

"You and a dog were walking that asshole Wolfe to an ambulance. I'm sure glad you caught him."

Brad poured a second coffee and added two cream and two sugar. "We're all safe now with that prick back in jail." He tossed change on the counter.

"Two cups? You expecting a rough morning?"

"Something like that. It's for my passenger."

Gerry looked out the window. "New partner? She looks young."

Brad was about to explain, then changed his mind.

"They're all looking young."

Brad slid into the Firebird and pushed the coffee to Annie. Finally, she looked over, hesitated, then took the cup.

"Thanks," she said.

"You're welcome."

"Double cream?"

"Yup."

"Double sugar?"

"Yup. Just the way you like it. A double-double. Ha! That's what they should call it."

Annie frowned and turned away.

Brad pulled out into the early rush-hour traffic. He thought about turning on the radio just to have a little noise in the vehicle. Instead, he said, "I'm not good at this. I don't know whether to leave you alone or ask questions. I can see you are worried. What can I do?"

Annie took a sip of coffee. "You're doing it."

"What?"

"You're here with me. You're staying with me. I am scared. I don't want to do this. But I know I'm safe when I'm with you."

Not the answer Brad expected. Again, he didn't know what to say. "You'd be safer if Lobo was here, too."

Annie smiled. "He likes me a lot."

"So I've noticed," Brad said. "He'd do anything for you and Maggie."

"He loves you, too. He took Wolfe down when Wolfe tried to shoot you."

"That he did. But, in his mind, his number one job is protecting you two. I guess he figures the two of you are more valuable."

"Or, he knows you can take care of yourself."

"Maggie might disagree. Still, it's nice to know he has our backs."

Annie turned back to the window and sipped coffee.

———

They took the elevator to the eleventh floor where the crown prosecutors had their offices. A dozen young lawyers were crammed into a space big enough for four. When Brad had worked here for Vaughn Matson, Brad had been relegated to the gopher farm. A prosecutor would come out of an office, shout a name and the young lawyer would pop their head up and get their orders.

As they passed Matson's office, Brad looked in but the room was unoccupied. They continued down the hall to Jenni Blighe's office. He knocked on the door.

"Come in."

Brad stepped aside and let Annie enter first.

Blighe stood and offered her hand. Annie shook Blighe's hand then slumped into a chair.

"Counselor," Brad said.

Blighe smiled. "Counselor. I'll probably be about two hours with Annie, so talk to the kids in the gopher farm or go grab a coffee."

"Actually, I'm staying."

"I'd rather talk to Annie alone."

"I know. But I'm here officially. I'm her lawyer."

"What?" Blighe said. "I can think of a dozen reasons that's unethical. Please let me—"

"If he doesn't stay, then I don't." Annie folded her arms across her chest.

Blighe looked from Annie to Brad and back and realized she wouldn't win the fight. She pointed to a chair. Brad sat, suppressing a grin.

"Annie, I'll try to make this as informal and short as I can. I have some questions that will be tough on you. I apologize in advance. If at any time you need a break, let me know. Can I get you anything?"

"Nope. Let's get this over with."

Blighe nodded. "Please state your name."

"Annie Hilliard."

"How old are you?"

"Eighteen."

"Are you familiar with a man named Jeter Wolfe?"

Annie swallowed hard. "Yes."

"How do you know him?"

"He held me captive in the Gypsy Jokers' Clubhouse and raped me."

"How many times did he rape you?"

"I don't know—almost every night. Sometimes more than once a night. Sometimes he brought other bikers and they took turns."

Annie's knees were bouncing, and she clasped her hands so tight they turned white. Brad didn't need to intervene yet, but it was getting close.

"You're doing great," Blighe said. "I have some specific questions. Are you okay to continue?"

"I think so."

"Good. Besides the rapes, it's my understanding that Wolfe did other specific things. Can you tell me what they were?"

"You mean the cigarette burns and bites?"

"Yes."

Annie slumped and looked at her hands. "When he was really drunk or high, he'd bite me—my breasts, the inside of my thighs, and my … my ass."

"And the cigarettes?"

"When he was done, he always had a smoke. Sometimes he'd sit on the edge of the bed and didn't say or do anything. After he finished the cigarette, he'd leave. But if he was furious, he raped me hard and then burned me with the cigarette. He'd light a second one, usually from the first. He'd pin me onto the bed. He'd get the tip red hot and then burn me. He got off on my screaming. Sometimes, he used several cigarettes —" Annie started crying.

Blighe handed her a tissue and said, "Are you okay? Do you want a break?"

Annie shook her head. "I want this done. He did other things."

"What was that?" Blighe asked.

"At the start, I fought him, but that got him more excited. So,

I stopped fighting but that made him furious. He wanted me to fight. If I didn't, he'd beat me." Tears flowed in a steady stream.

"Thank you, Annie, now—"

Annie stood. "I need a bathroom."

"Sure," Blighe said. "Straight down the hall."

Annie left the office.

Brad and Blighe sat in silence. Blighe looking at her notes, Brad fuming.

"You've got what you need," Brad said. "Let her go."

Blighe shook her head. "Not yet. I need to know if there was anything else. We don't have the forensics results from either the murder or rape. We won't get much from the rape of Billy-Lou. Any evidence there might have been was washed away in the river. If Billy-Lou doesn't regain consciousness, then Annie is the only link to Wolfe. I need to know everything if I'm going to push for similar circumstances."

"You've got fifteen minutes."

"That's not enough time."

"That's all you get. It took almost two years for Annie to move past what Wolfe did. She still has nightmares. Now you've opened closed wounds. I know you need to do this interview, but I think you've already got what you need. To prove similar circumstances."

"Based on what? Your vast experience as a trial lawyer?"

"Nice shot." Brad glared at Blighe. "It's based on me being with her on her darkest days. I don't want to see her go back there. I want Wolfe in jail until he dies. But today the cost is too high. You can use fifteen minutes or not. Up to you. But I'll shut this down and we'll leave the second I think you've pushed her too hard."

Annie walked in and took her seat.

"Ms. Blighe has decided she's almost done," Brad said. "Fifteen minutes or less."

Blighe scowled at Brad. He ignored her.

"Okay," Annie said. "I can do fifteen minutes."

CHAPTER TWENTY-EIGHT

Wednesday

WOLFE SAT ACROSS THE DESK FROM THE PSYCHIATRIST. *THEY'RE ALL the same,* Wolfe thought. Low, methodical speech, gray beard, and a stupid-looking tweed jacket with leather patches on the elbows. Wolfe looked around for a pipe. Paintings covered the walls. Just paint splattered on canvas. No doubt each represented some inner turmoil or repressed memory. He was learning the lingo. To him, they looked like the work of five-year-olds.

Wolfe was dressed in a white hospital shirt, pants and slippers. His hands and legs were shackled, with a chain connecting the two. At the door, two burly hospital orderlies stood guard.

This guy was the third psychiatrist to interview in the last three weeks. Was three some magical number? He'd practiced on the first two. He was ready for this one.

"Mr. Wolfe. Let's talk about your childhood," Professor Van Dyke said. "Would you say it was happy?"

Wolfe glared. "Fuck you."

"It is important that I understand your upbringing. Then we can work on the reasons you are here. Please bear with me. Tell me about your family."

Wolfe stared. Maybe this was the time to give him a little. Not a lot. But enough to explain how disturbed he was. "My father was a drunk and my mother was a slut."

"Please expand."

Wolfe thought carefully about his next words. "He was around when I was young. Maybe eight. He was a big guy. I guess I get the size from him. He'd come home drunk and stagger around the house. If I was awake, he'd be nice then hit me. When I cried, he told me to toughen up. Then he'd laugh and go to his bedroom. We'd hear Mom screaming from the other room and Dad laughing. I'd hide under the covers in the room I shared with my older sister. Later, he came out and was in a better mood."

"Your mother?"

"She never came out after Dad went in. The next day she had bruises or cuts."

"Did she ever talk about it?"

"Nope."

"How long did this go on for?"

"I don't know. When I was nine or ten, he left for a couple of years. I didn't get beaten, but Mom had other men over. Same thing. She'd be screaming and crying."

"What happened when he came back?"

"Same stuff with Mom. Except he started coming to our room."

"The room you shared with your sister."

"Yeah."

"What happened then?"

"He'd tell me to get out of the room. At first, I did, and I sat in the dark in the living room, listening. Then I got curious. So, I'd leave the bedroom, but leave the door ajar. Then I'd sneak back and watch from the door."

"What did you see?"

"He was on top of my sister. She tried to stop him. He liked that and laughed louder."

"How did you feel about your father hurting your sister?"

"Nothing at first. I figured she was old enough now, that it was time for her."

"How old was she when your father starting attacking her?"

"Twelve."

"How old were you?"

"About ten."

"What did you do?"

"Nothing. But I felt strange. There was excitement throughout my body."

"How did you feel about that?"

"I loved it. I watched whenever I could."

"Why did you like it?"

"Because I was learning how to handle women. I saw the power he had over them. I saw his excitement. I wanted that."

"Why did you want power?"

"Because it was a gift from Satan. Men are meant to rule. Especially over women. That's true power. Satan provided women for men to use."

"Why does ... *Satan* want you to have power?"

"Because I am his son!"

"You're the son of Satan?"

"Yes. I'm the heir. I will rule this world. The women will be mine and the men shall die. It is decreed." Wolfe struggled out of his chair. "Now it's your time." Wolfe dove across the desk. The guards dragged him onto the floor. The doctor shouted for a sedative.

Wolfe smiled. Soon the play would enter the final act. *God, manipulating these clowns is too easy.*

CHAPTER TWENTY-NINE

Thursday

BRAD, TINA, AND DEVLIN SAT BEHIND JENNI BLIGHE. JUDGE GRAY was seated and court was in session for Jeter Wolfe's second appearance.

"Before we begin, Mr. Bridge, you wish to address the court?" Judge Gray asked.

Bridge stood and buttoned his coat. "Yes, Your Honor. I have tried to interview and counsel my client over the past two weeks. At no time was I able to have a coherent conversation with him. I don't know if he understands the charges. I don't know if understands he needs to enter a plea. I have seen his psychiatric assessment, as has my learned colleague, and the three psychiatrists have consensus that Mr. Wolfe is having some sort of mental health breakdown. He believes he is the son of Satan."

"Thank you, Mr. Bridge. Ms. Blighe?"

Jenni stood. "Your Honor. I have read the reports from the psychiatrists and I have witnessed Mr. Wolfe's nonsensical outbursts. Frankly, I do not believe he is having a breakdown or that he thinks he's the son of Satan. I believe that faking a mental breakdown is part of his plan. This is theater to him. He does not want to go back to jail and has contrived this theater to remain in psychiatric care. It is obvious that he has been able to sway three professionals with his act. We should not, no, cannot get caught in this farce perpetrated by Wolfe."

Brad felt like clapping.

Bridge was on his feet. "Your Honor, does my colleague mean to say that she is better qualified than three experienced professionals with doctorates in psychiatry?"

"Ms. Blighe?" Gray asked.

"No, Your Honor, I am not better qualified in psychiatry. However, I am familiar with the criminal mind and the lengths they will go to ensure they are not incarcerated. If I may, the mistake the psychiatrists and my colleague are making is thinking that Wolfe lacks intelligence, that he is simple and slow. Nothing could be further from the truth. He is clever, deceitful, devious and manipulative. He knows exactly what he is doing."

"Thank you, Ms. Blighe." Judge Gray rubbed his eyes and sighed. "Thank you both for your comments. I would find it difficult to overrule the psychiatrists. Let's bring in Mr. Wolfe and see if he wants to enter a plea today." He nodded to the bailiff.

Brad turned to Tina. "I've got a bad feeling about this."

"Me too," she replied.

A couple of minutes later four guards escorted Wolfe into the courtroom. Brad was relieved to see that the shackles were in place on his hands and feet. Wolfe stared straight ahead.

"Mr. Bridge, do you wish to talk to your client?"

"Yes, Your Honor." Bridge walked over to Wolfe and whispered. Wolfe continued staring ahead, a blank expression on his face. He showed no reaction to Bridge. Shortly after, Bridge returned to his table. "Mr. Wolfe does not respond to my questions."

"Very well." Judge Gray turned in his seat toward Wolfe. "Jeter Wolfe, the court clerk will read the charges."

"Jeter Wolfe, you are charged with escaping lawful custody, then auto theft times three, first-degree murder, attempted murder, two counts of rape, criminal negligence while operating a vehicle, and assault with a deadly weapon. How do you plead? Guilty or not guilty?"

Wolfe's head slowly turned to the judge. "You ask me if I'm guilty? You're guilty!"

Wolfe's sudden outburst caught everyone by surprise. His guards took an involuntary step backward.

"Did I kill anyone? Did anyone see me do it? Did I assault anyone? Do you have proof?" Wolfe pointed to Blighe, and when he spoke his voice thundered in the courtroom. "You're mine! I've got it all worked out. For two years I woke up every day in jail planning our time together. The fantasies will be reality. I'll come for you, you bitch."

Wide-eyed, he scanned the courtroom then back to Blighe.

"I don't hate you, I could never do that. You misunderstand me. But I say this, we will be together. They can't keep us apart. They will go crazy trying to stop me. I see the future. You are mine and cops will die!"

"Mr. Bridge, control your client."

Bridge jumped to his feet and raced over to Wolfe, who lunged at him. Bridge backpedaled. The guards reached for Wolfe but he stepped aside. "The demons in my head tell me what to do. They whisper: revenge, revenge, revenge! Pain's not bad, it's good. If you're going to do something, do it well, enjoy it and leave others terrified! Do you think I should be remorseful? For what? You persecute me—want to crucify me! Doesn't that give me equal right to crucify you?"

Wolfe tried to shake the guard free.

"I'm one of the most dangerous men in the world. Those fearful that I might someday be released, should be terrified. I will escape and you will all pay! My life is not important here." Wolfe pointed at Tina. "You should fear for your life. I'll come for you, bitch. You'll die slow until you beg to be dead."

Wolfe smirked at Brad.

"You can't save everyone, Coulter," Wolfe spat. "From the world of darkness, I loose demons and devils to torment and drive you crazy and then you will kill yourself."

"Jeter Wolfe, be silent or I will have you removed from the courtroom," Judge Gray said.

"I'll have *you* removed if you don't stop this circus," Wolfe said. "You cannot hold me, you cannot punish me."

Judge Gray stood. "Remove the prisoner from my courtroom!"

The guards dragged Wolfe toward an open door. Wolfe screamed in devilish laughter.

Judge Gray sat and rubbed his eyes again. There was silence in the courtroom, the only sound a clock ticking on the wall.

Brad's heart pounded. He stared at Judge Gray and silently said to himself, "No, please no."

Judge Gray lifted his head and leaned forward. "Based on the report from three psychiatrists and Jeter Wolfe's outburst, I have no choice but to refer him for a thirty-day psychiatric evaluation."

CHAPTER THIRTY

Late Afternoon

BRAD STOOD OUTSIDE THE DOOR TO THE ST. LOUIS HOTEL BAR. Run down as it was, four years ago TSU adopted it as their debrief bar. Probably the chicken and chips. The team had changed quite a bit, but Brad had remained friends with Steele and Zerr.

He opened the door and headed down the stairs. Zerr and Steele were already there, a tray of draft on the table.

"About time, boss," Zerr said. "Thought you'd forgotten about us."

"Never." He sat and grabbed a beer.

"Well, that piece of shit is off the street, again," Steele said. "Good work." He held his glass out, and they tapped their glasses. "Do you know who shot the Mountie?"

"The ballistics report hasn't been released." Brad took a fortifying gulp of his beer.

"I have it on good authority," Zerr said, "that the bullet is Mountie issue. None of us carry a Colt 1911."

"Well, that should shut the Mounties up," Steele said.

"I hear the Mounties have a new motto." A big grin spread across Zerr's face.

Wait for it, Brad thought.

"What's that?" Steele asked.

The comedy team. The straight man Steele and comedian Zerr.

"Stop ... or I shoot the Mountie."

Brad shook his head and laughed. Black humor was a mainstay of policing. Sometimes it was the only way you could distract yourself and avoid thinking about what you saw on the job. Brad knew about the demons stored in his brain. They came out at night, vivid and real.

"That was a real cluster," Brad said. "We're lucky that first shot didn't start everyone shooting."

"That was just dumb luck," Steele said. "Dark railway tracks in the middle of the night. Bad enough we didn't know who Devlin had there, let alone Mountie UC guys we didn't even know were there."

"To dumb luck." Zerr raised his glass and they clinked again.

Brad looked at his friends. Over a beer it was fine to say dumb luck, but they were a good team. Well trained and disciplined. Even during an event that was in motion, they did their jobs, backed each other ,and didn't get caught up in all the peripheral shit. He missed them, but they were doing fine without him.

"Boss, hey, boss, you kinda zoned out there. You okay?"

"Yeah, sorry. What'd you say?"

"We were wondering if they'd tied Wolfe to the two rapes and the murder yet?"

"Not yet, but there isn't much doubt. I talked to Blighe after court today. She's going to prosecute for the escape from prison and then a preliminary hearing on the murder and rape. Then she'll take her time constructing a solid case on the murder and rapes. Blighe wants to put him away for life, no chance of parole."

"Blighe, the cute blond with short hair?" Zerr asked.

"Out of your league," Steele said. "You're playing single A ball and she's in the big leagues."

"I said she was cute, that's all." Zerr smiled. "You can't blame a guy for wishing. I'd let her cross-examine me."

"Can't argue with that," Steele said.

"You'd have to compete with Devlin," Brad said.

"Like that's a challenge," Zerr said.

It was like watching a family dinner. The kids picking on each other. All in good fun.

"So, I, um, have something to tell you."

"You and Maggie are getting married," Steele said.

"I knew it." Zerr nodded.

"Congratulations, boss," Steele said.

Brad held up his hands in surrender. "Slow down, that's not it."

"You dying, boss?" Steele asked.

"Would you guys shut up and listen. I got a letter today. I passed the bar. I'm officially a lawyer."

Steele grabbed a beer and raised his glass. "That's great, boss, or should I say counselor? Will you still drink with us lowly cops?"

"You guys are jerks. Yes, I'll still let you buy me beer."

"Screw the beer," Steele said. "We need to celebrate. Drinks, real drinks like rum, on me all night."

"I'd love to, guys, but I gotta get home."

"You might not be married, but you act like it," Steele said. "Call Maggie and tell her you're out with us, celebrating. She'll understand."

"I gotta go, too." Zerr stood.

"What the—" Steele stared at Zerr.

"Raincheck, guys," Brad said. "I've been away a lot this last month. I promised Maggie I'd be home early. I'm exhausted. But I'll hold you to the promise of rum. You guys stay safe."

"Will do, boss … counselor," Steele said.

Brad parked, walked up the sidewalk, unlocked the door, and stepped inside. Lobo greeted him, tail wagging.

"Hey, buddy. I'm glad to see you, too." He stepped back and stared at Lobo. Black and white ribbons were tied around his neck. "What the hell is with the ribbons? Maggie, what did you do to my dog?"

No answer. Lobo bounced happily at his side as he headed for the kitchen. Brad stopped. The blinds in the dining room were down and the lights off. Candles gave the room a soft glow. The dining room table was set with his grandmother's China and silver cutlery.

A set of court robes hung from the door. Then the stereo blasted *Pomp and Circumstance*. Lobo raced back into the room wearing a cape that looked like the robes hanging from the door.

Maggie followed Lobo into the dining room. "Welcome back, counselor." She stepped close for a kiss, then hugged Brad. "I'm so proud of you."

"How did you know? The letter came today. I was going to

surprise you tonight. Oh, wait. Your father, right?" Maggie's father had pushed Brad for three years to write the bar exam. It wasn't surprising Ethan had a contact in the Bar Association who gave him the news.

"Sit," Maggie said. "I'll bring you wine."

Lobo sat, tail wagging and eyes glued on Brad. "Were you in on this, buddy?" Lobo cocked his head. "Yeah, I'm sure you were."

Maggie came back with the wine. They clinked glasses and Maggie said, "You worked hard for this. I'll be back with dinner." She set plates of salad on the table along with Brad's favorite meal—meat and potatoes.

"This is great. Thank you."

"I'm glad you like it," Maggie said. "Are things finally going to settle down?"

"I think so. Wolfe will undergo a thirty-day psych assessment. If they find he's crazy, he'll be locked up in a mental hospital for fifteen or twenty years. If they say he's sane, then it's life in prison—at least twenty-five years with no parole. Either way he's out of our hair forever."

"Then what?" Maggie asked.

"Then Devlin and I will go after some other scumbag and throw him in jail as well. But I doubt the next guy will be as violent and remorseless as Wolfe."

"I still get chills when I think of him," Maggie said. "As long as this guy is still breathing, he's a killer waiting to kill."

"We don't have capital punishment. A life sentence is the biggest punishment we'll get."

"I know," Maggie said. "Annie's still shook up. It's going to take a while for her to get over this."

"I know. But she's got Auntie Maggie to watch out for her."

"And you."

"Oh yeah, I'll kill the next guy who messes with her."

"She knows that. That's probably why she hasn't told you about a guy at college she likes."

Brad dropped his fork onto the plate. "What? She never said anything to me."

"Of course not. She knows you'd react like you just said you would. You'd run his name, set up stakeouts. Then you'd get Steele and Zerr to go with you on a covert mission to scare him away."

"Okay, Mags, now you're just exaggerating," Brad said. "I'd just take Zerr."

Maggie shook her head. "Will you be that way with our kids?"

"Worse. Locked room until they're twenty-five. Maybe thirty. Have you ever heard of waterboarding? It would be perfect for ensuring any boyfriend would be respectful."

Maggie rolled her eyes.

They finished dinner and cleaned. "Just leave the dishes, I'll do them later." Maggie poured two glasses of wine, took his hand and led him to the living room.

"I have another surprise."

This room was lit with candles, too, with one addition: blue and pink balloons.

Brad's jaw dropped. "What … the balloons … does this mean …?"

Maggie drew Brad tight. "You are not only a card-carrying, robe-wearing lawyer, but you're also about to be a dad!"

CHAPTER THIRTY-ONE

A MONTH LATER

Monday

EDWORTHY PARK WAS A HALF SQUARE MILE OF WILDERNESS IN THE southwest part of the city. It was a favorite for hiking, biking, and dog walking.

Brad parked at the top of a hill next to a half-dozen marked cruisers. He jogged down the hill toward the police tape and a mass of cops. Griffin stepped away from the group.

"Dump site for some fuckwad," Griffin said.

"Nice to see you, too. What do you need me for?"

"Oh, it's what I'm doing for you."

"Cut the crap, tell me."

"You've got warrants out for three shitheads who jumped bail. You've got a missing dealer, Marcus Alvarez. I think this is your missing scumbag."

"Why do you think that?"

"Excellent police work," Griffin said.

"Bullshit."

"Okay, maybe a small part was good detectiving."

"Did you find ID?" Brad asked.

"No ID, but the timeline fits. He's been here about a week." Griffin nodded toward a man talking to a uniformed cop. A dog sat impatiently watching the conversation. "He's walking his dog this morning and the dog bolts. He chases the dog down here. The dog scrambles into the trees to a clearing and starts digging. The dog's tugging on something. The guy looks—it's a jacket—with an arm still in it. He hoofs it up the hill, drives home, and calls us. He meets the first cruiser, leads the cops down here. They confirm it's a body. Fuckin' amazing, the quality of guys on the street. Anyway, they protect the scene, I get the call and get Ident on the way."

"Makes sense," Brad said.

"What made you think Alvarez was missing and those three guys had something to do with it?" Griffin asked.

"Good detectiving." Brad grinned. "Devlin and I were looking for these three assholes after they skipped bail on aggravated assault charges two weeks ago. Last week, Alvarez went missing. His family was concerned but we didn't put resources to it. Then witnesses, other drug dealers, told Devlin they saw Alvarez grabbed on the street and thrown in a van which sped away. They described the van as green, old, with a badly dented passenger fender and a peace sign on the window of the side door. They described two of the guys who hauled Alvarez into the van."

"Where's Devlin?" Griffin asked.

"He's been skulking around the streets at night talking to his snitches, dealers, and hookers, trying to find out where those three are hiding."

"He takes the night shift and you take the day shift."

"Something like that," Brad said. "Are you assigned to this homicide?"

"Yup. Meet me tomorrow morning at the autopsy and I'll fill you in on what we find today."

"Oh great, I get to watch a week-old corpse being filleted– let's do it before breakfast."

Brad waited in the parking lot until the last minute, then strolled to the front door of the Medical Examiner's Office. He could handle all other aspects of the job, but autopsies got to him, right from his first autopsy in recruit training. Blood and guts on the street were fine, but there was something about the slow pace, the dissection of a body, and the odors that sent his head spinning.

With reluctance, he opened the door and entered the reception area.

"Detective Coulter for the John Doe autopsy. The Edworthy Park homicide—John Doe."

"Suite 2."

A door buzzed and Brad walked down a white hallway. Everything was white—the walls, the doors, even the floors. Griffin stood outside Suite 2. "You're just in time." Griffin pushed away from the wall and pulled open the door to Suite 2.

The overpowering odor of antiseptic cleaner oozed from everywhere. His head spun.

"Didn't expect to see you here," Sergeant Sturgeon said. "Let me get a padded mat for when you fall."

"I'll be fine," Brad said.

"I'd never have picked you for a queasy stomach," Griffin said.

"Let's get this over with."

"Seriously, Coulter," Griffin said. "If this is your guy, and you arrest those three dickheads, you clear this murder for me."

"I do the work and clear your case."

"Exactly–it's perfect."

Sturgeon nodded to a man entering the room. "Medical examiner. Showtime."

Brad stared blankly as the 'Y' cut was made, closed his eyes when the ribs were cut, and plugged his nose when the bone saw cut the cap of the cranium. He was no expert, but the back of the brain was mush, that much he did know—not consistent with life. Consistent with a gunshot to the back of the head, though. The ME glanced at the X-rays illuminated on the wall, selected a pair of forceps, and extracted a piece of lead. He rinsed the lead with saline and deposited it in an evidence bag.

"I'll take that." Brad was eager for the opportunity to leave. "I'll get that over to forensics and put a rush on identification."

"Without a murder weapon, you won't get much," Sturgeon said. "I can take it after the autopsy."

"You've got enough to do. I don't mind."

Sturgeon and Griffin glanced at each other and grinned.

CHAPTER THIRTY-TWO

Monday

JETER WOLFE LAY ON HIS BACK, STARING AT THE CEILING. HE WAS running out of time. His return to court was in two days. To make it worse, tonight was the fat orderly's last shift until Wednesday—too late.

Except for his mandatory counseling sessions, he was in this room. He exercised as best he could, push-ups, sit-ups, and stretching. He ate in this room. Prison had more freedom, and a gym. Mostly he stared at the ceiling, scheming.

Getting sent to the psych ward for a mandatory thirty-day assessment had been part of his plan. Now he wasn't so sure; escaping would not be easy. Whenever he was out of his room, two orderlies accompanied him. Big guys. Not as big as he was, but the two of them would be a handful. One orderly wore a permanent scowl, and the only thing he ever said was, "Shut the fuck up." He was Wolfe's kinda guy.

The other orderly was like a big teddy bear. He was in awe of Wolfe and begged him to tell stories of his biker days. Wolfe wasn't sure how yet, but this orderly was the key to getting out. If he failed, he'd be back in maximum security, isolated in his cell twenty-three hours a day.

Wolfe put the escape aside for now. He'd rather think about that bitch, Jenni Blighe. The fact she locked him up again made her more desirable. Somehow it added to the fantasy. Before, he planned to spend an hour or two with her, having his version of fun, then killing her. Now, he wanted to take his time, all day. Fridays she was home alone for at least six hours. He'd like a few days, but six hours was better than lying on this bed thinking about all the things he would do to her. The risk of moving her somewhere else was too high. He didn't need the cops stopping him and finding her in the trunk.

Wolfe had made big mistakes during his short freedom. Aside from the fact the cops got lucky finding him, he'd made it easy. What had he been thinking? Of course cops would check out a car with a single occupant in the park. Next time he'd find a place to call home.

Changing vehicles was a good idea, but he needed to find vehicles that hadn't been used for a long time. *Downtown is good —lots of apartment buildings with underground parking.* Once he got out, he'd fulfill his fantasy at the first opportunity. Then he'd leave the city. But then his mind wandered to the other bitches who'd had a part in his arrests. If the plan worked for Blighe, it would work for them, too. Wolfe liked that idea a lot. *I have to get out of here.*

CHAPTER THIRTY-THREE

Tuesday

BRAD WAS SITTING AT THEIR SHARED DESK WHEN DEVLIN BURST IN.

"I have a good tip. I leaned on a couple of high-end drug dealers. At first, they didn't want to cooperate, but then—with some friendly persuasion—they remembered some stuff."

"Do the paramedics have them now?" Brad asked.

"That hurts. That you think I would resort to violence to get the information I want."

"Remember the snitch, Lenny, two years ago?"

Devlin smirked. "Oh, yeah. The clumsy one. Kept hitting my fist with his face."

"Funny, that's not how I remember it," Brad said.

"Anyway, they eventually gave me the location where those three shitheads are hiding. I took a drive by, and the van was there. I checked a gas station close by. The manager said the van stops every day. Three guys get out and buy smokes and year-old sandwiches. The manager wrote down the van's license number. He thought it might be stolen, which it was."

"But he didn't think to call us?"

Devlin shrugged. "Minimum wage gets you minimum information. But we've got a problem. The house is in Springbank, outside the city limits."

"I'll get the warrants," Brad said. "You call TSU."

"We have to call the Mounties."

"Screw the Mounties," Brad said. "They don't respect our jurisdiction, why should we respect theirs."

"You know they were wrong," Devlin said. "We accomplish nothing by shutting them out. Our relationship with them will get worse."

"We give them the location of the suspects, and they get the credit."

"Something like that."

"Well, it's bullshit. I say we don't tell them anything unless they include us on the raid."

"I'm not sure they'll buy into that."

"Screw them," Brad said. "They don't buy in, we'll do it ourselves."

CHAPTER THIRTY-FOUR

Two hours later, Brad was back with the warrants. When he entered the detective bullpen, he saw Archer and Devlin—and Sergeant Stinson and his team.

Ah shit.

"Do you have the warrants?" Archer asked.

Brad held them up. "What're they doing here?"

"I called their inspector and we came to an agreement," Archer said. "Since the suspects are hiding in RCMP territory, they're lead."

Stinson grinned. Brad wanted to punch the smirk off Stinson's stupid face.

"Fine," Brad said. "But we use our tactical team."

"Not a chance," Stinson said. "I already have our Emergency Response Team on the way."

"I've seen Stinson's team in action." Brad looked at Archer. "Can we have a pre-raid briefing where we discuss whom we *can* shoot and whom we should *never* shoot?"

Before Stinson could reply, Archer said, "Enough, Coulter. Stinson has agreed that you and Devlin will accompany them during the raid. After the suspects are arrested, with your assistance, it's no longer your case and Griffin runs with it. No arguments or you're not on the raid."

Brad and Devlin hunched in the trees at the back of the house. Once Archer was gone, Stinson's attitude changed. Brad and Devlin were on the raid, but they'd been assigned security at the back door in case anyone escaped. Stinson said that was unlikely. Brad cradled an AR15 and Devlin held a shotgun.

So, Brad and Devlin waited as the RCMP ERT got ready. They heard the countdown on the RCMP portable radio Stinson had given Devlin.

ERT took positions around the house. The radio announced "execute."

Wood cracked as doors were kicked open. "RCMP, get on the floor," sounded throughout the house.

Brad and Devlin stepped out of the trees. Devlin took a position to the side of the back door, Brad to the side of a large window.

Shouting came from inside the house. It was hard to decipher the words. Then two shotgun blasts. Over the radio someone yelled, "Officer down. Officer down."

The shouts grew louder, then, "Stop. Stop. He's on the run."

The back window shattered as a suspect dove out the window onto the porch, rolled several times, then stood.

"On your fucking knees." Brad pointed the rifle. The suspect looked toward the front of the house.

Stinson ran around the corner of the house, gun at his side. The suspect raised his pistol. Two gunshots echoed through the trees.

The suspect fell to the ground—the pistol tumbled harmlessly beside him.

Brad ran to the suspect, knelt, and reached for a pulse. One of the guys they were looking for. Blood oozed from two holes in his chest. Brad glanced at Devlin and shook his head. Stinson stood frozen to the spot, eyes wide.

"You good, Stinson?" Brad asked.

"Yeah, ah, thanks, Coulter. You got this?"

"I'll take care of it," Brad said.

Stinson stumbled away.

"Nice shooting," Devlin said. "Stinson's fricken' lucky. What was he thinking, racing around the corner?"

"He wasn't thinking." Brad rolled the gunman onto his stomach and cuffed him. They weren't needed, but protocol was protocol. He rolled the gunman onto his back. Brad glanced at the pistol, looked around, grabbed the gun, and slid it into an evidence bag.

"You need to leave that here," Devlin said.

"My shooting, my evidence. Besides, this might be the murder weapon. If I let the RCMP have it, we'll never know."

Devlin grinned. "I didn't see a thing."

"I'll give it to Griffin. He can take it for ballistics testing. He can deal with the RCMP."

They walked to the front of the house as two ambulances arrived. The RCMP were in a full-blown panic and practically dragged Dixon and Thompson over to their injured member. They were seasoned paramedics and wouldn't take any crap from the Mounties. If Brad was hurt, he'd want them to take care of him. Not that Maggie wasn't a good paramedic, she was great, but she didn't need the stress of treating him.

The second ambulance came to a stop near him. Maggie got out of the passenger seat, looked over, raised an eyebrow, grabbed her kits and caught up to her partner, Rick Fola. They followed a Mountie to the house.

Stinson met them at the door. "Inside."

"Who's hurt?" Maggie asked.

"I've got one cop shot. He's not too bad. The first paramedics are looking after him."

"And the bad guys?"

"One scumbag is dead. Another with a gunshot wound to the shoulder."

"That's it?" Maggie asked.

"The third guy shot my cop," Stinson said. "He's under arrest. He won't need paramedics."

"Do you want me to check him out?"

Stinson shook his head. "He's fine."

"Are you sure?" Maggie asked.

"Yup."

"What about the guy you say is dead?"

"Ask the detective." Stinson pointed at Brad. "He's the one who plugged him."

Maggie glanced at Brad, then disappeared into the house.

"Hey, Stinson. I want to interview the two surviving suspects," Brad said.

"Not a chance in hell, Coulter. It's different now, they shot one of ours. Wait in line."

A few minutes later, Fola jogged out of the house and asked for a hand taking the stretcher inside. Brad waited until the stretcher came out of the house. The suspect had both arms handcuffed to the stretcher. An intravenous hung from a pole and an oxygen mask covered his face. When the suspect was inside the ambulance and the back door was shut, the Mounties walked away. Brad turned to Devlin. "Follow the ambulance."

"Where are you going?"

"I'm going to interview our suspect."

"What—" But Brad was already sprinting to the ambulance.

The ambulance was pulling away as Brad reached the side door, flung it open ,and jumped inside.

"Jesus, Brad." Maggie was injecting something into the intravenous line. "What the hell are you doing?"

"I need to interview this guy."

"I thought he was the Mounties' suspect?"

"Technically he was my suspect first," Brad said.

"Technically?" Maggie grinned.

"We had a warrant for him. But he was hiding outside the city limits."

"So, *technically* he's theirs, too," Maggie said. "There's going to be hell to pay, isn't there."

Brad grinned. "Yup. Can I talk to him?"

"Go easy," Maggie said. "He's shot in the shoulder. I just gave him morphine and I'll probably give more as the pain gets worse. So, get your questions in quick."

"You bet." Brad slid to the bench seat beside the stretcher and stared at the suspect. "How you doing, Oscar?"

"Mounties shot me."

"Yeah, they do that sometimes. Did you shoot at them first?"

"That wasn't me. No way. You gotta believe me."

"Shooting at a Mountie will get you big time in prison. Fifteen years. Maybe twenty-five."

"Jeez, man, I didn't shoot no Mountie."

"Convince me."

"We was just hidin' out here. Lorne said we'd be safe."

"Who's Lorne? Did he shoot the Mountie?"

"No, when the Mounties busted the door Lorne dove out the back window."

Ah, I shot Lorne.

"Howie had the shotgun and fired at the cops. I heard one cop scream, then heard a shot and my shoulder was on fire, then I got tackled."

"Okay, Oscar. I believe you. Tell me about the night Alvarez was shot."

"No, no. I ain't talking about that. No way."

"So, you were there when Alvarez got shot."

"That's not what I said."

"Well, you said you weren't talking about that. Maybe you should have said I don't know what you're talking about."

"Jeez, man. You're twisting my words."

"What do you think is going to happen when the RCMP come to the hospital. Do you think they'll believe you? Maybe they think you're lying and decide to use some persuasion to get you to talk."

"No, man. You gotta help me."

"Why would I help you? You haven't given me anything." Brad turned to Maggie. "Stop the ambulance. I'm going to sit up front. I'm wasting my time with this shitrat."

"No! Wait. Promise you'll keep the Mounties away from me."

"Not until I get something I can use."

"Okay. Alvarez owed Lorne a bunch of money. Alvarez bought drugs on credit with Lorne. Then he shot the profits into his arm. The debt kept getting bigger. Lorne offed him."

"That doesn't make sense. Why kill a guy who owes you? Make him hurt, sure. But killing him doesn't get the drugs or money back."

"Lorne wanted to send a message to his dealers. Bad luck that Alvarez was the example."

"Who killed Alvarez?"

"Lorne, man."

"How'd he do it?"

"Took Alvarez to a park. Lorne made him kneel and beg for his life. Then boom. Lorne shot him in the back of the head. Me and Howie had to dig the grave. Jeez that was hard diggin', roots everywhere. We went back the next morning and tidied it up."

"Where did you bury the body?" Brad asked.

"In that park below CFCN hill."

Brad nodded. "What kind of gun did Lorne use?"

"A pistol. I don't know guns too well. The kind that can shoot twelve or thirteen times."

Fola called back saying they were pulling into the hospital.

"Thanks for the help, Oscar. Good luck."

"Hey, we got a deal."

"The Mounties are mad at me. I'm not gonna be able to help you." Brad winked at Maggie and opened the side door.

"Coulter!"

Brad glanced over his shoulder. Stinson.

"What the hell are you doing in the ambulance?"

"In the big city we don't leave unarmed paramedics alone with possible killers—that's a little rule we have. And in the big city, emergency services are a team—we have each other's backs —and we rarely shoot each other."

"Screw you," Stinson said. "You had no business being in that ambulance."

"Actually, I did," Brad said. "Keeping continuity since none of your guys did. Gotta go. Good luck." Brad sprinted to the ambulance bay door.

"Coulter, damn you," Stinson yelled. "Stop."

A car screeched to a halt. Brad opened the door and slid in. The car peeled away.

"Did you get what we needed?" Devlin asked.

"Yup. He told the whole sordid story." Brad brought Devlin up to date.

"You killed the suspect, who turned out to be Alvarez's killer," Devlin said. "We didn't get to execute the warrants, but we solved a murder *and* pissed off the Mounties. That's a good day."

"That's a *great* day," Brad said. "Let's get a beer and pizza."

Brad walked over with three beers. He slid two across the table. Devlin and Griffin each grabbed one. "I ordered a pizza."

"I'm starving," Devlin said. "And exhausted."

"I feel great," Griffin said. "I solved a murder and didn't have to lift a frickin' finger. My kind of day."

"Are you forgetting who gave that to you gift-wrapped with bows?" Brad asked.

"Funny thing, I don't think that's how I wrote the report. I've got a few more cases you can work on."

"What? And do all your work?"

"You did just fine today. Tell Devlin to go to hell and come work with me."

"I'm not doing your work."

"I'm more fun than Devlin. Think about it." Griffin drank. "You guys got anything big to work on now?"

"I'm going to sleep for two days," Brad said.

"Saying that is a jinx," Devlin said. "Now we'll be lucky to get a couple of hours of shut-eye."

"Why're we sitting in a pizza shop in Bowness instead of The Cuff and Billy?" Griffin asked.

"Brad pissed off the Mounties," Devlin said. "He's scared, so he's hiding."

"Screw you," Brad said. "I'm simply avoiding confrontation. I'm not a fighter, I'm a lover."

"That's funny," Griffin said. "You've got two others looking for you."

"What?"

"Internal affairs detectives came to the bullpen looking for you. Deputy Chief Archer, too. You've got a day of meetings tomorrow. Archer's office 8 A.M. I hear the RCMP internal affairs will be there, too."

"Ah, shit," Brad said.

"I'll miss you." Griffin raised his beer.

CHAPTER THIRTY-FIVE

Tuesday Night

WOLFE SAT ON THE EDGE OF HIS BED. IT WAS ALMOST DINNER TIME. The orderly would be here soon with the crap they called food. The orderly, not as big as Wolfe, had been friendly, and especially curious about Wolfe's crimes. Wolfe knew this presented an opportunity to escape. He'd been friendly to the orderly, who hung on every word of Wolfe's fights, rapes, and murders. Wolfe described the rapes in detail. The orderly was clearly excited.

The three weeks in the psych ward made Wolfe crazier, not better. He was a caged animal pacing around his cell, needing his freedom. Daily counseling sessions with the psychiatrist asking about Wolfe's feelings, talking about his anger, the continual phrase, "How are you feeling today?" made his head ache with an overwhelming desire to reach out and choke the living shit out of the psychiatrist.

The few weeks on the outside were invigorating. The freedom, the food, and the women. Especially women. This time the cops wouldn't find him and he'd get revenge on everyone responsible for him being here.

There was a knock on the door. "Wolfe, step away from the door."

"I'm sitting on the bed."

Wolfe knew the orderly would look through the peephole to see where Wolfe was. The lock turned, the door opened, and the orderly stepped inside with a tray that he set on a night table.

"What kind of swill did you bring?"

"I think it's meatloaf, fake mashed potatoes, and broccoli."

"That's disgusting. Stay while I eat."

"I shouldn't. I've got more food to deliver."

"Just a few minutes. I thought of another rape I haven't told you about."

The orderly locked the door, sat on the edge of the bed and said, "Just for a couple of minutes."

"I was hiding out at the Stampede barns. When I woke up, this girl, maybe late teens, blonde hair in pigtails, was at the barns. She was all alone. I snuck up on her and put my arm around her neck, pulled her close. I was already excited. Then I choked her and within seconds she was unconscious. I dragged her to the barn and tied her up with baling twine. I stuffed a rag in her mouth. I pulled her boots off, then pulled down her jeans."

The orderly was hanging on every word. He leaned close to Wolfe and said, "Go on. Don't stop now."

Wolfe wrapped a big arm around the orderly's neck and used his other arm to hold the orderly's head. Then he squeezed. The orderly clawed at Wolfe's arms for a few seconds, then his arms went limp. Wolfe struggled with the shirt. It wasn't easy getting clothes off a dead person. With the women, he'd cut or rip the clothes, but he needed these.

The orderly stirred. Wolfe choked him and twisted his neck until there was a loud pop. The orderly wasn't breathing now. Oh, well. He'd served his purpose.

Wolfe tugged and pulled and finally had the white uniform off the orderly. He stripped out of his baggy green pants and a pullover shirt. The orderly's pants fit okay, but the shirt was tight, real tight. He heard seams rip.

Wolfe checked the orderly—still no breathing. Unfortunate, but who cares. Wolfe rolled the orderly on his side on the bed facing the wall. He wouldn't be able to get his patient clothes on the orderly. Instead, he laid the clothes over the body. To anyone looking through the small peephole, it would look like Wolfe was sleeping.

Wolfe checked the orderly's pockets and pulled out twenty bucks. That was a start. He found the cell key, walked to the door, and listened. The door was thick so that no sounds could be heard. He'd have to chance it.

As he stepped out, another orderly walked past to the security door at the end of the hall. Wolfe timed it so that when the door was almost closed, he stuck his hand in, preventing the door from closing, and slipped through. The hall led to another security door. *Shit!* He'd have to move quickly.

The door was almost closed when Wolfe stuck in his hand. Only his fingers caught the door and immediately pain shot up his arm. With his other hand, he pried the door open and stepped through into a regular hospital ward. The doors to the rooms were open and nurses moved between rooms. Farther down the hall, nurses came out of a room with trays with patient medication. He strode down the hall, like he belonged.

When he got to the drug room, he peeked in. No one was inside. On one wall was a cabinet with a glass door with a key in the lock. He stepped close—it was filled with narcotics. He grabbed a pillowcase and cleaned it out. On the opposite wall hung coats. He rummaged through the pockets and found a set of car keys.

He stepped out of the room and strode down the hallway to a bank of elevators. When the door opened, he got in and pushed the button for lower-level parking.

He stepped out into the parking garage and faced hundreds of vehicles. If he tried every lock, eventually someone would see him and call security. He didn't have that kind of time. They could find the dead orderly at any moment. He looked at the ring tag—Gremlin. That narrowed it down. The parking spots closest to the elevator would go to the doctors. So, the nurse's or orderly's car was likely in the middle of the parking lot. He weaved back and forth between the parked cars, looking for the Gremlin.

On the fourth row he found inside the car. He opened the trunk and threw the pillowcase of drugs. He slammed the trunk. The loud echo in the parking garage startled him. He looked around, then raced to the driver's door. With the door unlocked, Wolfe slid into the driver's seat. He pushed the key into the ignition and turned. The car fired up right away. Wolfe stared at the dash—it even had a full tank of gas.

Wolfe drove downtown. There were lots of low end bars to choose from. He'd fit in with the crowd in any of them. He passed the York and Calgarian. The problem with them was the lack of parking. He needed to ditch this car. Wolfe parked the Gremlin at the back of the Calgarian Hotel and slipped out of the car. He'd found clothes that fit in a laundromat. Fortune was on his side.

The bar lights were dim and about half the chairs were occupied. He walked over to the bar and ordered a beer. The bartender set the beer on the counter and Wolfe slapped a dollar down. The first beer in almost two months. Cool and refreshing. He emptied the beer and ordered another. With the second beer in hand, he turned to face away from the bar. The first thing he noticed was the waitresses. They looked old and well used. He wasn't that desperate. He scanned the bar, looking for car keys sitting on a table. He didn't see any, so he left his seat and wandered around the room. He passed a group of guys with short hair cuts. Maybe military.

On his way back across the bar, he saw two old men nursing their beers. A set of car keys sat in the middle of the table.

"Hey, old timers, mind if I sit and buy you a beer?"

One man stared at Wolfe, then said, "You're a big fella. You work the oil rigs?"

"Yeah. I work in Fort McMurray. Back for a few weeks of R&R."

"Sit down."

Wolfe caught the eye of the grizzled waitress.

"Don't you be ogling that waitress," the old guy said. "I get first shot."

"You better move quick, old man, or I'm moving on her."

The waitress wandered over, shoulders low, a defeated look on her face. "Whatcha need?"

"Three beers. For my friends and me. I'll have a burger and fries. You guys want anything?"

They shook their heads.

"That's it," Wolfe said.

"Okay. Coming right up." She walked away, clearly in no hurry.

"You guys regulars here?" Wolfe asked.

"Sure are. I'm George and this is Vic."

No need to leave a trail. It's unlikely the cops would ever look here for him, but why take a chance. "I'm Pickens. Slim Pickens."

"That's funny. You don't look like no cowboy and you ain't slim."

"My old man had a sense of humor. How'd you two know each other?"

"We grew up together, fought in the war together, and now we drink together."

"The second one?"

"We ain't that young. First one. Although, then we called it the war to end all wars. Didn't think there'd be another one."

"I appreciate your service." Wolfe nodded to each man.

The waitress set three beers on the table. Wolfe gave her a ten. "Keep the change and bring another round."

"Hey, George, I think this young fella is buying your girl," Vic said.

"Watch your step there, Slim." George stood. "I gotta take care of business."

Wolfe re-arranged the beers and his meal on the table, slipping the keys into his lap.

"Sure you don't want sumpin' to eat, Vic?"

"Nah, I don't eat too much no more."

George came back and Wolfe's burger arrived. He convinced the old boys to talk about the war while he ate.

George did most of the talking. Vic was content to drink beer.

"The news is coming on," George said. "Ain't that something about Mount St. Helens blowing its top. We're still getting that ash here. Can you believe that?"

"I've been away. What happened?" Wolfe swung around and looked at the small TV over the bar. The picture wasn't great, but he could see volcanic explosion and cars covered in ash.

"Hell," Wolfe said. "That's impressive."

The news moved on to other events. In the psych ward he didn't get a TV and the shrink said reading the papers would be bad for him.

The screen changed and showed a police ceremony. The chief was pinning medals on two cops. Wolfe walked toward the bar for a better look. The camera zoomed in on two uniformed cops. Wolfe's jaw clenched, his heart pounded, and he felt a burn up his neck. *Those fuckers. Those cock-sucking bastards.*

The caption on the bottom of the screen read, *Detective Thomas Devlin and Sergeant Bradley Coulter receive Medal of Valor.*

Eyes ablaze, Wolfe stared at the screen, his breath rapid, his pulse racing and rage building.

The next film clip showed Coulter with a pretty blonde. She was tight by his side and looked at him with love and pride.

Like Mount St. Helens, Wolfe exploded. He threw his beer at the TV, shattering the bottle and punching a hole in the screen. A waitress passed with a tray of draft beer. Wolfe swung at the tray, sending beer in every direction. Two large bouncers pushed between the tables toward Wolfe. The first bouncer reached for Wolfe, who stepped forward and landed a solid punch under the bouncer's jaw. His head snapped back, his eyes rolled upward, and he collapsed onto the floor, unconscious.

Wolfe swung an arm across the bar, knocking glasses, bottles and food to the floor. The second bouncer grabbed Wolfe from behind in a bear hug, then moved one arm around Wolfe's neck. Wolfe snapped his head back. There was a loud crack as Wolfe's head mashed the bouncer's nose flat. The bartender yelled the cops were on the way.

Rational thought returned, and Wolfe ran to the back door. No one dared follow. He ran to the Gremlin, opened the trunk and grabbed the pillowcase. He left the key in the trunk lock.

Under a streetlamp in the parking lot, he looked at the keys he'd stolen from the war veterans. He looked in the parking lot for an old man's car. He spotted a dark, four-door Oldsmobile at the back of the parking lot. He ran over, tried the key in the door —it opened. Wolfe slid in and started the car. He was backing out before he'd closed the door. As he pulled out of the parking lot, two police cruisers raced in.

Wolfe drove around the southeast looking for a place to stay. He passed a few drug houses where he could sleep and no one would ask questions. But if any of the dopeheads got picked up by the cops, they'd give Wolfe up in a second. He drove down a street of houses in bad shape. The house at the end of the block, maybe no more than a thousand square feet, looked vacant. He parked across the road and waited for an hour. No one came near the house and not a single vehicle drove down the road.

He got out of the car and wandered over to the house. The front door looked solid with glass intact in the front windows. He walked around the house looking for signs someone was squatting there. The yard was overgrown with wild grass and weeds. None of it seemed stomped down. The back door was locked. Wolfe leaned into the middle of the door with his full weight while pushing on the doorknob. The door popped open. He stepped inside and couldn't believe his luck. The house was in passable shape and it was furnished. He flipped a switch and the kitchen light came on.

Wolfe checked out the rest of the house, then closed the back door and stepped into the backyard. He wandered down the alley to get a feel for the area. Few homes had cars parked in the alley. The cars had current license plates and it was tempting to steal one, but if the owner reported the theft to the cops, Wolfe might be pulled over, or at the very least they'd check out this street. He'd need to find plates somewhere else. Now that he had a place to crash, he needed cash. Seventeenth Avenue was a haven for drug dealers. Tomorrow he'd find a dealer to buy some of the stolen drugs, then he'd have enough money to get some groceries, gas, and beer.

CHAPTER THIRTY-SIX

Wednesday

BRAD WAS PUTTING THE FINISHING TOUCHES ON BREAKFAST WHEN Maggie came home the next morning. Lobo abandoned Brad in the kitchen and raced to the door.

"Something smells good," Maggie said as she stepped into the kitchen.

"Eggs Benedict and coffee."

Maggie frowned. "A heavy breakfast and coffee after a night shift."

Brad pouted. "But I worked hard making this for you."

"Bullshit, that's your favorite breakfast."

"I'm willing to share."

"Okay. The eggs benedict, but not the coffee."

Brad set two plates on the table—orange juice for Maggie, and a big mug of coffee for himself. Lobo sat under the table waiting for something, anything, to fall to the floor. "How was your night shift?"

"You mean after you ran away from Stinson?"

"I didn't run. I had reports to write."

"Are you sure you want to know how my shift was at breakfast with your delicate tummy and all."

"Hey, that's not fair. I can handle most stuff. Just not the smell of autopsies."

Maggie described a motorcycle crash where the rider was ejected from his bike and impacted a brick wall with his head at about fifty miles per hour. Helmets don't always save lives. Then she described the homeless man who complained of foot pain. When they took off his boots, what little was left of his socks came too, as well as a layer or two of skin.

Brad picked at his breakfast.

"You going to finish that?" Maggie laughed. "I knew you couldn't handle it."

"No, I'm just full."

Maggie laughed again. "You and Devlin were on TV last night. You two were so dashing."

"You looked pretty good yourself," Brad said. "I hate that crap."

"It wasn't about you, darling. It was about the chief bragging and the city looking tough on crime."

Brad collected the dishes. "Yeah, well, I still hate it."

"What're you up to today?" Maggie asked.

"I have a meeting with internal affairs at nine. Archer after that."

"You should be used to that. You're practically best friends with them."

"It shouldn't be too bad. I have Devlin and RCMP Sergeant

Stinson as witnesses, but I'm sure they'll try to trip me up on something."

"Internal affairs has it out for you. But then again, you do get into a lot of shit."

"What's up for you after your nap?"

"Shopping for groceries."

"We're pretty well stocked."

"Not with the stuff I want."

"What's that?"

"Ice cream, cheezies, and chocolate—lots of chocolate."

Brad smiled. "Ah, the craving stage has begun."

"Yup."

"How long are you going to keep working?"

"What kind of question is that?" Maggie's voice grew cold.

"Well, you're over two months along so maybe this is a good time to take it easy."

"Two months is nothing. I plan to work until at least six months."

"Are you crazy?" Brad immediately regretted those words.

"Why not. I feel fine."

"Sure, you do now. What if you have to lift a heavy patient? What if you get another patient like Wolfe?"

"I'll be fine. I can get the firefighters to help lift heavy patients and you'll be there to deal with guys like Wolfe."

"How would I know you were in danger?"

"Because, my dear, I know you listen to the ambulance radio channel."

"What! Where did—"

Maggie held up a hand. "Before you say more stupid things, you forget that I still see Steele and Zerr. They had some interesting things to say."

"Those rat-bastards. Hey, wait. They said you paid them to look after me."

Maggie laughed. "I didn't, but that's a damn good idea. Someone has to."

"You know what I mean. Southeast and downtown—not the nicest areas. Your partner, Fola, is a rookie and a bit of a wimp."

"He's a good medic."

"I don't doubt that, but not the guy I'd like covering my back."

"Not everything is fights and shooting. That's your life, not mine."

"Still, I'd feel better—"

"Not open for discussion. You're overprotective."

"You're stubborn."

Maggie smiled. "Yup." She kissed Brad on the top of his head. "I'm going upstairs. You coming?"

CHAPTER THIRTY-SEVEN

BRAD RACED IN THE BACK ENTRANCE TO POLICE HEADQUARTERS AND took the stairs two at a time, then down the hall to the detective office. Devlin was waiting.

"What the hell happened?" Brad asked.

"I don't have many details yet," Devlin said. "Griffin is at the General Hospital, Psych Ward. An orderly is dead and Wolfe is missing."

"How does this happen? One of the most violent and sadistic criminals in Calgary and he escapes. He killed an orderly and then walked out. How is that possible?"

Devlin held up his hands in surrender. "You know him better than anyone. I need your help to catch him."

Brad stared at Devlin while his brain flashed thought after thought. Wolfe would rape and kill again. He threatened revenge on Annie and the crown prosecutor.

Brad raced out of his office to his car. He picked up his portable radio as he drove. "Briscoe, this is Coulter."

"Go ahead, Brad."

"Do you know where Annie is?"

"The detail dropped her off at her apartment about fifteen minutes ago."

"Are they still with her?"

"Nope. They're heading home."

Shit. "Meet me at the condo right away."

"What's up?"

"We'll talk when we get there."

Brad tried to make sense of the court system. On the one hand he understood why Wolfe needed a psychiatric assessment. But on the other hand, the man was a vicious killer. Sending him to a psych hospital was a mistake. *Obviously.* It's easy to look back and see what should have been done differently. Two years ago, when Wolfe was beaten almost to death, Brad immediately called the paramedics. *What if I'd waited a few minutes before bringing the paramedics in.* The scene wasn't completely secured, so he could have justified the delay. Would a few minutes have made the difference? Would Wolfe have died? How many lives would have been saved if he'd died? How many more would die before Wolfe was captured?

Briscoe parked outside the condo behind Brad's car. They exited and met up on the sidewalk leading to the condo.

"What's the deal?" Briscoe asked.

"Wolfe escaped from the psych hospital."

"Ah, shit," Briscoe said. "The stupid frickin' court system. They got suckered. He's about as crazy as me."

Brad raised an eyebrow.

"Go screw yourself. This was predictable."

"We keep underestimating Wolfe," Brad said. "No more."

"What do you think his first move will be?"

"I don't know, but every scenario I think of isn't good. He was really pissed in court. He threatened Annie, the crown prosecutor, Maggie, female reporters, the judge, and me. Just about everyone in the room."

"That's a lot of people to protect."

"Blighe has personal protection," Brad said. "Annie has protection when she is at college. Maggie and Annie will be okay at home. My place is secure. I have the new alarm system, Lobo, and Maggie can defend herself, but—"

"But what?" Briscoe asked.

"Maggie's pregnant."

Briscoe's jaw dropped. "Congratulations. But, uh, the timing is a little bad."

"I know. I just talked to Maggie about getting off the street."

"I can guess how that went."

Brad chuckled hollowly.

The doorman opened the door for them.

"Sergeant, Detective, what brings you gentlemen here today?"

"We've come to move Annie," Brad said. "Have you seen anyone hanging around here, or a vehicle parked close by with someone inside?"

"No, nothing like that. If I did, I'd call you or the sergeant right away."

Brad and Briscoe took the elevator to the third floor and headed down the hall to Annie's place. Brad knocked.

"Who is it?" Annie asked.

"I know you can see me through the peephole," Brad said. "Open the door."

"Can I see some ID? Step back from the door."

"Annie, quit screwing around."

"You don't have to get so pissy."

A deadbolt unlocked, then another deadbolt unlocked, and finally Annie opened the door.

"You're a grump today," Annie said. "I was doing what you taught me to do."

Brad pushed into the apartment. Briscoe stayed at the door.

Brad looked around. "Get your stuff, you're coming to my place."

"Why? You're scaring me."

Brad turned to Annie. "Wolfman escaped again."

Annie's hand covered her mouth. "No ... please no. Tell me you're joking."

"I'd never joke about this. Pack up. You might not be back here for a while."

Annie packed a suitcase of clothes and toiletries, and a gym bag of schoolbooks.

Briscoe grabbed the suitcase and Brad took the gym bag.

"This weighs a ton," Brad said.

"Summer semester starts tomorrow. Gotta have the textbooks. The professors have already assigned reading."

"Have you done the reading?" Brad asked.

Annie glared and headed to the elevator.

When the elevator door opened, two uniformed cops stood in the lobby. One cop led them out of the building, the other bringing up the rear.

On the street, two more cops stood on alert.

They threw Annie's bags into the back of Brad's Firebird. Annie climbed into the passenger seat.

"These guys will follow you home, just in case," Briscoe said.

"I appreciate that," Brad replied. "I'll get Annie settled in, then go after Wolfe."

"You know this guy better than anyone," Briscoe said. "What do you think his next move will be?"

"He'll pick up where he left off, and we'll have another body to deal with—soon."

"Let me know if you need help with Annie. I can hang out at your place while you're at work."

"Thanks. We're okay for now. But you'll be the first one I call."

Brad slid into the driver's seat and they pulled away from the curb.

Annie stared out the window, silent. Brad left her alone.

"Do you think he'll come after me?"

"I hope not. But this time I'm not taking any chances."

"What about school?"

"You'll have your own security detail, just like the president."

"They'll follow me everywhere? What about the restroom?"

"There'll be a lady cop on the detail. She will be with you in the restroom."

"That's creepy."

"I thought you ladies always went to the bathroom in pairs."

"That a little judgmental, even for you. What about my brother?"

"He's safe with his foster family."

"Maybe we should get him, too."

"The foster family is the best place for him. Heck, I don't even know where he is."

Annie turned to Brad. "You know that's a bunch of shit."

"Language."

"I'm not a child. You've always been honest with me. Don't feed me crap now. Where is he?"

Brad hesitated, then said, "You're right. I know where he is. I also know he's safe. You have to trust me on that. When this is over, I'll make sure you see him."

Annie stared out the window again.

Brad parked in front of his house—one cruiser parked in front of them, and one behind. Brad waited while the cops left their cruisers. Two of them walked around the house. When they came back, one cop nodded.

Brad and Annie got out of the car. Brad grabbed her bags and they headed up the sidewalk. Brad stopped and turned to the cops. "You guys can go now."

"No can do, sir," the older cop said. "We've got instructions from Sergeant Briscoe. We'll be out here if you need us."

As they approached the door, they heard loud barking. When Brad opened the door Lobo rushed out, stopped next to Annie and let her pet him. Then he raced off to check out the cops.

Brad disarmed the security system and took the bags upstairs to Annie's room. She'd stayed there numerous times over the past two years. This was her second home.

Brad walked through the house, making sure all the windows were closed and locked. He tested the deadbolts on the doors. Then he headed outside. Lobo was sitting beside a cruiser getting the attention from a cop.

"Lobo, come." Lobo ran to Brad's side and sat. "I sometimes

take him to work. Now he thinks a cruiser means we're going to chase bad guys."

"He seems pretty friendly," the cop said.

"He's nice and calm now. He recognizes the uniform and your boot polish. But he can go into attack mode fast."

"I'll be sure not to piss him off," the cop said.

Brad and Lobo wandered around the yard. Brad checked the padlock on the tool shed. Lobo sniffed at the ground but didn't indicate anything suspicious. The motion sensors were intact and the floodlights weren't broken. Tonight, after dark, he'd check to make sure they were still functioning.

Brad and Annie were sitting in the living room. Lobo jumped up from sleep and raced to the entrance. The door opened and Maggie stepped inside with grocery bags.

"Why is a police cruiser parked in front of our house?"

"Hey, Maggie, welcome home."

"Don't, 'hey Maggie' me. Now I know for sure you're up to something."

Annie stepped out of the living room. "Hi, Maggie."

Maggie glanced from Brad to Annie then back to Brad.

"Let's go to the kitchen," Brad said. "We'll be back in a few minutes, Annie. Keep Lobo out of trouble."

They sat at the kitchen table and Brad told Maggie about Wolfe's escape and the danger to Annie.

Maggie sat quietly for a few moments. "How does this happen?"

"I've asked that question a bunch of times myself. We've underestimated Wolfe."

"What do you mean?"

"We've treated him like he was just a big, dumb biker. He's a lot smarter than we gave him credit for."

"Crazy like a fox?"

"Yeah, exactly. Not many people escape from jail—few escape twice. You might be lucky the first time—things just fall into place. But the odds are against it happening twice. Yet he's roaming free. The second escape required detailed planning. We're dealing with a cunning psychopath."

"Are we in danger?"

"Wolfe is too smart to come here. Until we get him, there'll be uniforms outside. The alarm system is the best there is and Lobo is our secret weapon. He'd never let anyone hurt you or Annie." Brad stood. "I need to go back to work for a couple of hours. Set the alarm when I leave. The cops will be here until I'm home."

Brad met the cops beside the cruiser.

"Thanks for doing this," Brad told them. "I can't emphasize enough how dangerous Wolfe is. He's very smart, too. If you see or hear anything suspicious, call for backup right away. Don't take any chances."

"We've got this, Detective," a young cop said.

"I'm serious," Brad said. "Don't be a hero. Everyone goes home to their family tonight."

CHAPTER THIRTY-EIGHT

When Brad arrived back at his office a detective told him to report to the briefing room.

"About time," Deputy Chief Archer said.

Brad grabbed a chair and looked around the room—Devlin, Davidson, and Griffin.

"You four are assigned to find Wolfe," Archer told them. "Ideally, we find and arrest him."

"That hasn't worked out well so far." Brad immediately regretted saying it. Sometimes stuff just slipped out.

Archer glared at Brad. "I said *ideally*. If he puts up any resistance, well … do what you need to do."

"Four of us isn't much of a team," Brad said.

"You four are the brains of the operation. If you need more people, then tell me. I'll get them. TSU knows Wolfe is out there and they're on alert. If anyone gets a sighting or a confirmed location, we surround the scene and let TSU take him down."

"I've got a request," Brad said.

"What's that?" Archer asked.

"We need more than four of us. I'd like Sam Steele and Charlie Zerr to join us tomorrow."

"If I do that, then the TSU is short guys."

"True, but if we're going against Wolfe, we need to have a little more muscle on our side. No offense to this group, but Steele and Zerr won't be afraid to head into the seamier places. They can handle themselves. If TSU is needed, then they join their team."

Archer nodded. "That makes sense. I'll have them report here tomorrow."

"We need a name for our group," Devlin said. "How about the Silver Bullet Team."

"Silver bullets are for werewolves, not wolfmen," Brad said.

"Close enough," Devlin replied.

"There's no team name." Archer stood. "I'll leave you to figure out how we're going to find Wolfe."

Tina leaned forward in her chair. "Where do we start?"

"Last time we got lucky and found Wolfe within eight days," Brad said. "He won't make that mistake again. We need to write down every aspect of this case, then work on them one at a time."

Griffin shrugged. "Sounds like a plan."

"He doesn't have many friends here," Devlin said. "They're either dead or in jail. But he may still contact the Hells Angels, if he hasn't already. We need to keep pressure there."

Brad wrote *Friends* on a whiteboard followed by *HA*. Then he wrote *Hideouts*.

"That could be anywhere," Devlin argued. "If he's looking to contact a biker, he will try the biker bars—Beacon, Town & Country, Bowness, maybe even the Shamrock, but that's too close to the HA."

Brad added the bars under the hideout heading. "I think we leave Shamrock in, to cover all bases."

"Sure," Devlin said. "I've been thinking about this. I'm more use on the street, checking the bars and underbelly of our wonderful city. I can go places none of you can. I'll take the bars and strolls. I'll get the narcs looking as well."

Brad nodded.

"I've got two murders to follow up on," Griffin said. "I still have my file from the hooker murder. I'll talk to Sturgeon and find out what he knows about the murder of the orderly."

Murders went on the whiteboard with *Threats*.

"Wolfe threatened everyone in this room," Brad said. "I think the top three are Jenni Blighe, Annie, and Tina."

"You should add Maggie there too," Devlin said. "He was pissed when she was bandaging the dog bites."

Brad wrote on the board. *Protection*. "That takes us to the next discussion. Whom do we give protection to and how?"

"We've already got a team on Blighe," Griffin said. "Same guys as last time."

"Lovely," Devlin said. "Frickin' Starsky and Hutch."

"I've got Annie covered," Brad said. "She's staying with Maggie and me. I have a team taking her from my house to Mount Royal College. They stay close in the college, then they bring her back to my place. I have a new alarm system and an eighty-pound German shepherd. And Maggie knows how to use a gun. When I'm not home there'll be a marked unit out front."

"Davidson, we need protection for you," Griffin said.

"No way." Tina straightened. "I can hold my own. I don't want guys following me around."

"I thought you'd enjoy the attention," Devlin quipped. "Maybe a strong TSU member."

Tina waved her middle finger at Devlin and mouthed, "Screw you."

"I get why you want your independence," Griffin said. "But don't be foolish. If Wolfe catches you by surprise, there's no way you could stop him."

"I won't let him get close. So, let's move on. Let me tell you what I found out about Wolfe last month. We caught him before I could tell you guys what I'd found."

"Sure," Brad said. "As good of a time as any."

"Wolfe got screwed up as a kid. His father was abusive and a drunk. He got off on violent sex with his wife, then later his daughter. He started with his daughter when she was about twelve. Wolfe told the psychiatrist that he shared a room with his sister and that he watched his father rape his sister. Wolfe said it excited him."

"Did Wolfe rape her?" Brad asked.

"I don't know," Davidson said. "But when she was fifteen, she ran away. There are some arrest reports for solicitation, then she completely disappears—no mention of her anywhere. No missing person report was filed. Wolfe's father was killed in a bar fight over a waitress and his mother died of an overdose of heroin. Wolfe was seventeen when that happened. He started hanging out with the Bandidos Motorcycle Club in Hamilton. You guys know most of this. He was the enforcer for the president, Felix Keaton. Then three years ago the two of them came west and took over the Gypsy Jokers' Club. What you didn't have two years ago were the reports from the Hamilton police. We knew Wolfe was rough on the ladies, but it's worse than we thought. Hamilton police have at least a dozen missing persons reports. None of them were found. All were young, blonde and vulnerable. A few other women made complaints against Wolfe for rough stuff, but those charges never went anywhere. But the Hamilton police were watching Wolfe close, then he came west."

"Would have been nice of the Hamilton cops to give us a heads up," Devlin said.

"They didn't say shit when we contacted them," Brad said. "The sister, was she blond?"

Davidson nodded.

"Son of a bitch," Brad said.

"In January, I went to Quantico to take a course the FBI was teaching. It was taught by two FBI instructors, Howard Teton and Patrick Mullany from the Behavioral Science Unit. Teton had designed a method for analyzing cases where the offender was unknown. He analyzed at every facet of the case: forensics, autopsy, similar death investigation, and psychiatric knowledge. He looked at the crime scene for evidence of mental disorders or other, specific personality traits. He looked at everything he could get his hands on."

"Is this going somewhere?" Griffin asked.

"When Wolfe escaped the first time, and after the second rape, I contacted Teton and told him what we were working on."

"I thought his process was for unknown suspects?" Brad asked.

"I'm getting to that. Cool your jets. I figured he'd be interested in what we know about Wolfe, his past and recent events, and I hoped he could give an insight into what Wolfe was thinking, his motivations. I told Teton everything we knew about Wolfe. He was interested and wants to add this case to his database. However, from what I told him, Wolfe doesn't fit into a single category or serial type."

"So, you've got nada," Griffin said.

Tina stood, a hand on her hip. "Do you want to know this or not. If not, I've got other things to do."

Brad glared at the others. "We'll be quiet. Right?"

"Here's the problem. Wolfe's attacks are for different reasons every time. His rapes of Annie and Sissy were of convenience. Annie practically walked into his arms the night her mother was killed. Wolfe took advantage of that. Sissy was one of their hookers that Wolfe liked. Again, opportunity. No doubt there are multiple rapes we don't know about. If they were hookers, there's no way they'd report that to the police. Who'd listen? Then he gets beaten nearly to death and has a major head injury. For most of the time during his trial he was quiet. We all thought it was because of the head injury. Teton thinks the opposite is true. That Wolfe used that time to scheme and plan. We already knew he liked blondes, so he turned his attention to Blighe. It's possible he was fantasizing and planning something horrible for her. But he was sent to prison for life. All he had in jail were his fantasies. He needed to get out, so he planned his escape."

"If he spent all this time planning a fantasy, why didn't he go after Blighe as soon as he got out?" Griffin asked.

"As much as he wanted Blighe, he didn't go after her right away because it had to fit the fantasy. But his urge was strong. Gail Wilson was a target of opportunity. So was Billy-Lou Hanlon. The bottom line is, he has Blighe as the target, but he won't pass up any opportunity with a young blonde."

"Shit," Brad said. "Until he gets to Blighe, he's gonna rape any target of convenience."

"Not any target," Tina said. "Young blondes."

"How the hell do we stop that. It's not like we can go on TV and say, if you are a young blonde, don't go out of your house or you'll get raped."

"But I can go on TV and warn everyone. And plead for any sighting of Wolfe."

"Maybe a reward would help," Devlin said.

Tina shook her head. "That would overload our phones from everyone who needs cash. We'd get hundreds or thousands of calls and waste most of our time chasing bad leads."

"So," Brad said, "we hope that honest law-abiding citizens see Wolfe and call us. The chances of good citizens being in the same world Wolfe is hiding in is slim."

"True," Tina conceded. "But if he's after Blighe, he won't be hiding all the time. If he's in the southeast, and Blighe is in the northwest, he has to cross the city twice each time he stalks Blighe. That's a lot of time for him to get stopped for traffic violations. He needs gas, cigarettes, food. We got lucky catching him last time. Maybe luck will be on our side again."

Brad shook his head. "No, it's going to take more than luck this time. But I don't have a clue what that is."

There was silence in the room as they mulled over Tina's information.

"There's one more thing we need to do," Davidson said.

"What's that?" Brad asked.

"As I mentioned earlier, we need to go public. Television, radio, and newspapers."

Brad nodded. "Last time we were wrong. We should have gone to the public right away."

"I'll get a news conference for tomorrow afternoon," Tina said.

"Why so late?" Devlin asked.

"We have to give the media notice if we want this done right. And I need time to put it together. Sorry."

"Don't give out details we've held back. You can say that we think he's in the southeast."

Three knocks on the door, then it opened. Sergeant Sturgeon entered. "Am I interrupting something?"

"No, we're done," Brad said.

"I've got some of the forensics back on the murder of Gail Wilson and some matches to fingerprints at the scene."

Brad sat up. *Maybe some good news for a change.* "Grab a seat."

"A lot of this stuff you already know. We collected quite a bit from the murder scene that we've been analyzing. That room had hundreds of fingerprints, so that was going to be a big task searching them all. I decided we'd take a shortcut. First, we compared Wolfe's fingerprints with those we found. Bingo. A match. That doesn't mean he raped and murdered Wilson, but it means he was in that room at some time. We're still going through every fingerprint looking for matches. Maybe it wasn't Wolfe. Maybe he had an accomplice. Maybe there's another unknown suspect. It's going to take a few weeks to work through that."

"We know it's Wolfe," Devlin said.

"You think it's Wolfe," Sturgeon said. "You need to prove that beyond a reasonable doubt. We have to check everything. Most evidence of the rape of Billy-Lou was washed away. But we found the barn where she was raped. We found two blood types. Billy-Lou's and another. There was some skin under her nails, so she fought back. Both victims had different blood types, but we also found a third type, and it matches Wolfe. *That's* evidence you can use."

"I have the Wilson autopsy report. It's nasty. I don't want to talk about it. I'll leave a copy and you can read it if you want to. I'd recommend you not read it. At least not now. That's stuff you don't need floating around in your head."

CHAPTER THIRTY-NINE

BRAD HAD COME HOME EXHAUSTED. FOR TWO DAYS HE'D WORKED with Steele and Zerr checking every hotel bar, corner bar, and tattoo parlor in the southeast. They didn't find Wolfe and, not surprisingly, no one remembered seeing him. Too late Brad realized it was a waste of time. No one was going to talk to the cops. And anyone who knew Wolfe would go to great lengths to keep quiet. Wolfe's revenge was far worse than anything the cops would do.

Dinner was finished. Maggie and Annie were in the kitchen planning a shopping trip on the weekend. Brad reclined in a chair in the living room and read the financial pages. It was the first time he'd relaxed in days. He tried to concentrate on the paper, but his mind wandered to Wolfe. Then his eyes grew heavy and he worked to keep them open. When the six o'clock news came on, Brad turned up the volume. The lead story was about Wolfe.

Wolfe's picture appeared on the screen. The reporter gave

background on Wolfe's involvement in the Gypsy Jokers' Outlaw Motorcycle Club two years ago and his conviction on murder and rapes of two teens.

The reporter talked about Wolfe's arrest a few months ago for murder and rape and his subsequent thirty-day psychiatric assessment.

The screen changed to Davidson's press conference and ended with a note at the bottom of the screen to call the police if Wolfe was sighted. Maggie walked into the living room and sat next to Brad. Wolfe's picture came back onto the screen.

Annie stood in the doorway. She gasped. Tears flowed.

Brad turned off the TV. "I'm sorry, Annie. I should have shut that off." He stood in the middle of the room, color draining from his face, feeling like a jerk.

Annie wrapped her arms around her chest, sobbing. Maggie jumped off the couch and put her arm around Annie's shoulder.

"I'm scared," Annie said. "He did horrible things to me. He's a monster. Do you think we're safe here?"

"Yes."

"Are you forgetting the night the bikers blew up your car?" Maggie asked.

Brad glared at Maggie, his you're-not-helping glare. "It's different now. The house is alarmed, Lobo is trained, and there will be cops here anytime I'm not here."

Annie turned and ran out of the room.

Maggie glared at Brad. Her you're-an-idiot stare. "What were you thinking, watching the news here?"

"I wanted to see how it went."

"You knew it was going to be on TV tonight?"

"Yeah."

"It's bad enough for Annie without you bringing it right into our home. For a bright guy, sometimes you're stupid. I'll see if I can settle Annie." Maggie stormed out of the room.

He collapsed into a chair, deflated. A tightness cramped his stomach, weight pressed on his shoulders, and an overpowering guilt for hurting someone he loved swarmed his mind. He'd made her cry. Maggie witnessed his stupidity. This was supposed to be Annie's safe place. For Annie's sake, he needed to make this right.

When Brad and Lobo got home from a run later that night, the house was quiet. He got Lobo settled with some fresh water and leftover hamburger, then tiptoed upstairs. The door was closed to Annie's room. In the master bedroom, Maggie was in bed, her back to the door. He stood in the doorway waiting to see if Maggie heard him or knew he was there. He felt like he should say something. Maybe apologize or agree he was an idiot or hit his head with a hammer or pull his fingernails out. He decided to let time pass and maybe in the morning he'd be out of the doghouse. Not that Lobo wouldn't like the company.

He showered and shaved and walked back into the bedroom. Maggie hadn't moved. He slid into bed as carefully as he could. He was torn between wanting to talk to Maggie and dreading they would talk. Rather, he'd do a lot of listening. Lobo wandered into the bedroom and took his spot at the end of the bed. Brad stared at the ceiling. Nothing they learned today about Wolfe was good and they were no closer to finding him. Lobo snored and Brad tried to settle his mind so he could sleep.

Wednesday Night

Brad awoke with a start, wide awake, soaked in sweat, his heart racing. He was eye to eye with Lobo. Brad glanced at the clock. 0100 hours.

"Hey, buddy. I guess I woke you up."

Brad swung his legs off the bed and stumbled downstairs, Lobo at his side.

He sat in his den in the dark. For almost a year the nightmares stopped. That was when he was off the street and studying. After less than two months back on the street, the nightmares had returned.

Lobo watched every move Brad made. "I can always count on you. My security blanket after a nightmare. You keep me sane."

He wasn't sure what the trigger was this time. Single event, the first murder or the rape of Billy-Lou. Maybe it was past horrors, his partner dying, killing his murderer, the senseless violence with the bikers. Or Jeter Wolfe. He'd barely touched the surface of the crap he'd seen over the years. Briscoe had told him to suck it up four years ago. That was the police mentality. Was it right? Was there another way? Telling anyone you were struggling would get you front-counter duty or prison transports. No thanks. He lived with the nightmares.

He turned at the creak on the stairs. Lobo jumped up, raced out of the room and growled. Then a scream. Brad flipped on the den light.

Annie stood on the second-last step, arms tight around her chest, shaking.

"Annie, are you okay?" Brad asked.

"Yes—well, no. Lobo scared me."

"What are you doing up?"

"I had a nightmare," she said.

"You have them often?"

She nodded.

"About Wolfe?"

"Seeing his face on TV terrified me." Annie burst into tears.

"I'm so sorry you saw Wolfe on TV. I'm an idiot." Brad put an arm around her shoulder and led her to the living room. He switched on a lamp and sat beside her on the couch. Lobo sat in front of her, then licked her hand.

Annie sobbed into his shoulder. A few minutes later she sat up and rubbed the tears from her face. "Why're you up?"

"The same reason as you, a nightmare."

"What? You get nightmares?"

"Yup."

"How often?"

"They stopped for a while, now they're back."

"Because of him?"

Brad nodded.

"Two years ago," Annie said, "after I was rescued, I had nightmares every night. The counselor helped me and after about a year they stopped. I was okay the first time he escaped, because I didn't know. When you told me I had to talk to the prosecutor and testify, the nightmares came back."

"I'm sorry. How often?"

"Every night until he was sent to the psych ward. Then they were fewer, but my subconscious knew he'd escape again. That was the theme of the nightmares—he came for me."

"I'm not going to let that happen. Nor will Lobo."

Annie wiped at her eyes. "How do you handle the nightmares?"

"Not very well. You're doing better than me."

"Do you go to counseling?"

"No," Brad admitted.

"You should."

He chuckled. "And here I thought I was comforting you."

"We can help each other."

CHAPTER FORTY

Thursday Morning

WOLFE WOKE AT DAWN AND GLANCED AROUND THE STRANGE ROOM. For a moment he couldn't figure out where he was. He sat on the edge of the bed and rubbed his eyes. *Right.* The abandoned house. He grabbed a cigarette and headed to the can. There were even towels, so he had a shower.

Thirty minutes later he headed out. He stopped at a 7-Eleven for a coffee and a couple of hotdogs, then headed northwest. Traffic was still light—the rush-hour traffic wouldn't start for another thirty minutes.

He drove past Blighe's house and was about to pull to the curb when he saw a gray Crown Victoria. The same car, probably the same cops. They paid him no attention. Wolfe parked at the end of the street next to a newspaper box. He slid out of the car and bought a paper. He was careful to keep his back to the cops. Back in his car he sipped coffee and read the newspaper. He spewed coffee when he saw the date—July 2—his court date. *I guess I get to keep my appointment with the crown prosecutor.*

He lowered the paper and focused his eyes on her house. First, check her routines—see if they'd changed.

He'd just finished his coffee when he saw her car back onto the street and drive in the opposite direction. If he was quick, he'd catch up to her by circling the block. He pulled up to the stop sign as she drove past, the Crown Victoria close behind. There was no need to follow her close—she was heading to work.

He took the back streets into downtown, parked in China Town and jogged to the corner. He was waiting at the lights when she drove past and into the car park. The unmarked police car stopped briefly on the street, then drove away. Wolfe was sure they were supposed to escort her to her office but after all night surveillance they were cutting corners. Good to know. Instead of crossing the street he leaned against the wall. Less than five minutes later she came out of the parking structure, briefcase in hand, and strode toward her office.

Wolfe crossed the street and followed a block behind. She entered the courthouse. Jenni Blighe was at work. For a second, he thought of going into the courthouse and catching a closer glimpse of the crown prosecutor. That was stupid. If the court security didn't recognize him, Blighe certainly would. The quick glimpse as she entered the courthouse would have to do. But soon, she'd be his.

That evening, Wolfe sat in a small bar on Seventeenth. He'd

pounded away three beers and two hot dogs. He was still hungry—maybe another dog or two. As he walked to get the hot dogs, he looked up at the TV. There was a good-looking blonde giving some report. The volume was low so it took him a moment to figure out what was happening. He knew the chick from somewhere. The camera pulled back and showed police headquarters in the background.

He leaned closer to the TV so he could hear what she was saying.

"We want to make the public aware of a fugitive who escaped custody and we believe is in Calgary. His name is Jeter Wolfe. He's a former member of the Gypsy Jokers' Motorcycle Club. The bikers call him Wolfman. The nickname is from his appearance." The screen changed from the chick to a picture of Wolfe. "We believe he is in the southeast, likely the Forest Lawn area."

Wolfe stared at the screen, jaw clenched, wide-eyed. He felt the burn move up his neck to his face. *The fucking bitch!*

"Wolfe escaped from both Edmonton Max and a psychiatric hospital. He was serving time for rape and murder. He's a suspect in one death and two rapes. Do not approach this man. He is extremely dangerous. If you see him, call police immediately."

Wolfman drove with the window down through the city center to the northwest. Those fucking cops. They'll pay. Fuck, his picture on TV. He was pretty sure he'd made it out of the bar before anyone connected him to the mugshot. Let's face it, none of those in the bar were there to catch the news.

He pulled into a 7-Eleven, grabbed scissors, shaving cream, a razor, and a pack of blades from the shelves. After he paid, he asked the clerk if he could use the restroom.

Inside, he locked the door and leaned over the sink. The long hair and beard had to go.

The scissors weren't the best. He hacked away randomly, the sink filling several times with hair and beard. He scooped up the hair and tossed it in the garbage bin.

Thirty minutes later he was down to skin. He rubbed the shaving cream over his face and shaved. It was weird with the beard gone. He'd had the beard for more than ten years. His face felt cold.

Shaving his head from the ears forward was easy. Shaving behind the ears was a disaster. He struggled with the opposite image in the mirror. When he thought he was shaving toward the middle of his head, he nicked his ears. Other times he twisted the razor sideways and cut his scalp. Finally, he was done. His head, particularly at the back, was a mess of razor cuts. In a few days he'd find a barber and get it done right.

He rinsed his head and face. The store clerk stared open-mouthed as Wolfman walked past.

Wolfe calmed while shaving. It was bad luck the cops showed his picture on TV, but what the hell, he'd easily fixed that.

Wolfe drove north on Crowchild Trail. As he neared her place his heart rate increased and he vibrated. After he'd escaped max, seeing her again was thrilling; the second time, he almost blew a wad. Then the fucking cops took it all away. This time he'd be more careful. This time he'd move around—never too long in one place. He drove toward her street and parked down the block.

Cigarette smoke drifted out of his window as he watched the house. He worried he was too late, but she was later. He chain-smoked while he waited.

The BMW turned right at the T-intersection and pulled into her driveway. She didn't look his way.

He focused his binoculars on the car—same routine as before. The driver's door opened, legs on display. Around to the passenger side and the kids jumped out. The three of them walked to the house.

The light was wrong tonight and the setting sun reflected off the picture window.

Fuck it. He opened the door and strolled toward her house— just a guy out for a walk. Well, a mountain of a man clean-shaven with a bald head. He looked like Mr. Clean.

He stopped just before he reached the corner of her yard, pulled out a pack of cigarettes and slid one out. He turned toward her house as he slowly slipped the pack into his pocket and lit a fresh cigarette. The sun still reflected off the glass. He couldn't see anything. *Shit.*

He walked to the end of the block, crossed the street, and walked back toward his car. The Crown Victoria was in its usual spot. He walked past the car as casually as he could. This was the real test of his new look. He walked past the cops, listening for a door to open, the sound of footsteps behind him. His brain shouted, "Run!"

In the car, he turned the ignition and slowly drove away.

For the next ten minutes he was sure the cops would stop him. Finally, he relaxed, but not much, and pulled to the curb.

He lit a cigarette and thought about his next move. He needed to visit in the morning, know that routine. Common sense said leave. His groin said to take her now. His brain said, "Not yet."

The cigarette burned to the filter and scorched his finger. *Damn.* He tossed the butt out the window.

He had a lot of pent-up tension from the TV report, her, and the cops. He needed a release. He knew just the place.

CHAPTER FORTY-ONE

Brad awoke to the ringing phone. He grabbed the receiver. "Coulter."

"Detective, it's dispatch. We got a homicide, downtown on Third Avenue."

"Hooker stroll?"

"Yeah, in the alley north. Detective Griffin wants you there."

"All right. I'm on my way."

Brad snuck into the spare bedroom where he kept his clothes for work. Late night callouts were routine now and changing in the spare bedroom let Maggie sleep. She slept like a log at home. At work, however, she slept in the shallow point just under consciousness, ready for the next medical call. Sleep to fully awake in seconds.

He crept down the stairs, Lobo at his side. Lobo went to the kitchen door and whimpered.

"Lobo, I have to go to work."

Lobo whimpered again.

All right. He let Lobo outside. Might as well make some coffee. Not like the hooker would get deader. *Where the hell did that come from?*

The coffee was ready at the same time Lobo wanted in. He shooed Lobo upstairs, then headed to his car.

———

Brad drove into the alley to the police tape and stopped. He showed his badge to a uniformed cop and ducked under the tape. Griffin stood by a dumpster.

"Morning," Brad said.

"Ah, did I wake you up? Why didn't you say you were in your jammies? We could've held the investigation until you were ready."

"That would have been more thoughtful. But I'm up now—what ya got?"

"You still sound sleepy. You need coffee."

"I had a cup."

"Obviously not enough."

"You going to yank my chain all morning or do you want to tell me what happened?"

Griffin shook his head. "Whiny to let's-get-going in ten seconds. Impressive."

Brad glared at Griffin.

"About an hour ago a driver came to pick up the dumpster," Griffin said. "As he pulled in, his headlights lit up the area and he saw someone sleeping next to the dumpster. Not unusual for downtown. So, he got out to wake the person up. When he reached the dumpster, he realized it was a naked woman. When he kneeled to roll her onto her back, her body moved one way, her head the other."

"What?"

"Her head is almost cut off from her neck. He called 911. The first cruiser and EMS showed up, all agreed she was dead. In some absolutely outstanding police work, the cops figured the death is suspicious. So, I got called. If I get called, so do you."

"Thanks, pal."

"Oh, no problem."

Sergeant Bill Sturgeon ambled up to them. "Why are you arseholes calling me out at this ungodly hour?"

Brad shrugged. "Griffin said if he gets called out, so do I. I'm just sharing the invite."

"You're an arsehole, Coulter. What do you have?" Sturgeon asked.

Griffin brought Sturgeon up to date.

"You're contaminating my crime scene," Sturgeon said. "Go get a coffee or breakfast. Don't come back for at least an hour."

Brad and Griffin sat at a table in the back corner of the restaurant. A mom-and-pop operation with about eight tables. Griffin said the breakfast special was to die for.

They sipped coffee in silence. Halfway through the second cup, Brad asked, "How do you do it?"

"Do what?"

"Every call for you is a body. Some, like this one, is pretty violent."

Griffin sipped his coffee, set the cup down, and stared at the liquid. "Dark sense of humor helps. Ragging on my partner. You, my friend, make it too easy."

The waitress set breakfast in front of them.

Brad ate quickly.

Griffin smiled. "You're half the way here."

"What do you mean?"

"You're eating after seeing a body."

"I've always been able to do that."

"For you in TSU it was boredom, then absolute terror. As a detective the pace is slower. I'm not saying we don't need to move quickly, but it's planned, methodical. As a homicide detective you arrived after the chaos—no adrenaline rush. She's dead. But she's also helpless. If we don't care about her, no one else will. That's wrong. I can't bring them back from the dead, but I can do everything I can to put the son of a bitch away and stop them from killing again. That's how I do it. I care when no one else does."

Brad spread strawberry jam on his toast. He chewed as he analyzed what Griffin said. In TSU, it was different. Split-second decisions come one after the other. A wrong decision and someone got hurt or dead. Maybe the slow pace was good for him.

"I like that," Brad said. "Caring when no one else does."

"It's not always that way. Often there are people who care. Then I'm doing it for the victim and their family and friends. I'm the only one who can give them some closure. Not much, but some."

Brad and Griffin headed back to the crime scene in silence.

Sturgeon met them by the dumpster. "This one is messy. Whoever did this is vicious. Worse than the other two, but a lot is the same. So, I'd say it's Wolfe. You know her head was almost cut off. But not with an axe. It was hacked off. He spent a lot of time with a knife, sawing at her neck. It's hard to tell in this light, but I'm pretty sure there are cigarette burns on her thighs. A lot of blood around her groin. I don't know what he did there. I don't even want to think about it."

"So, she wasn't killed here," Brad said. "This is a dump site."

"Good work, Coulter," Sturgeon said. "You figured that out on your own. Autopsy today about eight. Meet me there." Sturgeon smirked at Brad. "I know you love that part of the job."

———

Brad stopped at the Medical Examiner's Office at nine, after he got a coffee from Gerry's. He signed in and headed to the autopsy suites.

Sturgeon was waiting in the hallway. "Chicken shit."

"Slept in, sorry."

"Bullshit."

"Just give me the details."

"Fine. Maybe we should move close to the trash in case you need to hurl."

Brad glared.

"Most of the stuff I said at the scene the ME confirms," Sturgeon said. "There are cigarette burns on her thighs. Now the nasty stuff. You ready?"

Brad nodded. "Continue."

"She didn't die there. Wolfe, if it's him, dumped her there. The reason the ME knows for sure is she lost a lot of blood."

"If she bled, she was still alive."

"Yup. The reason for the bleeding wasn't the rape. Afterward, while she was alive, he violated her with a knife."

"Oh shit." Brad swallowed hard as bile assaulted his mouth. "Wolfe is escalating. This isn't about sex or domination. He's inflicting pain, torture. Worse each time. We gotta find him."

CHAPTER FORTY-TWO

Friday

Brad was seated at a diner near the Hells Angels' Clubhouse drinking coffee and eating the Friday morning breakfast special when Pickens came in. His two goons took up positions by the door.

Pickens slid into the booth across from Brad. "Let's make this quick."

"Sure," Brad said. "Same as last time: where is he?"

"Shit, Coulter," Pickens said. "Same as last time, I don't fuckin' know where he is."

The waitress brought a cup of coffee.

"I don't need that," Pickens said. "I'm not gonna be here long."

"You don't know where he is," Brad said. "Does that mean you've talked to him?"

"I'm not here to play word games with you," Pickens said.

"If I knew where that son of a bitch was, I'd let you know. I'm tired of his shit splattering on me. I don't need the attention."

"Is Wolfe bad for your business?" Brad asked. "That's gonna make me cry. If he's such a problem for you, then we need to work together."

"Since I took over, there's been no street war, no attacks on cops or judges. We've kept our noses clean."

"All you've done is take it underground," Brad said.

"Two years ago, we learned an open war is stupid. Back then everyone was against us—cops, judges, politicians, and the citizens. We were news every day. Now the only things the media sees are us doing good stuff, Christmas toy drives and helping neighbors. I don't want heat from the cops. If I knew where Wolfman was, I'd tell you."

"I'm supposed to take your word on this. Not this time, Pickens, no way. If I find out you know where heis, or that you're protecting him, putting the HA's out of business will become my fulltime job. We'll come down hard on your club."

"Your threats two years ago didn't bother me, and they don't now. I have a business to run." Pickens stood. "Good luck, Detective." He walked out of the restaurant—his goons followed.

Pickens stomped into the clubhouse, door slamming in the face of his driver and bodyguard.

"That son of a bitch. I told him to get out of town. Did he listen? No! Now Coulter thinks he can call me anytime he wants. He thinks I'll drop everything to meet him. I told Wolfe he'd draw heat on us. Motherfucker."

Pickens slumped into the chair in his office. His boys stood quietly at the door.

Pickens leaned forward, hands on his desk. "The cops want Wolfe. As long as he's out there, we're gonna be watched."

"What are we gonna do, boss?" the driver asked.

"We find Wolfe for the cops."

"What? Like catch and deliver him to the cops?"

"No. We find Wolfe, kill him, and leave his big fuckin' body to rot."

"If the cops can't find him, how're we gonna do it?"

"We've got better connections than Coulter has. Get the rest of the boys, get out there on the street and in the bars. Find Wolfman."

"What do you want us to do when we find him?"

"Kill him, slowly," Pickens said. "Leave him where the cops will find him. My gift to them."

CHAPTER FORTY-THREE

Friday Night

WOLFE SAT AT THE BAR ENJOYING A COLD BEER AND THE BARTENDER. She was late twenties, long brown hair, tight jeans and a quick, sarcastic wit. She wasn't intimidated by him. She'd said his head looked like a big white bowling ball. When he pushed too hard, she shut him down immediately.

She glanced down the bar and nodded as Wolfe held up the empty bottle. She slid a fresh beer in front of him and leaned forward, elbows on the counter, head in her cupped hands. "You've been staring at my ass all night and now your eyes are glued to my tits. What color are my eyes?"

Wolfe looked up from her breasts that threatened to pop out of her low-cut T-shirt. "You put it on display, I'm gonna look." He stared into sparkling blue eyes then took a long drink of beer. "I've heard the guys call you Linda. Is that really your name?"

"As far as anyone in this bar is concerned, that's my name. What's yours?"

"Slim."

She laughed. "You don't look slim. I doubt anything is slim."

From the end of the bar a group of guys in cowboy hats shouted for more beer.

"Be right there," Linda said, eyes boring into Wolfe's. "You gonna be here for a while?"

"If it's gonna be worth the wait."

"Oh, big boy, you don't know what you're in for." As she walked over to the group of cowboys, she exaggerated her walk.

Mighty fine. Mighty fine.

"Hey, he's not the only thirsty guy here," the loudest cowboy said. "We need another round."

"Cool your jets, rodeo clown. I'll get your beer."

"Move it a little faster, bar bitch." The cowboy looked to his pals who all laughed.

Wolfe started to get up, but Linda shook her head. She turned to the loud-mouthed cowboy. "You got some kinda problem?"

The cowboy grinned and winked to his buddies. "I sure do, honey. We need your sweet ass to move a little faster while you get our beer."

"Did you call me honey?"

Wolfe shook his head and took another drink of beer. This should be good.

"I sure did, sweet cheeks. How about we go somewhere and I ride me some cowgirl."

The cowboy nodded to his buddies and they slapped him on the back. When he turned to face Linda, her fist struck him on the nose, knocking him off his bar stool. His head hit the floor with a dull thud.

"You boys better get this asshole out of here before I decide who's next."

The cowboys dragged their friend out of the bar.

Linda strolled back to Wolfe. "Where were we?"

"I was about to ask you when you got off work."

"You were? Well, you should sit there and drink for another hour."

"I like your spunk. We could go somewhere and have a few drinks and get to know each other."

"You've been watching my ass all night. Does this have anything to do with getting in my jeans?"

"Everything."

Wolfe sat on the edge of the bed and reached for a package of cigarettes on the nightstand. He lit the smoke and inhaled deeply. He turned and stared at Linda. Bands of light from the streetlights filtered through the blinds, illuminating her face and her tousled hair. As she slept, it looked like she was smiling. He certainly was.

He was used to being the aggressor—in control. But not tonight. From the moment they'd stumbled into her house, she'd taken charge. He'd never let any woman do that before. She'd taken him places he'd never been. He was confused. What the hell happened last night? Had he lost his edge? It wasn't so much that she took charge, he gave that to her. Now as he looked at her, he had no urge to hurt her and he certainly wasn't going to kill her. He took the last puff on his cigarette and lit another from the red ash.

He slid off the bed and wandered to the kitchen. He opened the fridge, pulled out a beer and popped the cap. The beer tasted good. He'd drunk most of the bottle before he stopped. He leaned against the counter and stared into the bedroom. Linda had moved and the sheet had fallen off. The light shone on her breasts. He felt a stirring.

The back door burst open. Wolfe was showered with glass and pieces of wood. As he turned to the door, he was struck hard in the stomach by something solid. He doubled over and sank to his knees. As he looked up, a fist crashed into his temple. Pain blazed through his brain. He struggled to get up, but was hit across his back. He tried to fight past the new pain. If he didn't, he was a goner.

"The boss wants you dead," a voice said from the darkness. "But he said we could have some fun first. You know, a little batting practice."

Wolfe's eyes finally focused in the darkness. Two men stood over him. One held a baseball bat high, then brought the bat down. Wolfe put up his arm to defend against the blow. He screamed out in pain. He struggled to stand. With his right arm he grabbed a chair and pulled himself up, staggering as he fought to stay on his feet.

The kitchen lights came on, blinding them for a moment. He grabbed the counter for balance and willed his eyes to adjust to the light. Linda stood in the bedroom doorway, eyes wide.

"Shit." One attacker pulled a gun out of his belt.

Wolfe staggered away from the counter. He moved in slow motion. "No!"

The gun fired twice. Red circles formed on her chest, quickly expanding. She looked at Wolfe—the sparkle was gone from her eyes. She grabbed for the wall as she fell. Her body lay crumpled on the floor, her blank eyes staring.

CHAPTER FORTY-FOUR

Saturday Night

Brad and Devlin sat at a back table in a pizza restaurant. Brad looked over to Devlin, who appeared as defeated as Brad felt.

Devlin sipped a beer while Brad nursed a double rum and Coke.

"How does a guy six-foot-five and two hundred and fifty pounds disappear?" Brad asked, a question they kept coming back to time and again.

"Hell if I know," Devlin said. "Everything is coming up goose eggs."

"Steele and Zerr got nothing from the tattoo parlors," Brad said. "Not surprising."

"The undercover guys aren't doing any better." Devlin leaned back in his chair. "It's like we're chasing a ghost. Maybe Wolfe is long gone."

"I'd like to believe that, but he's got unfinished business here," Brad said. "He really wants Blighe."

"We've got her under twenty-four-hour protection. He can't get close to her."

Brad nodded. "Wolfe will find other victims until he gets Blighe. If it were just about sex or perversions, he'd leave. He's here and he's waiting for the right opportunity to get Blighe. He'll wait months if he has to. And he'll rape and kill when he needs to. At some point we'll stop her protection, then he'll pounce."

Their pagers beeped at the same time. Brad glanced at the number, then headed to the front of the restaurant and borrowed a phone. Dispatch gave him a message and he hung up. "Devlin, we gotta go."

In the car, Devlin asked, "What's going on?"

Brad hit the lights and siren. "Two bodies found at the city limits."

"Wolfe one of them?"

"Not sure. The cops on scene say they're big guys."

"If it's Wolfe, who's the other one?"

"Guess we'll find that out when we get there."

Brad had to park well back from the scene. The road was blocked by a dozen cruisers, a couple of ambulances, and a fire truck. They jumped out of the car, ducked under the police tape and jogged down the road to cops shining their flashlights at power poles.

Brad followed the flashlight beams to a man nailed to the pole. "Ah, shit." His face was severely beaten, with caked, dried blood. His arms and legs hung limp at weird angles.

A cop walked over to them. "Same thing on the next pole."

"Who called this in?" Brad asked.

"Dispatch says it was from a pay-phone a few miles back," the cop answered. "A guy said the cops would be interested in something left on power poles at the city limits. When the first cruiser got here, they saw the body and called for backup. We didn't find the second body for about twenty minutes. We were all kinda focused on this guy."

"Who are they?" Brad asked.

"Not sure, we didn't want to disturb the scene. Homicide and Ident are on their way."

Brad looked at the power pole and then to a cop standing at a cruiser. "Can you pull that cruiser closer and shine your spotlight on the body?"

"Sure."

He pulled the cruiser to the edge of the road and used the cruiser's powerful spotlight.

Brad stared at the body. Big guy, dressed in jeans and a tight T-shirt. Long hair tied back. His face was bloated, like a basketball. Brad moved as close as he dared. "Shit."

"What?" Devlin asked.

"That's one of Pickens' bodyguards."

"Are you sure?" Devlin asked. "Hard to tell from here."

"I know. I saw him earlier today with Pickens. Let's check the other guy."

At the next power pole they had a cruiser pull close and use the spotlight.

"That's the driver," Brad said. "I'm sure."

"Well damn. Wolfe's work?"

"I'd bet on it."

They waited until Griffin and Ident had investigated the scene. Sturgeon walked over. "You boys are keepin' me busy. I wouldn't mind a night off."

"They're Hells Angels," Brad said. "Any identification on them?"

"No wallets, no credit cards, or driver's licenses," Sturgeon said. "They both have large tattoos on their backs, Gypsy Jokers. Hells Angels tattoo on their shoulders. Someone was pissed with them."

"You think?" Devlin said.

"I don't know where to start. You could probably see from here that their arms and legs were broken. The probable cause of death was a thin wire. They were both garroted."

"Shit." Brad swallowed hard. "How'd they get here?"

"There's only one set of tracks to and from each pole, and drag marks. They were dead before they were nailed to the posts."

"One guy," Devlin said. "Those are two big suckers."

"Yup," Sturgeon said. "It would need to be someone bigger than them."

"Jeter Wolfe" Brad said.

"A couple more things." Sturgeon turned to them. "They were castrated and their tongues were cut out—before they were killed."

"Ah, jeez," Brad said.

"And the tongues are missing."

CHAPTER FORTY-FIVE

Sunday Noon

IT WAS NOON WHEN BRAD MET GRIFFIN OUTSIDE A HOUSE.

"What's up?"

"Call came in as a check on the welfare of the occupant," Griffin said. "First cops on scene met a lady who said she was a friend of the occupant, Linda. Linda missed two shifts of work, which was unusual for her. Linda's friend called a bunch of times and no one answered. So, she came here today, but no one answered the door either."

Brad shrugged. "We do dozens of those calls."

"First responding cops found the front door locked and no one responded. They walked around and looked in the windows. Then they saw that the back door was broken with shattered glass. When they pushed the door open a foul odor wafted out. They called for backup, then stepped into the house. As their eyes adjusted, they saw dried blood on the floor. Then they saw a body in the bedroom doorway—obviously dead. They backed out and called me. Sturgeon is inside with his techs."

"What do we know about her?" Brad asked.

"She works at a little bar on Seventeenth. She has always been a regular worker. She's late twenties, long brown hair. Might have been pretty in a hardened way."

"Are you thinking it was Wolfe?" Brad asked.

Griffin shrugged. "Too early to tell, but I'm suspicious of everything that happens out here. As far as I can tell, there was a big struggle in the kitchen. That's where the blood is, a *lot* of blood."

"From Linda?" Brad asked.

"No, I don't think so," Griffin said. "She's ten feet from the kitchen and there's no trail of blood between her and the blood in the kitchen."

"Two separate events?" Brad asked.

"That's the way I see it. Two days ago we found two of Pickens' thugs beaten to a pulp and missing tongues. Tongues that were cut out while they were alive. That would leave a lot of blood."

Brad nodded. "That makes sense."

"Is this where Wolfe has been hiding?" Griffin asked. "Did he shack up with Linda? Pickens' guys find him, they shoot Linda and Wolfe goes berserk?"

"That's a good timeline," Brad said. "Most of that fits. What's bugging me is Linda."

"How so?"

"She's got brown hair and she's older," Brad said. "As far as we can tell, she hasn't been abused in any way."

"She was shot," Griffin said.

234

"Sure, but I don't think that was Wolfe. That was Pickens' goons."

Griffin nodded. "You're right. He's been consistent in his targets. This was a pure and simple hookup. Maybe he's had a bunch of hookups. If he didn't rape or beat them, we'd never know. Maybe he's been with her for weeks. Knows her from before he went to prison. They got reacquainted when he escaped."

"That's a lot of guessing," Brad said. "It's hard for me to accept that Wolfe has a normal side. Have you talked to Linda's friend?"

"Not yet. I was waiting for you. She's over at that cruiser."

"Well, let's talk to her." Brad approached the woman standing with a uniformed cop by the cruiser. "I'm Detective Coulter. This is Detective Griffin. What's your name?"

"Alice."

"Last name, Alice?"

"Alice Leggett. Am I in trouble?"

Brad shook his head. "Not at all. We have a few questions for you."

"Okay." She chewed on a fingernail.

"How do you know Linda?"

"We work together."

"How long have you worked together?"

"About two years."

"Are you friends?"

"No—well, kinda, I guess."

"What does that mean?"

"We hung out sometimes. Not like we went shopping or got our nails done together, but sometimes after work we'd go to a better bar for a drink or two and look for guys."

"Did she have a boyfriend?"

"No. She'd hang out with a guy for a week or two, then she'd dump him."

"Did any of the guys get mad? Did they threaten her?"

"Nah. They just chased another skirt."

"Has she been friends with any guys lately?"

"Yeah. A couple of nights ago she was chatting up this big guy."

"Do you know his name?"

"No, I don't think she told me. She just said they were going out for drinks after work."

Brad felt his heart racing. "This big guy, did he have long dark hair and beard?"

"No," Alice said. "He was completely shaven, hair and face. Linda said he looked like a big bowling ball."

Brad's heart sank. "Did you see the TV press conference about the guy we're looking for, Jeter Wolfe?"

Alice nodded. "Oh, yeah. He was a mean-looking fuc … monster. Oh, I see, you think Linda was with him. No. Her guy was a lot different. His name wasn't Jeter. It might have been Jim."

Deflated, Brad looked to Griffin, who shook his head.

"Alice, did you give your name, address and phone number to the officer?"

She nodded.

Brad turned to the officer. "Be sure it is in your report and send me a copy." He turned back to Alice. "I'm sorry about your friend."

Alice shrugged, but Brad could see the tears forming in the corners of her eyes.

CHAPTER FORTY-SIX

Sunday Night

THAT NIGHT THE TASK TEAM DROVE AROUND THE SOUTHEAST looking for Wolfe. They hit every dive bar, massage and tattoo parlor, and cruised the alleys. Devlin had talked to hundreds of dealers.

Just after midnight, Brad, Griffin, and Devlin met with Tina for a coffee. As Brad looked around the table, he saw exhaustion, defeat. They'd been working twenty-hour days without any success. He'd barely been home in the last four days, and then only to catch four hours of sleep before hitting the streets again. Even strong coffee couldn't keep him focused. He was sure the others were the same.

"You guys look like crap," Tina said.

"And you think you're ready for a fancy ball?" Griffin asked. "Have you looked in the mirror lately?"

Devlin sniffed. "You all smell bad."

"That's funny coming from you," Brad said. "You ever wash those clothes?"

"Not since I bought them at a thrift store."

"When was that?" Tina asked.

"About ten years ago," Devlin said.

"That would be funny if I wasn't so tired." Brad sighed. "This was a waste of a night."

"Not completely," Devlin said. "A bunch of dealers I talked to are real happy. A week ago a big dude sold hospital-grade drugs to them. They're making a fortune demanding a high price for the real stuff. They bought more off him Thursday, but haven't seen him since."

"Wolfe?" Brad asked. "The hospital drugs he stole."

"Yeah, I think so."

"Look, we're all exhausted and no good to anyone," Brad said. "If Wolfe walked in here right now, we likely wouldn't recognize him. I say we pack it in for the night. Sleep in late and we can be back here in the late afternoon and keep looking."

"I'm all for that," Griffin agreed.

"It's still early," Tina said. "Maybe a couple more hours."

"No, Tina. I'm bagged," Brad said. "See you tomorrow."

"One more hour?"

"Sure," Devlin said. "Let the pretty boy go home and get his beauty sleep."

"Thank you," Griffin said.

"Not you, asshole. I meant Coulter."

"Now I'm hurt," Griffin said. "I'm outta here."

"Let's go, Tina," Devlin said. "I'm good for a few more hours."

Pickens was working late in his office. Hells Angels National wanted a report on his business and they wanted it tomorrow. On the good side, they were doing well, very well. National would be happy with that. On the negative, the cops were making things difficult in their hunt for Wolfe. He dropped his pen, leaned back in his chair, and rubbed his eyes. The cops would do more and more raids and hassle dealers and hookers until they found Wolfe. That was not good for business and next month's report would not make National happy.

A knock at the door interrupted his thoughts. Pickens rocked forward. "Come."

A young biker whose name he didn't remember came in. "Sorry to bother you, boss, but this package was at the front door. It's addressed to you and marked urgent."

Pickens sighed and reached for the package. It was smaller than a shoebox and light. "All right, thanks. You can leave."

Pickens placed the box on his desk. It was addressed to him, but there was no return address or postage. Curious—and suspicious.

He carefully examined the packaging. On the outside he found nothing amiss.

Cutting the tape on the brown paper wrapping, Pickens slid it away. Still nothing.

He sliced the tape holding the lid in place and slowly lifted the top.

A putrid odor escaped. Gagging, he put the lid aside and peered into the box.

Set in a bed of tissue were two chunks of brown, rotting meat.

Pickens recoiled and his stomach rolled. After a few deep breaths he dared look in the box again. He'd seen this before—a message about traitors—their tongues.

CHAPTER FORTY-SEVEN

TINA AND DEVLIN DROVE AROUND FOR AN HOUR. THEY SAW FEWER and fewer people on the streets. "Even the bad guys are asleep," Devlin said.

"Are you bailing on me?" Tina asked.

"Not yet, but soon. It looks like Brad is taking to this detective gig."

Tina stared ahead and nodded. "He does what he likes and gives it his all."

"True, he took to TSU. That first team was excellent."

"Do you miss it?"

"Nah. It was fun, but narcotics is my thing." Devlin shifted in his seat so he was facing Tina. "I hear you and Zerr have been on a few dates."

Tina swung her head to Devlin. "Where'd you hear that?"

"I wasn't sure, but you just confirmed it."

"Ass."

"So, how's it going?"

"What's with the personal questions?"

Devlin grinned. "You're the one who wanted a partner for tonight, so I'm getting to know my partner."

Tina drove in silence, then said, "It's early, but we get along. We're both kinda feeling this out. Cops dating cops or cops marrying cops seldom ends well."

"Wow! You've talked about marriage!"

"That's not what I said! We aren't rushing into anything."

"But?"

Tina turned to Devlin and smiled. "But it's going great. He's hard to read. Most cops don't do emotion well. Add into that his military experiences and it's even worse. But I'm breaking down a few walls."

"That's awesome. He truly is a great guy. He's very dependable and honest." Devlin's head jerked to the side. "Stop here."

Tina stopped at the curb. Devlin rolled his window down and waved a woman over.

She leaned on the roof of the car and looked in. "You lookin' for some company—" She leaned in, saw Tina, then looked back at Devlin. "Ah, shit. Cops."

"We don't want you," Devlin said. "I need you to look at a photo. Tell me if you've seen this guy."

"You ain't gonna arrest me?"

"Nope." Devlin passed Wolfe's picture to her.

She turned the picture toward the streetlight. "Yeah, I seen this guy around. I seen him late at night selling drugs to dealers. The dealers tell me it's good shit. Real shit, like from a pharmacy."

"When did you last see him?" Devlin asked.

"Maybe three days ago, I guess."

"Do you know where he lives? Or a bar he hangs out in?"

"No clue where he's stayin'. Can't say about the bars. I'm mostly on the street."

Devlin nodded. "Thanks for your help. Stay safe."

The woman leaned into the car again. "I seen him a couple of times hanging out at the convenience store a half mile east. I think that's where he meets the dealers."

Devlin grinned. "Thanks."

Tina pulled away from the curb, drove down the street, and pulled into the store's parking lot. "Let's see if the night clerk recognizes Wolfe."

"You go," Devlin said. "I got the info. You confirm it."

"You lazy shit."

"I'll wait here. Unless you get something really good, we're calling it quits for the night. Nothing is happening out here." Devlin slumped in the seat and closed his eyes, arm hanging out the window.

"Fine." Tina walked to the store.

CHAPTER FORTY-EIGHT

BRAD WEAVED AROUND THE SOUTHEAST. HE'D SAID HE WAS BEAT, and he was, but he couldn't bring himself to head home. He could barely keep his eyes open. Finally, he turned toward home. He was crossing Deerfoot Trail when the radio blared "Code 200, officer down. Seventeenth and Thirty-Sixth Street."

He swung his Firebird in a U-turn and sped across the city. The minutes passed. All he could do was listen to the radio and reports as cops arrived at the scene.

The first crew on scene said they found one officer outside the car unconscious. He requested EMS.

When Brad arrived, the scene was filled with police cars and an ambulance.

He jumped out of his car, raced over to the ambulance and yanked open the back door. Paramedic Willie Dixon glared as Brad looked in. "A little busy in here, Coulter. Wait outside."

Brad's eyes stared at Devlin, unconscious on the stretcher. "How is he?"

"He took a nasty beating. He was unconscious when we arrived. We gotta get out of here and get him to the hospital. Come with us if you want, but we gotta go."

"I'll catch up to you later." Brad jumped out of the ambulance and closed the door.

He wandered over to a group of cops standing around the unmarked police car. "Who's in charge?"

A sergeant stepped away from the group. "I am."

"Briscoe. What happened?"

"The owner of the store called it in. He said a cop was in his store showing him photos of a guy she was looking for. There was a scuffle outside. She told him to call 911 and say a cop is code 200. After the call, he looked out the window and saw a man on the ground beside the car. A big guy was fighting with the lady cop."

"Tina?" Brad's gut rolled. He already knew the answer.

"Yup. He tossed Davidson into a van through the sliding door. Then he went back and put the boots to Devlin. He jumped in the van and peeled out of here."

"Do you have a description of the van and a plate number?"

"Yeah, not much to go on. He said it was a van with a sliding door and dark blue or dark gray. He wasn't sure. The van left the parking lot and headed east. That's all we've got so far. I put a BOLO out on the partial plate number. Got cops cruising around the area doing what we can."

"Was it a robbery?" Brad asked.

"Not likely."

"Anything missing?" Brad asked.

"Tina's badge and radio. Devlin's gun, too."

"Where's Tina's gun?" Brad asked.

"I found it under the car on the driver's side."

"Mind if I take a look around?"

"It's all yours."

Brad walked over to the open passenger's door. Blood was spattered on the inside. Outside the car on the ground was the debris left behind by the paramedics. He wandered around to the driver's side. This door was open as well. Tina's purse was on the driver's seat. He shone his flashlight in and waved it around. On the floor mat he saw lip gloss, tissue, keys, a brush and gum. He searched the rest of the car, but didn't find a badge case, radio, or Devlin's gun.

A few feet away from the car he saw what remained of a pager—smashed.

Brad parked outside the emergency entrance and rushed toward the trauma rooms. As he passed the triage desk, a nurse said, "Can I help you?"

Brad showed his badge and kept walking.

"You can't go back there," the nurse said.

He continued down the hallway. Dixon stood outside a trauma room.

Brad watched the emergency staff buzz over Devlin. From where he stood, Brad could see Devlin's face bruised and bloated beyond recognition. Bruises and scrapes showed on his exposed chest. An alarm sounded. Activity around Devlin increased. He heard someone say *tension pneumothorax*. He knew what that was, and it wasn't good. They assisted Devlin's breathing and put a tube into his chest. Activity slowed.

Brad's jaw clenched, his gut tightened, as he opened and closed his fists. Five minutes with Wolfe. That's all he needed.

"How's he doing?"

Dixon looked over and shook his head. "He was roughed up pretty good. You can see the bruises to the ribs and stomach. Probably a few broken ribs. I think his face might've been smashed into the pavement a couple of times. His nose is broken, a couple of teeth are missing. The left arm looked broken. He was unconscious the whole time we had him. Docs say it's highly likely that he has a bad concussion. Maybe a brain bleed, but they're leaning more toward a concussion. That's all we got. He'll go for X-rays soon. Hopefully they know more when they get the X-rays back."

Shit. Brad pointed down the hall. "Can we go to the coffee room? I've got some questions for you."

Dixon nodded. They took seats in the coffee room.

"What did you see when you arrived?" Brad asked.

"We followed the first cruiser in," Dixon said. "Before we got our kits out there were cops everywhere," Dixon said. "The car doors were open. Devlin was lying on the pavement beside the passenger door. A couple of cops were kneeling next to him. He was unconscious. There was blood around his head."

"Where was he bleeding from?"

"Most of it was from his face—nose and mouth, also from lacerations to his head. His pupils were uneven so we thought head injury right away. Thompson grabbed two cops and they helped him with the stretcher. We rolled him onto a spine board then onto the stretcher. We were getting ready to race to the General Hospital when you opened the back door."

"Did anything stand out as suspicious or out of place?"

Dixon nodded. "Yeah. Both front doors were open, but Devlin was the only one there. I asked if there was another injured cop. The cops looked at each other, like there was something they weren't telling me. One cop said, 'No.' That seemed weird, but Devlin was in bad shape, so we focused on him. Was there another cop injured?"

Brad nodded. "Tina Davidson. We don't know if she's hurt, but she's missing."

"Missing?" Dixon asked. "Like she walked away from the scene?"

"No. We think she was kidnapped." Brad pulled out a business card and handed it to Dixon. "You guys hear anything, anything at all, have dispatch page me."

CHAPTER FORTY-NINE

BRAD SKIDDED HIS CAR TO A STOP, OPENED THE DOOR, AND slammed it shut. He sprinted up the sidewalk. He pounded on the door and waited. No answer. He hit harder this time, and waited. Still no response. He battered on the door continuously until finally it opened.

A burly Hells Angels biker filled the door and frame. "What do you want?"

Coulter stepped close. "I need to talk to Pickens, now."

"Fuck you, he's busy," the biker said.

Brad jabbed a finger into his chest. "Tell ... Pickens ... Coulter wants to see him now."

The biker stood his ground and stared back.

Brad pulled out his badge and shoved it into the biker's face.

The biker smirked. "That doesn't impress me."

Brad grinned. "No?" He drew his pistol and thrust it into the biker's chest. "Does this impress you? How about we go inside and talk to Pickens, now?"

The biker backed away and started down a hall. Brad followed. Other bikers, sitting around a table, started to get up. Brad swung his pistol in their direction. "Sit down."

They stopped, frozen in motion, and stared at Brad. Discretion being the better part of valor, they sat.

Brad followed the biker to the end of the hall. He opened the door and stepped aside. Brad glanced into the room. Pickens sat at a desk.

Brad smiled at the biker, said, "Thank you for your cooperation," and stepped into the office.

Pickens stood, jaw clenched, eyes ablaze, veins pulsing at his temple. "What are you doing here, Coulter?" His eyes dropped to Brad's pistol. "Are you crazy? Walking into my clubhouse flashing a gun."

Brad smiled. "I asked nicely but your boy didn't understand nice. So, I asked in a way he'd understand."

"Put the gun away," Pickens said. "It'll be best for your health. What the hell do you want?"

"I came to talk to you about our friend, Wolfe. I thought we had a deal. I thought you were going to let me know when you found him. I thought you knew to let me take care of it."

"I don't know what you're talkin' about," Pickens said.

"Bullshit. You found him and you sent guys to kill him."

This time Pickens grinned. "Coulter, you're always making up crazy shit."

Brad holstered his gun and sat across from Pickens. "How about we start over. Tell me about Wolfe."

Pickens sat. "Okay, we found him."

"How?" Brad asked.

Pickens grinned. "We've got better contacts than you. It wasn't that hard when we put our minds to it."

"We had a deal," Brad said. "You said you'd call."

Pickens leaned back in the chair with his hands behind his head. "Yeah. I changed my mind."

"You changed your mind and ordered a hit on Wolfe," Brad said.

Pickens shook his head. "I'm not admitting anything. All I'm saying is we found him."

Brad leaned forward, eye to eye with Pickens. "Here's what I think. Your story is good to a certain point. You put out the word. Your boys found him and tried to kill him. How did that work out?"

Pickens swung forward in his chair. "Fuck you, Coulter."

"We both have a reason to want Wolfe dead. Tell me where he is."

"I don't know."

"What will your boys say if I asked them?"

Pickens shook his head. "You know they won't say shit. That's the biker code."

"I want to know where he is," Coulter said. "Get your boys out there again. Find him. Then call me."

Pickens stood and glared at Brad. "Not a fuckin' chance. He made this personal. He killed my bodyguards. They were my closest friends—were with me from the start. Maybe you remember them from our first meeting. We *are* looking for Wolfe. When *we* find him, *we* will take care of our problem, and yours. I'm going to give you one minute to get out of my clubhouse. I'll hold my boys off for one minute. After that, you're fair game."

CHAPTER FIFTY

Monday Early Evening

BRAD PEELED THE POLICE TAPE OFF THE DOORFRAME. HE USED Tina's key and unlocked the door. He hadn't been in the apartment for over four years. It looked the same—very clean, with a woman's touch.

Griffin followed Brad into the living room. "Any idea of what we're looking for?"

"No. I hope we know when we see it."

"Roger that. I'll take the living room and kitchen."

Brad walked to the bathroom. Like the rest of the place, it was spotless. He opened the medicine cabinet and examined the contents. The usual stuff: Tylenol, Advil, birth control pills and a box of condoms with a few missing.

For the few months they dated they'd always come to her place. He'd been surprised the first night they slept together by the variety and quantity of condoms. They'd done a pretty good job of testing out the various brands.

He closed the medicine cabinet and walked to the bedroom. The bed was made with at least a dozen pillows. Nothing looked out of place, except ... on her dresser a picture lay on its face. He turned it over. It was a picture of Tina and him from four years ago. They were dressed in western wear for the Stampede Rodeo. Her face glowed. He set the picture upright on the dresser then sat on the bed. He opened the top night table drawer—a few novels, a fashion magazine, and two Guns and Ammo. There were a few research papers, mostly from the FBI, about the science of criminal profiling, and a sleep mask. The bottom drawer contained more novels, more research papers and condoms. He closed the drawer. She wasn't right for him, but she was an intelligent and beautiful woman. Even after they'd split, she remained devoted to him, something not lost on Maggie. She'd finally found a good guy. Brad could tell this was killing Zerr.

Griffin walked into the room. "Nothing of interest out there. You find anything?"

Brad nodded. "I feel like I'm intruding."

Griffin glanced at the photo. "I knew you two were friends, but it was more than that, wasn't it?"

"That's from a long time ago. Doesn't mean I don't care."

"We have to find something to lead us to her. Maybe Wolfe sent her something, a threatening note."

"She would have told us—me, for sure," Brad said.

"Are you done in here?"

"No. I haven't checked the closet or dresser drawers. You take the closet."

Brad felt weird, creepy-weird, going through her underwear and clothes. He found an envelope. It contained more photos of them together. He suddenly had an ominous feeling trickle down his back, his chest tightened and his breath came in gasps. They weren't going to find Tina alive.

CHAPTER FIFTY-ONE

Monday Late Night

ZERR JUMPED OUT OF THE CAR AND MADE A BEELINE FOR THE TOWN & Country Bar. Steele sprinted after him. "Charlie! Charlie, slow down, buddy. Let's talk about this."

Zerr ignored Steele and walked faster.

"Come on, Charlie. Jeez, come on, buddy. I know you're hurting but there's no sense getting us killed."

"If there's any killing, it'll be by me."

Steele looked over his shoulder. Two marked cruisers pulled into the parking lot. When the officers got out, he frantically waved them over.

Zerr burst through the door of the T&C and stopped, letting his eyes adjust to the dull light.

Steele was at his side. "Okay, let's slow down. Let's look around and make a plan."

Zerr stared around the bar. His eyes came to rest on a group of Hells Angels in the far corner. "There they are."

"Slow down, big fella, slow down. There are about a dozen bikers there. You, me and …" He glanced back. Four rookies stood nervously about ten feet behind them. "Uh, you and me."

"Sounds about right," Zerr said.

"Now you sound like Coulter."

Zerr grinned. "That's about right."

Zerr strolled over to the bikers, Steele hot on his heels. The rookies scrambled along behind, not sure what to do.

Zerr looked down at the bikers. "Okay, motherfuckers. I've got one question and one question only. Answer my question, I leave. You don't answer my question—things are going to get nasty."

The biggest, ugliest biker stood. "And who the fuck are you?"

Zerr smiled. "Calgary Police."

"This is a biker bar. So, why don't you and your buddy take your scared deputies out of here and go to your own club. What's it called, the pig and whistle?"

"That's good," Zerr said. "Really funny. All right, to the question. Where's Jeter Wolfe?"

The bikers looked at each other.

The big guy said, "Don't know nothing about a wolf. I heard a good story about werewolves. Was you looking for werewolves?"

Zerr grinned and stepped toward the big biker. "You should be doing comedy. I'll try again. Where is Jeter Wolfe?"

The biker grinned. "Jeter Wolfe. He's the Gypsy Joker that almost died a couple of years ago. Big head injury. Crazy motherfucker. Don't know nothin' about him."

Zerr stepped closer. "That's weird. I heard he killed a couple of your boys. I thought you'd want to know where he is instead of hiding here. I thought you'd be out looking for him. Maybe you're all scared and worried you'll be next."

Red crept up the biker's neck as he clenched and unclenched his fists. "Look, pig, you need to leave now or this won't end well."

Zerr grinned again. "I want that SOB. I don't care how many of you I take down to find him."

The biker shook his head. "I got no beef with you, pig. I can't help you. Why don't you and your buddies get out of here and we'll call it square. We'll pretend like you never came here."

"That's not going to work for me," Zerr said. "That's not going to work at all. You guys found him once and I think you'll find him again. You know places he might be. Tell me and I leave or keep talking shit and we'll have a problem."

The biker folded his arms across his chest. "Well, then I guess we got a problem."

Zerr's left fist came in a fast uppercut. The biker's head snapped back, his eyes rolled, and he collapsed to the floor. Eleven bikers were on their feet in an instant.

Zerr squared off against the next closest biker and fired a couple of jabs to his head.

Steele and the rookies were quickly surrounded by the other bikers. Too dangerous to draw their guns in the crowded bar— suicide to leave them in a holster.

The bikers were content to let their friend duke it out on his own. Zerr was getting in some good shots but the biker was getting in just as many. Zerr's head snapped back a couple of times as the biker connected with a left and a right, and then another left and right.

Zerr staggered backward. Steele was sure Zerr was going to drop. His shoulders sagged and he wobbled on unsteady legs. Then Zerr stood tall, his fists flying and pounding the biker. He fell to the floor beside his buddy.

The bikers enjoyed watching Zerr fight their man. But they weren't accepting that their buddy lost.

They turned on Steele and the rookies. The fight was on. The first biker stepped too close to Steele, who punched the biker once in the throat, collapsing his windpipe. The biker dropped to the floor, clutching his throat, his mouth opening and closing like a fish out of water.

Another biker swung a beer bottle that glanced off the side of Steele's head. He saw stars and his vision blurred. A second bottle crashed against the side of his head. A chair disintegrated on his back. He dropped to his knees.

Through his blurred vision he could see the rookies fighting with the bikers, but they were no match. It was going to be a massacre.

Steele pushed himself into a kneeling position and tried to stand but couldn't. He collapsed onto the floor and rolled onto his back. When his eyesight cleared, he saw four big guys wailing away on the bikers. They looked like construction workers. In the distance, Steele heard sirens and then the bar was full of cops. Twenty or more.

One of the construction guys lifted Steele off the floor and dropped him into a chair next to Zerr.

A couple of the rookies stood, dazed. The others grinned through puffy lips and spit blood.

The fight was over. The big construction guy was talking to Sergeant Briscoe, who was nodding his head.

The bikers were cuffed and marched out. Paramedics rushed into the bar. Briscoe sent them over to Steele and Zerr.

Steele turned to Zerr. "What the hell was that about?"

Zerr looked back with two glazed eyes, dark circles already forming. "I thought if I took them down one at a time, we might have a chance."

Steele shook his head. "One at a time? You barely got two down."

"Yeah, well—" Zerr's grin was lopsided. "How many did you take out?"

"One."

Zerr laughed. "I guess I'm ahead."

They stopped talking while the paramedics shone a light in their eyes, checked their grip, took blood pressures and pulses. The paramedics gave them ice packs for the bruises forming on their faces. Zerr got extra icepacks for his swollen knuckles. They cleaned a large cut on the back of Steele's head and told him he'd need stitches.

They leaned back in the chairs.

"We didn't get any information, did we?" Steele said.

"Nope. Zero."

"Explain to me why we did this?" Steele asked.

Zerr shrugged. "I had some frustration I needed to work out."

Steele nodded. "You got that out of your system?"

Zerr smiled. "I think so. For now."

"What were you thinking?" a new voice boomed.

They turned at the same time. Brad Coulter.

"Hey, boss," Steele said. "Good of you to stop by."

"Yeah, boss," Zerr said. "It's okay. We got it under control."

Brad shook his head. "Under control, my ass." Brad nodded

to the big construction guy. "You're lucky these guys jumped in when they did."

Steele shrugged. "I guess we owe you guys big."

The construction guy nodded. "You owe us way more than that."

"Why?" Steele asked.

"You screwed up a two-year undercover operation."

Brad's eye grew wide. "What are you talking about?"

"We're narcotics undercover. I'm Mitchell. We've been working this bar for over two years. First it was a Gypsy Jokers and Satan's Soldiers. Now it's the Hells Angels. But the operation is busted."

Zerr's head dropped. "Sorry."

"It was time to shut this down anyway." Mitchell smiled. "This is the second time our operations have been interrupted by cops too big for their britches. The first time we didn't have to intervene, so we kept our cover. This time we didn't have a choice."

Brad turned to them. "What do you mean the first time?"

Mitchell grinned. "Two years ago, the sergeant for TSU came into the bar. He wasn't in uniform, but we recognized him right away. He picked a fight with four bikers playing pool. For some reason he thought he could take them. They got the better of him. We called for backup. We were ready to intervene if needed. But the bouncers stopped the fight. Before the bouncers kicked the shit out of him, the first cops arrived."

Brad laughed. "Ah, crap. You guys saved my ass two years ago."

Mitchell grinned. "Yeah, we did. The bikers gave you a good beating. It was kinda fun to watch. I guess sooner or later you guys were gonna blow our cover."

"We're a little hotheaded right now." Brad glanced at Zerr, then back to Mitchell. "You guys hear anything about Jeter Wolfe?"

"Only that he wasted two Angels," Mitchell said. "They're looking for Wolfe harder than you. My money's on them finding him first. When they're done, there won't be anything left to identify."

"All right," Brad said. "Thanks again. When this is all done, Zerr owes you a night of free beer."

The big guy grinned. "We like beer."

CHAPTER FIFTY-TWO

Tuesday Early Morning

Brad slipped quietly into the house. He reset the alarm, kicked off his shoes, and hung his jacket on the coat hook by the door. He turned and gasped. Lobo was sitting there in the dark, eyes shining, tongue hanging.

Brad knelt. "Jeez, Lobo. Don't you know it's not nice to sneak up on someone. Especially someone as exhausted as me." Lobo followed Brad to the kitchen. He opened the fridge and stared at the contents. *Screw it*. He grabbed a beer and popped the cap. "Lobo, come." They walked out of the kitchen and down the hall to Brad's office. He plunked into his chair and took a long drink of the beer. *Ah, that hits the spot*. Lobo sat at his feet and was snoring within seconds.

How could things have gone so horribly wrong? He couldn't piece it together. How was Wolfe ahead of him? How did Wolfe know what they were doing? And how the hell had Wolfe found Tina and Devlin.

He took a big breath, leaned back in the seat, and closed his eyes. Mistake. He could see their empty car. Blood on the passenger side, and in his mind, he could see Devlin lying on the ground. Blood pooling around him.

On the driver's side he saw the struggle. Wolfe attacking. Tina putting up a valiant fight. But there was no way she was going to stop him. Maybe Wolfe hit her. Maybe he choked her. Maybe Wolfe simply overpowered her and threw her in the van. Who knew? This was screwed up.

He opened his eyes. Maggie was standing in the doorway. "You're home late. Well, early, I guess. It's almost sunrise. I didn't even see you yesterday."

"It was a messed up day."

"Are you okay?"

"Tina was kidnapped."

Maggie gasped. "When? How?"

"She was working with Devlin. I thought we should call it a night late Sunday evening. Tina wanted to keep looking for Wolfe. Devlin said he'd work with her for an hour or two. They stopped at a convenience store. The clerk called 911 saying cops were being assaulted."

Maggie sat in a chair opposite Brad. "Wolfe?"

Brad nodded.

"You said she was with Devlin. How is he?"

Brad shook his head. "Not good. When the first crew got there, they found him unconscious. Dixon and Thompson rushed him to the hospital. He was unconscious the whole way."

"Let me call the hospital. I'll find out what's happening." Maggie started to get up but Brad shook his head. "Not now. You won't find out anything. I was at the hospital in the morning. They're running tests. They're not going to know for a while."

"You need to sleep. It's been days since you've slept."

Brad stood, took Maggie's hand and pulled her up. "A few hours. Then I need coffee. Lots of it. Something to eat and a shower. Then I go after that son of a bitch."

"I know you're upset—"

"Frickin' right I'm upset. I have one job. Find Wolfe and put him back in jail."

"What happens now?" Maggie asked.

"I'm going to kill him."

CHAPTER FIFTY-THREE

Tuesday Late Night

Late that night, Brad and Griffin leaned against the car sipping coffee.

"We've been searching the southeast for two nights," Brad said. "Half the cops in the city are searching for Davidson. We haven't found the van. We don't know that she's even in this area. If we don't get a decent tip soon, it won't be good." Brad drank some coffee.

Griffin stared at the dark liquid in his cup. "I don't know what to say. You're right. We've covered this area so many times I know it like the back of my hand."

"How is Wolfe eluding us? He's the size of the Sasquatch, about as ugly, and probably stinks worse. He would standout everywhere, yet no one has seen him or recognizes his picture. Do we still focus on the southeast?"

"What little we have points here," Griffin said.

The radio came to life. "All units southeast, from EMS dispatch, they've lost contact with one of their ambulances. Last known location was Seventeenth Avenue at Sixtieth Street southeast for a 'man down' complaint."

Brad flung his coffee onto the asphalt and jumped into the car. He had the car squealing out of the parking lot before Griffin had the door shut. The car bounced over the curb as he raced toward Seventeenth Avenue. A quick right turn and he accelerated.

"Slow down," Griffin said.

Brad kept his foot on the accelerator, eyes sweeping the road. He grabbed the mic. "Dispatch, get any close unit responding now. Treat it as a code 200."

"Oh shit," Griffin said. "Is Maggie working tonight?"

"Yeah."

"I'm sorry," Griffin said. "Keep going." He braced his hand against the dashboard.

"Update from EMS," dispatch said. "They're still unable to get in contact with the crew."

Griffin keyed the mic. "Do you know what ambulance unit/station or who the crew members are?"

"Sorry," dispatch said. "We don't have that information. I'll check."

Brad slammed his hands against the steering wheel several times. "Shit, shit."

A few blocks ahead they saw the red-and-blue lights of police vehicles. Brad caught up and was tempted to pass, but stayed close behind. They were going just as fast as he was.

Up ahead they saw the red flashing lights of the ambulance parked at the side of the road.

One police vehicle pulled in front of the ambulance, another to the side and Brad pulled in behind. He'd barely put the car in park when he was opening the door and racing toward the ambulance. He opened the back door. No one was inside. The cupboards were empty, and the medical supplies were strewn on the floor.

Brad raced to the driver's door. The cab was empty. He turned to the responding cops. "We're gonna start a search. Two guys each side in the ditch. Go slow. We gotta find the paramedics."

They walked down the ditches, Brad and two cops on the left, Griffin and two cops on the right.

Brad found Sharma, conscious, with his arms and legs bound with tape. A wide strip of tape covered his mouth. Brad ripped the tape off his mouth.

"Is Maggie your partner?"

"Maggie's with Fola on Medic 12. I'm working with a new guy, Jay. Did you find him?"

Brad shook his head and cut the tape off Sharma's hands and feet.

Sharma sat up and rubbed his wrists. "Our assailant dragged him over to the ditch. I couldn't tell where they went. It was too dark."

"Griffin," Brad yelled. "A paramedic is missing. Get some guys and start a search in the ditches."

"What the hell happened?" Brad asked Sharma.

"When we got here a big guy was lying in the middle of the road. We almost didn't see him it was so dark. He was lying on his stomach. I asked if he was okay but got no response. We rolled him onto his back. Next thing I know he's got a knife to my neck. He demanded our drugs. I told him the drugs were in the ambulance and he was welcome to them.

"The guy told my partner and me to lie down on our stomachs, then used tape to secure my arms and legs. When he tried to tape my partner, Jay fought. I yelled for him to relax, but he kept fighting. The big guy slammed my partner's head onto the road a bunch of times. Jay stopped fighting. The guy taped Jay's arms and legs, then put tape over our mouths.

"He dragged me into the ditch, Jay somewhere else. Then he went to the ambulance. I heard a lot of crashing and banging in the ambulance.

"Then he came back. He pulled the tape off and held the knife to my neck. He asked for the keys to the drug safe. I told him they were on my belt. The guy put the tape over my mouth again and grabbed the keys. I heard his boots crunch on the gravel, the ambulance door opened, and then silence. About a minute later I heard the ambulance door shut. A vehicle started and he was gone."

"Hey, Coulter," Griffin yelled. "We found the other paramedic. He's unconscious. We're gonna need EMS."

Sirens sounded in the distance. Brad looked back toward Seventeenth Ave. The ambulance and several cruisers were heading toward them.

Brad stood. "What did he look like?"

"Not sure," Sharma said. "It was dark and he was wearing a jacket with a hood. I don't think I ever saw his face. But he was damn big."

"Do you think it was Wolfe?" Brad asked.

"I wish I knew for sure, but I don't."

"Okay. Another ambulance is pulling up."

Brad waited as the ambulance stopped in front of him. The passenger door opened—Maggie.

He stepped toward her and pulled her into his arms. "Thank

God you're okay." He released his grip. "I was worried. Dispatch couldn't tell us who the paramedics were."

Maggie stepped back. "Are the paramedics all right?"

"Sharma is good, but his partner, Jay, is unconscious. You need to check him out first."

"Okay. I'll have Fola check Sharma just to make sure he's fine. There's another ambulance on the way. They can take over when they get here."

Brad watched her walk off with her kit, ready to help as she always was.

Maggie stopped as if sensing his eyes on her, turned, and mouthed, "I love you" before walking away.

Brad and Griffin watched the ambulances leave and slid into their car. "How's Devlin?" Griffin asked.

"Not good. He has internal bleeding and a half-dozen broken ribs. He's on a respirator to help him breathe. The bones in one hand are crushed. He's in ICU. They're waiting and watching for him to wake up."

"Devlin's tough." Griffin shook his head. "How the hell did that happen? Two great cops, and Wolfman got the drop on them."

"We'd called it a night," Brad said. "I should have made them go home."

"We were all tired." Griffin rubbed his eyes. "It could have been any one of us. Every one of us would have done the same thing."

"That's the problem, we were all tired," Brad said. "The only one getting any sleep is Wolfe."

"Probably the only one getting any action, too," Griffin said.

Brad glared. "Okay, there's dark humor and then there's that. That's way too dark."

Griffin shrugged. "Yeah, you're right. See. I'm saying stupid stuff. We're not functioning as well as we need to."

Brad did a U-turn and headed to Seventeenth Avenue. "I'm going home and getting five or six hours of sleep—if I can. Then I'll take Lobo for a run and try to clear my head. I'll meet you tonight at nine. Check and see if there's anything new then head out."

"Sounds like a plan—my wife's at work. The kids are in school. The house will be quiet. I got a bedroom set up in the basement. Cool, quiet, and dark during the day. I'm looking forward to that."

CHAPTER FIFTY-FOUR

Wednesday Morning

BRAD AND LOBO WERE RETURNING FROM A RUN AS MAGGIE ARRIVED home. They walked into the house together. Maggie headed upstairs to change while Brad took Lobo to the kitchen for his breakfast.

Maggie returned wearing flannel pajamas.

"If you're trying to turn me on you might want to rethink your sleepwear."

"After the night I had, sleep is the only thing on my mind."

"Well that hurts. And here I got all sweaty for you. How's Sharma's partner?"

"He's okay. On the way to the hospital he woke up and then vomited all over the ambulance and me."

"Yum. Do you want some breakfast?"

"Maybe a banana and milk."

"Really?" Brad cringed. "After getting barfed on?"

"Aw, does that make the tough cop nauseated?"

"Shut up and eat your banana."

They sat in silence for a few minutes.

No time like the present, Brad thought. "I was wondering how long you plan on working?"

Maggie looked up. "What?"

"I was wondering, you know, how long you planned to stay on the street as a paramedic?"

Maggie shrugged. "I don't know. I thought five or six months would be good, but I guess until I don't want to, or the baby says I can't."

"After last night, you know, Sharma getting attacked and all. It could have been you."

"But it wasn't."

"If Wolfe attacked you, and if he figured out who you were, you wouldn't have been as lucky as Sharma."

"There're a lot of *ifs* in there. It wasn't me. Wolfe didn't attack me. The chances of that happening again are astronomical."

"But it could."

"I *could* get hit by lightning. I *could* get in an accident. I'm not going to live my life based on *could*."

"Wolfe is a real threat. He made threats to you after Lobo and I arrested him. I love your independence. I love how hard you work. I love how you are an excellent paramedic. But this time I insist. Until Wolfe is caught you can't go back to work."

Maggie glared at Brad. "You insist?"

"It's the smart thing."

"Most of the time I like you being a gentleman. But today you're taking it too far. You can't tell me to quit work. It doesn't work that way. I'm not some little girl you need to protect. I'll

272

know when the time is right to stop working. When that time comes, I'll let you know." She stood. "I'm tired. Good night."

Brad watched her walk away. He loved Maggie's independence and toughness. He just couldn't shake the feeling that they were all in danger.

CHAPTER FIFTY-FIVE

Friday Morning

Wolfe woke early—the sun creeping over the horizon. Today was a special day. He set his duffel bag on the table and checked the contents. He'd used a lot of his supplies on the cop. Yesterday he'd stopped at the army surplus store and restocked, picking up a few extra items.

The days with the cop had been the most exhilarating he'd ever had. She'd started defiant, but at the end, she was begging —not to be released, but to die. Wolfe had been more than willing to comply. He'd learned a lot torturing her, but that had been over days. He wouldn't have that much time today. From that experience he knew how to get the best results in as little time as possible. Of course, the torture was second. That he'd have her every way possible came first. Thinking about it, that it would finally happen, had Wolfe aroused.

The cops had been all over the southeast searching with no

luck. When they found the blond cop, they'd do anything to capture him. It would only be a matter of time until they did. Today the plan was to go northwest, where she lived.

The package should reach Coulter tomorrow. He'd lose his mind. Too bad Wolfe couldn't see that. Even better would be the look on Coulter's face when he found the bitch. No doubt the cops would swarm the bars and streets with Wolfe's photo. Not that it would do much good. No one had seen him without the long hair and beard. It was like hiding in plain sight.

He loaded the car, took one last look at the house that had served him so well, then drove away. He stopped at a 7-Eleven and bought three hotdogs and several packages of Polaroid film. It was a special day. Driving northwest, Wolfe was tempted to grab a beer from the twelve-pack in the back seat, but held off. Those were for the performance later today. He could wait.

A few blocks from her house he stopped and bought a paper and a coffee. He parked at the other end of the crescent. The view wasn't as good, but it was a new parking spot. It was a different car, too, so he wasn't too worried about being spotted. A marked police cruiser and the Crown Victoria were parked out front.

He sipped the coffee and ignored the paper. Heart beating rapidly, his breath came in gasps and his body shook. The anticipation was thrilling. Today was the day.

Her front door opened—right on schedule. He grabbed the binoculars. She herded the kids out of the house and down the sidewalk. His breath caught. She wore a tank top, shorts, and her hair was pulled back into a ponytail. Wolfe was on the verge of hyperventilating. His heart pounded in his ears. He set the binoculars down.

Instead of heading to her car, she walked the kids to the

Crown Victoria. The back door was held open by a big guy in a suit. She and the kids got in the back and the Crown Vic pulled away, the cruiser following behind.

This was a little different, but if she stuck to her routine, she'd drop the kids at school and be back in fifteen to twenty minutes. Enough time to get set up.

As soon as they were out of sight, Wolfe grabbed the duffel bag, slid out of the car, and hustled to the house. If anyone noticed, he'd look like he belonged. At a used-clothing store he'd found a jacket with the words, "Gas Company" on the back. He walked past the house and down the steep path to the backyard. Sliding doors would be easy to force open. He'd brought the right tools. He rounded the corner, glanced around and, seeing no one, stepped to the glass doors. He stopped. Heavy bars covered the glass, the doors held closed with a thick piece of metal. Wolfe could break the glass, but there was no way to get inside. It would take better tools and too much time to get into the house this way. He took the stairs up to the deck. He might be able to force the door there. Again, he stopped. *No!*

The door he'd seen on his last visit had been replaced. Instead of a wooden door, there was a solid metal-framed door. He checked his watch. Ten minutes had passed. He couldn't use the front door. Windows were out as well. Mind racing, he couldn't think of a viable option. He thought about forcing the front door. When the cops came in, he'd be waiting. It would be easy to kill them quickly, then carry on with the plan. But the cops would call for backup when they saw the door. In minutes the house would be surrounded by cops. Even if they tried to negotiate for hours, and he raped her during that time, in the end they'd capture him. All the planning would be wasted. This wasn't something he wanted to hurry. It was too important.

He walked down the stairs and up the side of the house. A couple of houses away he heard cars behind him. He peeked over his shoulder. The cops were back with her. *Damn!*

Wolfe drove around the northwest for a while, then drove into Bowness and past the old hotel and bar. He stopped at the lot where the Gypsy Jokers' Clubhouse had stood. Two years ago, the city got a court order and had it demolished. He had a lot of memories from that place. The parties were beyond amazing. All the booze you could drink, food and women—lots of women, there to do whatever you wanted. He preferred the feisty ones. Like Annie. He'd had too little time with her. That would change. She was on his list, too. The lady cop was actually third on his list, behind Blighe and Annie. Circumstances had changed the order, but not the details. Once he was done with Blighe, the young blond was next. Sometime soon he'd need to kill Coulter, too. That cop was a big pain in his ass. He'd spent so much time planning what he'd do to the women he hadn't thought about getting revenge on the cops. He'd gotten a bit of that frustration out on Devlin already. The day had gone to shit but thinking about killing cops brought a smile to his lips. Yeah, that would be cool. Figuring out how to make Coulter pay. He'd work on that tonight. Since Coulter didn't live too far away, Wolfe decided to swing past the house.

Two years ago, Wolfe had blown up Coulter's car. The rival club, the Satan's Soldiers, got the blame. If only Coulter had been in the car. Things would be much different now. He slowed for the playground zone and that gave him a reason to take his time as he passed the house. *What the—*

A police cruiser was parked out front and a Crown Victoria was parked behind. Two uniformed cops were talking to a guy in a suit and a chick in a pantsuit—cops. Why the hell would Coulter need protection?

Wolfe drove to the end of the road and did a U-turn. He stopped on the opposite side of the street, three houses away from Coulter's place. He watched the cops talking. They seemed pretty relaxed. Then they all turned toward the house at the same time. Two women were walking toward the cops. Coulter's bitch!

Why hadn't I thought of this before? A perfect way to get at Coulter—do his bitch like I did the cop.

If seeing the bitch was a surprise, then seeing Annie was unbelievable. Coulter was protecting Annie at his house. Wolfe admired Coulter's thinking. Fuckin' brilliant. Too bad that idea was blown now. Wolfe was already thinking of the possibilities.

Annie got into the back of the Crown Victoria and the cops in suits sat up front. The car pulled away from the curb and drove past Wolfe. They didn't look at him. He touched the gas and casually pulled onto the street. Once he was past Coulter's house he sped up, made a quick right and then a left turn. He'd almost been too quick. The cops had just cleared the intersection as Wolfe arrived. He pulled in behind them and stayed well back. He wondered where they were taking Annie. To another house? To court? No, she was carrying a gym bag. To play sports? All the guessing in the world wasn't going to help. He relaxed and followed as they headed south. Ten minutes later he was sure of where they were going—Mount Royal College. That made sense. Books and other shit in the gym bag.

Wolfe pulled into the parking lot of Mount Royal College and watched as the Crown Vic pulled to the curb at the southwest entrance. The lady cop got out of the car and opened the back door. Annie stepped out and walked with the lady cop into the college. The Crown Vic pulled away from the curb. Wolfe guessed he was going to park the car.

Wolfe jumped out of his car and raced across the parking lot to the entrance. He entered and was immediately surrounded by students rushing to class. This place had to be filled with young pieces of ass — a regular smorgasbord of young pussy. A group of girls—well, teens—giggled their way past. They glanced at him and kept walking. How the hell would he find Annie in this crowd? He also realized he didn't fit in. He was in his thirties, big, bald, and mean looking. He wasn't a professor and certainly not a student. A caretaker's cart was sitting against a wall to his right. He glanced around but didn't see the caretaker. He grabbed the cart, walked farther into the college, caught up to the girls, and followed. He couldn't make up his mind which one was best. A blonde, always his favorite, caught his eye. But a brunette had the nicest, tightest ass he'd seen.

The girls turned into another hallway. Wolfe followed, then stopped. Walking toward him was a group of cops. *What the hell.* How could they know he was here? He started to back away, looking for an escape route. But something wasn't right. They were all young, walked casually in a tight group, and were smiling and laughing. They had nothing on their belts, nothing at all. Then they stopped at a concession. None of them paid any attention to him.

This was too good to be true. Wolfe grabbed a mop and slowly worked his way toward the cops. While they waited for food or drink, they talked about the class they'd been in. Wolfe realized they were recruits. Even more fun. He mopped toward them, then asked them to step back while he mopped at their feet. Not one of them glanced at him. Wolfe cleaned his way back to the cart and set off down the hallway. The group of girls were gone, but there were many more to take their place. Another time. He needed to find Annie.

Ahead of him a girl came out of the restroom. Blond, slim, and confident. Annie.

He watched as she walked away, mesmerized by the sway of her hips and the bounce of her ass. Oh, how he remembered that ass. He pushed the cart toward her. As he reached the restroom, the lady cop came out. She looked left and right, then followed Annie. Wolfe slowed and looked around. On the other side of the hall, the cop in the suit was jogging to catch up. He looked across the hallway to the lady cop. She nodded.

Wolfe followed, but kept his distance. Annie turned into a classroom. The man continued past but stopped about three classrooms farther. The woman stopped across from the classroom.

That fuckin' Coulter. He had no reason to think Wolfe would find her, let alone at college, yet he'd planned just in case.

For the next hour Wolfe worked his way up and down the hallway, cleaning. Ten minutes to the hour the classroom door opened and the students flowed out. Annie came out with the last group and walked to another classroom. Her protectors followed, and Wolfe followed them. Annie entered the class-room and the cops took up the same positions. He'd seen enough. No sense following them all day. Eventually the cops would get suspicious. After all, Wolfe knew where they'd be later in the day.

There were two roads that the cops could take to get back to Coulter's house. Fortunately, both of them led to the house. Wolfe stopped and picked up a newspaper, a couple of hotdogs and a large soda. He parked several blocks away and waited.

He'd almost drifted off to sleep when the Crown Vic raced by. He followed a couple of blocks back. When the cops parked outside Coulter's, Wolfe pulled to the curb. His view was hampered by the cars parked in front of him, but he couldn't risk getting out and being seen. He decided he would risk using the binoculars.

Annie and the lady cop got out of the car. They were met by the paramedic bitch and a dog. The fuckin' dog that attacked him! Killing him would be a pleasure.

The three women stood at the curb talking. A smile crossed his face. Nice to have options—two in one place. He had a new plan.

CHAPTER FIFTY-SIX

Friday Afternoon

MAGGIE AND ANNIE SAT ON THE COUCH. BRAD PACED AROUND THE living room. "Tell me exactly what happened."

"Annie came home from school upset," Maggie said.

"I need to hear it from Annie," Brad said.

Annie had her knees up to her chest and arms around her legs. She was shaking. "I don't know how to describe it. The morning was fine. But then in the afternoon, before two, I felt a chill. I looked around, but I couldn't see anything wrong. I'd gone to the restroom and I was fine. When I came out, I don't know, I just felt something was wrong."

"Did you tell your detail?"

"Not right away. I figured I was being silly. I was safe at school. When I went to the restroom, Brenda came in, too."

"But you didn't feel weird when you were in the restroom."

"No. But right after I got out and headed to my next class, I felt something was wrong. I looked around, but nothing was different. Lots of students were heading to their next class. Lots of instructors, caretakers, and delivery guys. It's always busy between classes."

"When you looked around, did you see a familiar face? Anything threatening?"

"No. That's why I think I'm overreacting. But Maggie said we should tell you."

Brad turned to a knock at the door. Brenda Edwards and Lou Houghton entered the living room.

"You wanted to talk to us?" Edwards asked.

"Yeah," Brad said. "Annie got a bad feeling at college today. Did you two see anything out of the ordinary?"

Edwards shook her head and glanced at Annie. "We didn't see anything suspicious. Annie didn't say anything to us. When did this happen?"

"About two this afternoon," Brad said. "She wasn't sure if it was anything."

"It would have been better if she told us right away," Edwards said. "We could have checked it out."

"So, nothing caught your eye?" Brad asked.

"Sir," Houghton said. "Other than quite a few guys looking her over there's been nothing out of the ordinary."

"You're sure?" Brad asked.

Houghton's face flushed. "We know what we're doing. That's why you hired us. If there were a threat, we would have seen it."

"I don't mean you didn't do your job. I'm a big believer in gut instinct. Something triggered a gut reaction in Annie. I'm trying to figure out what that was."

"I understand, sir," Houghton said. "Perhaps if this happens again Annie will let us know right away."

Brad glanced at Annie. "I can assure you she will let you know if she has the slightest suspicion."

Houghton nodded. "We'll be extra vigilant now that we know something is triggering a gut response. We both believe in following our instincts."

"I'll keep closer contact with Annie," Edwards said. "She wanted us in the shadows. Perhaps it's best if I'm with her all the time. Even in classes."

"No way," Annie said. "That's not gonna—"

Brad held up his hand. "That is a great idea, Edwards. Annie, you will not give Edwards any grief and you will let them know if you get that feeling again."

"But—"

"No buts." Brad turned to Edwards and Houghton. "You know how to contact me."

"Do you want us to stay tonight?" Houghton asked.

Brad shook his head. "We're good here tonight. I'll stay home and we've got Lobo. I appreciate the offer. Sorry if I came across like I doubted you. Annie means a lot to us. Have a good night."

CHAPTER FIFTY-SEVEN

Saturday July 12

THE BOARDROOM WAS SILENT. BRAD FACED THE WALL OF VICTIMS. He didn't need to look, he had them memorized—images that would haunt him forever. He'd never be rid of them.

Steele slept, his head on a desk. Griffin flipped through the tips that had come in over the past week. Zerr paced around the room.

There was a knock at the door. Zerr sprinted over and opened it.

A uniformed constable poked his head in. "Got a package here for Detective Coulter."

"I'll take it," Zerr said.

"The sergeant gave me strict instructions to give it to Detective Coulter directly."

"It's fine. He can bring it to me."

"If you say so, sir."

Zerr grabbed the package and was about to hand it to Brad when he stopped.

"What's wrong?" Brad asked.

"Since you've been a detective, how many packages have been delivered to the station for you?"

"None."

"The entire time you've been a cop, how many packages were delivered to you at work?"

"One."

"What was in the package?"

"Women's underwear."

Griffin popped his head up. "What?"

"I had a stalker for a while."

Griffin shook his head and went back to his paperwork.

"There, that's my point," Zerr said. "We're deep into this investigation and out of the blue, you get a package. Something's not right."

"Easy way to figure it out: we'll open the package." Brad reached out.

"I'm going to check it first," Zerr said.

"You think it's booby-trapped or something?" Brad asked.

"You don't know till you look," Zerr said. "If we assume this is a threat, then it makes no sense for us all to stand here. Everyone out. I'll call you when I'm through. Or you'll hear a boom and that also means I'm finished."

"Fine." Brad followed the others out of the room but stayed near the door, watching.

Zerr set the package, wrapped in brown paper and big enough to hold a sandwich, on the table. He used his knife to slit the tape, then used the tip of the blade to pull back the paper. Nothing suspicious.

Zerr lifted the package off the table and held it out in front of him, then used the knife to cut the tape on the bottom. The paper came free and he let it fall to the floor. On the lid was a picture of a postcard. The box was used to ship postcards to stores and was taped closed. Zerr cut the tape and slipped off the lid.

Inside the box was a note that said *Coulter*. An elastic held the note holding it to a two-inch stack of paper.

"All clear," Zerr shouted. He handed the box to Brad. "All clear, boss."

Brad pulled the stack out and slipped off the elastic band. He unfolded the note.

Beneath the word *Coulter* were the words:

You'll find her where she belongs, with the trash.

Brad dropped the note and grabbed the stack—Polaroid pictures. Tina. Barely recognizable, but it was her. His guts rolled as he choked back the bile rising into his mouth. His breath caught, throat tightening. Brad reached out a hand to steady himself, vision blurring as tears formed.

He flipped through them numbly, one by one—each picture more gruesome than the one before.

"What's up, boss?" Steele asked. "You got awfully pale."

He couldn't speak. He flipped through the twenty or so pictures again.

"Boss?" Steele said.

Griffin looked up from the papers. "Coulter, what's up?"

Zerr stepped toward Brad.

He found his voice. "No. Sit."

They stared, puzzled.

"What's going on?" Steele asked. "You got to tell us, boss."

Brad cleared his throat. "Griffin. I need to talk to you." Brad grabbed the package and raced out the door.

Griffin followed.

Brad sprinted down the hall, stepped into a vacant interview room, and slammed the door after Griffin.

"For Christ's sake, what the hell's going on? Coulter?"

Brad stopped pacing the room and threw the stack of photos on the table. He staggered to the corner and punched the wall. "Failed. I goddamn failed."

Griffin flipped through the photos. "Motherfucker. He killed her, he…he killed her."

Brad pressed his head into the wall, his breath coming in gasps.

"But not right away."

"Not right away." Brad picked up a chair and threw it against the wall. "Fuck!"

Griffin flipped through the pictures one more time then threw them onto the table. "You can't let Zerr see these."

"You think?"

"Send him home," Griffin said. "Get him as far away from this investigation as you can."

"I can order him to stay away. But he's going to do his own thing. It's easier having him where I can keep an eye on him."

Griffin grunted. "Like the other night?"

"Steele said he could keep Zerr under control."

"Didn't work, did it?"

"Didn't work." Brad hung his head. "I'm going to the board-room to talk to Zerr and Steele."

Griffin grabbed Brad's arm. "Clean yourself up. They see you like this, you won't have to say anything—they'll know."

Brad glanced down at his bloodied knuckles and took a deep breath.

When Brad entered the boardroom, Steele and Zerr looked up.

"What's going on, boss?" Steele asked.

Brad pulled out a chair and sat across from them. He didn't know how to say this.

He looked at his two best friends. "Tina's dead."

"What?" Steele yelled. "How do you know?"

"I know."

"Fuck!" Zerr jumped to his feet knocking his chair to the floor. "It's the photos, isn't it? I want to see them."

Brad shook his head. "No."

"That wasn't a fucking question. Give me the photos."

"I heard you. I said no. Sit … down."

"Fuck that." He leaned on the table and glared at Brad. Zerr's jaw clenched, the veins in his temples pounded, and his face turned scarlet. His breath came in short huffs.

"Both of you, go home," Brad said. "Griffin and I will handle this. As of now, both of you are off the case. Is that clear?"

They were silent for a moment, then Zerr stomped out of the room, slamming the door.

"You need to stay with him," Brad said.

Steele nodded, then paused in the doorway. "The pictures. She suffered, didn't she?"

Brad ignored the question. "Keep him away from radio and TV, and especially away from work."

"I'll do my best."

Griffin entered the boardroom after Zerr and Steele left. "I talked to Deputy Chief Archer. He's ordered the afternoon shift in early and he'll keep day shift as long as we need. All K9 officers are coming in to help with the searches."

"Thank you," Brad said. "I sent Zerr home with Steele."

"How'd he take it?"

"About as you'd expect. We need to upgrade the protection on Blighe. Double the protection and have K9 there at all times."

Griffin nodded. "What about your place?"

"I've been sending the uniformed cops home when I get there. I'll keep them 24/7."

"What about K9 at your place?"

"Lobo is there. He'll shred anyone who comes into the house."

"What's our next step?"

Brad slid the note across. "It says we'll find her where she belongs. The trash."

Griffin studied the note. "Well, there are lots of possibilities. Dumpsters come to mind."

Brad nodded. "Yeah, I thought of that."

"There're thousands of dumpsters in the city. Even if we only look in the ones in the southeast, that's still, I don't know, twenty-five thousand. If we used every cop on the job it might take weeks."

"Wolfe's pointing us at something specific. In the trash where she belongs."

"I don't know," Griffin said. "Is there some special meaning in the word trash?"

"Like take out the trash or toss out the trash."

Griffin nodded. "What do you do with trash?"

"Throw it in the garbage can," Brad said. "Or just throw it away."

"We're going in circles."

"Yeah."

"But if you throw your stuff in the trash, it goes in the garbage can. Garbage cans get picked up and go to the dump."

"Forest Lawn dump in the southeast," Brad said.

"Holy shit," Griffin said. "We've got to stop the city from dumping there."

"At all the city dumps."

"I'll let Archer know and arrange briefings for everyone on duty or called in." Griffin raced out the door.

CHAPTER FIFTY-EIGHT

Saturday Evening

Darkness fell and the search continued into the night and early morning. Generators with light stands were pulled into the landfill to illuminate the trash.

Brad looked over at the ambulance on standby. They weren't going to need the paramedics. He slowly walked to his Firebird and opened the back door. Lobo lifted his head from the bed he was lying on. Brad had used Lobo for the search for the better part of the day. When he realized the dog was exhausted, Brad took him back to the car, gave him some food and water, and let him sleep.

Brad tried to nap, but every time he closed his eyes, he saw the photos. He'd never seen anything like them. The terror in Tina's eyes. The cuts, the bruises, the bleeding. The worst were the sex acts. Brad's eyes popped open. He wasn't sure he'd ever be able to close his eyes again.

An hour later he gave up on sleep and attached the harness to Lobo. They headed back to the landfill. Brad reached into his pocket and pulled out an evidence bag containing one of Tina's shirts he took from her apartment. Lobo tugged at the leash and anxiously sniffed the shirt. He was ready to go to work.

Brad pulled a doctor's mask over his face. It didn't eliminate the odors, but at least it filtered them a bit. Lobo didn't mind the smells.

During the day they created a grid search pattern based on information from sanitation on where the trash had been dumped yesterday. That was their best guess as to when she'd died. If Tina's body had been thrown in the trash yesterday, then dumped here, they might find her. It was all guessing though. Maybe Wolfe had dumped her here himself. If that was the case, she could be anywhere. Maybe she wasn't here at all.

Brad's shoulders were tight, and his jaw ached from being clenched for the better part of the day. Blood pounded at his temples.

Two other K9 cops and their dogs were searching as well. In over twelve hours of searching they'd found nothing.

Time dragged on and Brad willed his feet to keep moving. Lobo, full of energy from his nap, was tugging at the leash. He was doing what he liked best—working with Brad.

Brad's chin bounced off his chest a few times. He willed his body to keep going. He was vaguely aware of someone calling his name. The voice got louder. A flashlight shone in his eyes. "Shit."

"Sorry," Griffin said. "Dispatch got a call from a trucker a few miles from here. He said he'd pulled into a truck stop to catch a few hours of shuteye. As he walked to the restroom, he saw a rolled-up carpet and a wallet by the door. He kicked the carpet and it unrolled a few feet. That's when he saw the body."

Brad was instantly alert. "What?"

"Come on," Griffin said. "He's waiting for us."

Cops stood silent as Brad approached. He shone his flashlight where an officer was pointing. He saw a hand, dropped to his knees next to the carpet.

An arm and shoulder were exposed. Brad repositioned himself and unrolled the carpet further. There were no clothes on the body. The face was unrecognizable, framed by blonde hair. His gut rolled and he fought back the urge to vomit. He was flooded with emotion—hate, rage, sadness, and failure. *Tina, I'm so sorry.*

He stood and stepped back. "Get this area cordoned off and let Ident do their job."

Griffin followed Brad back to his truck. He stared into the night at the stars and followed a jet as it trailed across the sky. He thought about the night Curtis died. They'd stopped outside a 7-Eleven. That night, too, he'd stared into the sky, watching a jet leaving the city.

He turned to the sound of squealing tires—Zerr and Steele. Zerr jumped out of the passenger seat and sprinted toward Brad.

"Where is she?" he asked.

Brad stepped in front of him. "It's a crime scene, Charlie. There's nothing you can do here."

Zerr tried to push past Brad, who blocked him.

"How the hell did you know we're here?" Brad asked.

"It's all over the radio," Steele said. "Every radio station is saying a body was found here."

"Shit," Brad said.

"I need to see her." Zerr's voice trailed off. "I need to. I need to."

Brad stood his ground. "No, Charlie. No, you don't."

"Why are you so cold about this? Why so emotionless. Don't you care?"

Brad stared at Charlie. "You know that's bullshit. You know I care. You know I care a lot. There's one thing I can do: protect you. And that's what I'm going to do."

"Protect me! Where the hell was Devlin when he was with her? He was her partner. He should have protected her. He's the one who got her killed."

Zerr attempted to step around Brad, but he moved with Zerr. "No, Charlie. This isn't on Devlin. This is on Wolfe. Don't forget that."

"On Wolfe? Really? When you were assigning the protection details, did you assign one to Tina? No. No, you didn't."

"Tina refused protection," Brad said.

"She didn't want one so, that was it? You went along with her?"

Brad nodded. "At that time, we didn't think Tina was a target. We were pretty sure it was Blighe. It's easy to look back and second guess and say I messed up. But I can't change that now."

Zerr's hostility lessened. His shoulders slumped and he stared at his feet. "Sorry, boss. I know it's not on you. I should have protected her. I should have been there for her. It's, well—"

Brad put his arm around Zerr's shoulder and guided him back to the car. "I'm sorry, Charlie. I'm sorry, buddy. Steele's going to drive you home and stay with you tonight. Take tomorrow off. Take the next couple days off. Take as much time as you need."

Zerr nodded.

"Get some sleep. If anything comes up, I'll let you know. I promise. If I have to keep looking over my shoulder to make sure you're okay, that's going to take me away from the task."

"I want to be there."

"You want to be where?"

"When you find him. I want to be there. I want to kill him."

"There's a long line of guys wanting to kill him, Charlie. Including me. If the situation is right, we'll take the shot. It might be you. It might be with me. But one of us is going to take him down. Get some sleep. I'll talk to you tomorrow."

Steele guided Zerr into the passenger seat and then closed the door.

Brad watched them drive away. Wolfe would die, and it would be soon.

CHAPTER FIFTY-NINE

Sunday Morning

BRAD PULLED TO THE CURB IN FRONT OF HIS HOUSE, KILLED THE ignition, and rested his head against the steering wheel. He needed to get out of the car, into the house, and then to bed. But that twenty feet seemed too far. The night had taken everything out of him.

Taking a big breath and leaning back in the seat, Brad closed his eyes. Mistake. He saw the arm sticking out of the carpet. The small rose tattoo on the left shoulder. At that moment he knew it was Tina. Her naked body covered in bruises, face unrecognizable. He wanted to open his eyes. He couldn't. The images took hold. They ran over and over. With a gasp, he opened his eyes.

Brad opened the car door and stumbled to the front of the house. He fumbled with the key and finally slid it into the lock and opened the door. He stepped inside and closed the door behind him, resetting the alarm.

Lobo came bounding over, running circles around Brad's legs. Lobo sat and stared. Brad slid down the wall onto the floor. Lobo leaned close. Brad grabbed him in a tight hug.

He'd thought all his energy was gone, but here, sitting on the floor with Lobo, the last morsel escaped. He had nothing. He felt empty. Nothing in his head. Nothing in his heart. Just an incredible weight on his shoulders.

He looked toward a noise on the stairs. Maggie. She was wrapping a housecoat around her. "I thought I heard you come in."

"Sorry. I tried to be quiet."

"Are you okay?"

He didn't answer.

She stepped closer. "Are you okay?"

Brad looked up, like he was seeing her for the first time. "No, I'm not."

Maggie sat next to him on the floor. "What happened?"

Brad shook his head.

"Brad, please talk to me. What happened?"

He put his head back against the wall—and the tears flowed. A steady stream at first and then a torrent. Tears he'd held inside for years, now came out in a flood with chest-racking sobs. Lobo looked up and whimpered.

Maggie slid over and pulled him close. "Oh my God, Brad. What happened?"

He leaned against her. The tears continued, the sobs became cries of anguish.

"Please tell me. I don't know what to do. I don't know how to help you. Please, tell me what happened."

Brad sniffled back the snot and wiped the tears from his eyes. "Tina's dead."

"What?"

"We found her. She'd been raped and tortured. Probably for days."

"Oh my God. Wolfe?"

Brad nodded.

Maggie held him close in silence.

CHAPTER SIXTY

Monday Morning

BRAD STEPPED INTO THE RECEPTION AREA OF THE MEDICAL Examiner's Office. He showed his badge to the receptionist. "Davidson autopsy?"

"Suite 2."

The door buzzed. He pulled it open and walked down the hall. As he approached Suite 2, the door opened and Sergeant Sturgeon came out.

"Did they start already?" Brad asked.

"Yup," Sturgeon said. "They're wrapping up."

"What? You told me they'd be starting at nine."

"They moved it up."

"Why didn't you call me? I needed to be here."

"You don't need to be here," Sturgeon said. "I get it that you wanted to, but this is for the best. I can tell you what we found, but it's better you weren't here. Trust me."

Sturgeon grabbed Brad's arm and guided him to a quiet room used by family members of the deceased. They sat and were silent for a few moments. Brad hunched over, head in his hands. Sturgeon waited. Brad sat up and took a deep breath. "Okay, tell me."

"When you found her, she'd been dead about twenty-four hours. Likely dumped there the night before."

Sturgeon paused and stared at Brad. "Are you okay to continue?"

Brad nodded.

"There were ligature marks on her hands and legs. There were other marks on her wrists, probably from her handcuffs."

"Ah, jeez."

"She was raped and tortured, and then killed with a bullet to her head. We'll check ballistics, but I'd bet it was her gun."

"How was she tortured?"

"The details aren't important."

"The hell they aren't!"

Sturgeon described the horrors Tina had endured at Wolfe's hands. Brad leaned forward, head between his knees. *Oh, God.*

Sturgeon paused, chewed on his lip and exhaled deeply.

Brad sat upright. "What else?"

"A couple of things were different. Her hair was cut short and there were lacerations to her face and breasts."

"That's something new."

"Yeah, I wondered about that," Sturgeon said.

"It didn't matter with the other victims. This was personal because it was Tina." Brad stood and paced. "Jeez, Tina. I'm so sorry." He placed his hands against the wall and rested his head against it. "Did she fight?"

"We found skin and blood under her fingernails. At some

point she fought. Wolfe was three times her size. I doubt he let her fight for long. Might have happened when he was tying her to the bed."

"Anything else?"

"Nothing about the assaults and death. We found a receipt under her right arm. It might be garbage, or it might have fallen out of Wolfe's pocket. It's for a convenience store not far from there." Sturgeon handed Brad an evidence bag.

"Can I take this?"

"Not yet. I'll take it back to the office and dust for prints. I can develop a photo if you want."

"Sure." Brad pulled out his notebook, wrote down the information on the receipt, then looked up. "That it?"

"That's all I have for now."

"Call me the second you get anything else."

"I should have the fingerprints and ballistics done by early afternoon."

CHAPTER SIXTY-ONE

Tuesday Morning

THE NEXT MORNING BRAD AND GRIFFIN PICKED UP THE PHOTO OF the receipt from Sturgeon. He confirmed that Tina was murdered with her gun. He only found partial prints from the receipt. A probable match to Wolfe and an unknown second set.

They drove to the southeast in silence. Brad parked outside the store and led the way to the counter where the clerk stood reading a newspaper. Without looking up, he said, "What do you want?"

"I want you to look at me," Griffin said. The clerk exhaled loudly and took his time. When he looked up, he was staring at Griffin's badge.

"Do I have your attention now?" Griffin asked.

"Yeah, sure."

Griffin showed the clerk the picture of the receipt. "Is this from your store?"

The clerk peered at the photo. "It's not very clear, but yeah, I think it's ours."

"It's dated, four days ago. Were you working then?"

"I'm always working."

Griffin slid a photo of Jeter Wolfe across the counter. "Does this guy look familiar?"

"Nope." He slipped the photo back to Griffin.

Griffin pushed it back. "Why don't you take a good look this time."

The clerk stared at the photo. "Nope."

He pushed the photo toward Griffin, then pulled it back. "Is he a big guy? Like Andre the Giant?"

"I wouldn't say that, but bigger than any of us."

"I ain't seen a guy with long hair and a beard, but there's a big bald guy and he's clean-shaven."

"What?" Brad asked.

"Yeah. He started coming here a couple of weeks ago. July 1st holiday, I think. He comes in almost every day."

"What does he buy?" Brad asked.

"Cigarettes. Junk food. Soda, chips, and porn magazines."

"That's all?"

"Yeah. No, wait, about a week ago he bought four packs of Polaroid film. I thought that was a lot. With him buying porn mags I figured he was into something kinky. When he left I went out for a smoke. He walked down the sidewalk and then up to a house."

"Do you know which house?"

"Not sure. One of the last two on the left, I think."

"Do you know the people who live in those houses?"

"No. This whole block was bought by a developer. All the

houses will be torn down. They're building a big condo complex."

"Are the houses is still occupied?"

"Some are. Most of the people moved out. Then the junkies moved in. The cops kick them out, but they're back the next day."

Griffin picked up the picture. "Thanks. Have a nice day."

They left the store, walked to the curb, and surveyed the road. It was a dead end. There was no way to tell if the last three houses were occupied.

"We need the addresses for the warrants," Brad said. "Do we drive by or walk by?"

Griffin laughed. "I know you're growing your hair long, but you still announce 'cop' with neon lights."

"You're no better."

"At least I look older than twenty."

"Okay, so what's your plan?" Brad asked.

"We get a cruiser to drive by. In this area marked police cars are common. Our Crown Victoria shouts detectives. I'll get dispatch to keep cruisers in this area until we get the warrant."

Brad nodded. "We can get Blighe to help us with the warrant. Judge Gray will sign right away."

At dusk, Brad, Griffin, TSU, K9, and about twenty uniformed cops met a few blocks from the convenience store.

Brad and Griffin described the plan and split the group into two teams. K9 would stand by near the middle house, ready when called.

Brad and Griffin, with Steele and Zerr, took the last house.

Sergeant Knight and TSU, the second last. The uniformed cops were sent to the alley behind the houses in case someone decided to run.

Darkness had settled in. Everyone was in place and waiting. Griffin gave the command. "Execute."

Steele ran to the last house with Brad, Zerr, and Griffin close behind. Steele swung a ram at the front door lock. Zerr entered to the right, Steele to the left. Brad followed Zerr, and Griffin backed up Steele.

Brad's flashlight swept over the living room. At first pass, nothing seemed out of place. Couch, stuffed chair, coffee table, and junk food wrappers and containers everywhere. They worked their way to the kitchen. That's when Brad recognized an odor—dried blood. In the kitchen, their flashlights lit a chair in the middle of the room. Ropes hung from the back struts and the chair legs. The smell came from under the chair—blood, lots of blood. Brad's stomach rolled.

"Brad. Come to the far bedroom."

In the bedroom, the odor was overpowering. Brad swung his flashlight around the room. Suddenly the ceiling light came on.

"Always check about power," Griffin said.

Brad wished the light hadn't worked. He faced a blood-soaked bed. Ropes hung from the headboard and footboard. Blood spattered the walls and window. "Oh shit. He killed her here. We need to back out and get Ident here."

Zerr pushed past Brad and Griffin. Brad reached to hold him back, but was too late. Zerr stopped at the side of the bed, staring at the blood-encrusted detective badge.

CHAPTER SIXTY-TWO

Wednesday Late Afternoon

WOLFE HAD WAITED SEVERAL BLOCKS AWAY FROM BLIGHE'S HOUSE on a stolen Honda motorcycle. Not as nice as his Harley, but the Honda was less likely to draw attention. The full-face helmet was a bonus. He followed the Crown Victoria as they passed. He rode slowly and glanced as she got out of the car and was escorted to her house. He continued down the street and rode for about five minutes. He stopped in a small strip mall and slid off the helmet.

The prosecutor's security detail drove her to work and back now. Her routines had changed. The cops likely changed them. After he escaped the first time, she was never home before seven and the family dinner was never before eight. Now she was home by five at the latest. Cops drove the kids to school and back. Wolfe guessed they stayed with the kids all day. Instead of two cops watching the house, now there were four. K9 circled the house continuously when she was home.

He looked at his watch. About now the night shift was talking with the day shift. Soon the night shift would start their patrol of the neighborhood. But the fuckin' K9 would still be there.

He was out of options. He mulled over the idea of grabbing her near her office. That might have worked when she was driving herself, and the protection was lax, leaving her alone when she parked. He could have grabbed her as she got out of the car, tossed her in a van, and taken her to an abandoned place like he did with the cop. He shook his head. That might have worked then. Not now. He'd never get close. Lucky for him there was another option.

CHAPTER SIXTY-THREE

Brad parked and keyed his portable radio. "Dispatch, Coulter. I'm off duty at my house."

"Roger," dispatch said.

He grabbed the files off the passenger seat and got out of the car. Two uniformed cops walked toward him.

"Welcome home, Detective," one cop said.

"Thanks," Brad replied. "I'm glad to be home."

"All quiet here," the cop said. "Nobody's been by all day. We walked around the house different times throughout the day. Nothing to report. Well, except your dog barks at us every time we walk around the back."

"He's like a roving alarm system," Brad said. "Thanks for your help, guys. Are you guys here all night?"

"Until we're relieved at eleven."

Brad nodded. "We might order pizza. If we do, I'll buy you guys one."

"That's great," one cop said. "No pineapple, though."

Brad trudged up the steps to the front door, pulled out his keys, unlocked the door, and stepped inside. He turned to the alarm panel on the right and canceled the alarm. He closed and locked the front door then reset the alarm.

"Hey Maggie," Brad said. "I'm home."

Lobo came bounding from the back of the house, tail wagging. He jumped up and down on his paws and ran around Brad.

"Hey buddy." Brad knelt. "I am so happy to see you."

Lobo ran circles around Brad. "Sorry, boy. I can't take you for a walk tonight. I'm exhausted."

Lobo ran around Brad a couple more times, then sat by the front door.

"Not tonight, sorry." Brad tossed his keys onto a table.

Lobo cocked his head to the side, stared at Brad, then headed to the back of the house.

Maggie stopped at the front door, holding a laundry basket. "Well this is a treat, you're home early. I didn't make dinner."

"We decided to shut it down early. Everybody is dead on their feet. We'll get a good sleep tonight and tackle the problem tomorrow."

"Still no leads?" Maggie asked.

Brad shook his head. "The girl from the barn, Billy-Lou, regained consciousness today."

"That's good news. What did she tell you?"

"She doesn't remember anything about the attack. Last thing she remembers is carrying a bag of feed into the barn, then nothing until she woke up."

"Is she going to be okay?" Maggie asked.

"I'm not the one to ask. But I think it's a blessing she doesn't remember the attack. Doesn't help us convict Wolfe, but I'm glad she's awake."

Brad held up a stack of files. "I'm gonna look at these for half an hour. Then I'm done for the night."

"Do you have to?" Maggie said. "Leave it for the night, please."

"Half an hour," Brad said. "I promise."

"Half an hour, no more."

"Half an hour," Brad confirmed. "What do you want to do for dinner?"

"I'm not sure," Maggie said.

"Why don't you order a pizza in about twenty minutes. Get one for the guys outside, too. I'll be in the study."

"Okay," she said. "I'll feed Lobo and put him outside."

Brad took the files into the study and set them on his desk. The top file was Tina's autopsy report. Nothing he didn't already know. He needed to put it aside, but he kept re-reading it. Finally, he threw it to the floor. For the next half hour, he flipped through the folders, reading the reports, not that he needed to. Everything was etched into his memory. There had to be a clue here somewhere, something he was missing. He shut the last file, sat back in his chair and closed his eyes.

His mind flipped through the pages of the autopsy reports, crime scene photos, and worst of all, Jeter Wolfe, grinning.

He leaned back in his chair. He was startled awake when Maggie called, "I've ordered the pizza. You better be done with work."

He picked the autopsy file off the floor and set it on top of the others. Then dispatch called him on the radio.

"Go ahead, dispatch."

"We have a reported sighting of Wolfe around the crown prosecutor's house."

Brad sat upright, grabbed the radio, and raced out of the study. He scooped up his keys as he ran to the front door and keyed his radio. "I'm on my way. Let the rest of the team know."

"I'm working on that, Detective," dispatch said.

"Maggie," Brad yelled from the front door.

She rushed to the door. "What's happening?"

"Wolfe's been spotted. I'm heading to Blighe's place. I don't know when I'll be back. Be sure to reset the alarm when I leave."

The cops started toward him.

"I've gotta go. Keep your eyes open."

Brad ran to his car, opened the door, jumped in, and raced away.

"Dispatch, I'm en-route. Six minutes away. Do you have any more information?"

"The protection detail is checking the area, but they don't have any sightings," dispatch said. "The prosecutor is safe in the house and under guard now. I have district units on the way."

"What's the ETA on my team?"

"Griffin will be there in about eight. Zerr and Steele should arrive at the same time you do."

The exhaustion he felt less than thirty minutes ago was gone. Senses were on high alert. Traffic was light as he raced toward the prosecutor's house. His brain was firing. This might be the opportunity to finally get Wolfe. His hands clutched the steering wheel tighter. His heart pounded. Anticipation and excitement changed to anger as his mind ran through the possibilities of what he would do when he found Wolfe. *I hope you will have a gun, bastard.* He knew that revenge wasn't enough. It didn't take away the pain and didn't take away the sadness, or the anger.

But taking that nan permanently off the streets was something he would do without hesitation.

Brad turned right toward the prosecutor's house and the red-and-blue lights of the district cars. He pulled to the curb, slammed the car into park, and raced toward the cops. "What've you got?"

One cop shook his head. "We have nothing, sir. We've walked around the house a dozen times. Wolfe's not here. We've expanded our search into the neighborhood, spreading out from the house. But no reports of anybody seeing Wolfe."

Shit. Brad's eyes roamed over the house and yard. He turned a full 360 degrees. The cop was right, there was nothing suspicious.

Brad turned to the senior guy on the protection detail. "I want to see inside."

"I'm telling you, there's nothing to see."

"I need to look for myself."

"For Christ's sake, suit yourself."

Griffin followed Brad into the house. Blighe stood by the kitchen counter, wine glass in her hand.

"Are you okay?" Brad asked.

"What do you think? We're getting ready to have dinner and a hundred cops descended on my house."

"We're cautious."

"Well, you scared the shit out of me and terrified my kids."

"Where are the kids now?" Brad asked.

"They're in the basement watching TV with a couple of cops watching them."

"Griffin and I are going to check your house."

"The other cops already did that."

Brad nodded. "I know. I'll feel better if I check."

Blighe waved her glass in the air. "Suit yourself." She took a big gulp of wine.

Brad and Griffin searched every room, checked every window and looked in every closet. Nothing.

They walked around the outside of the house with K9 following. Whoever had replaced the doors and secured the windows knew what they were doing. Blighe was safe.

They headed back to the front of the house.

"What do you guys have?" Brad asked Steele and Zerr.

"Nothing," Steele said. "We checked the outside a couple of times, and we checked a few blocks in each direction. Either it was a false alarm, or Wolfman is long gone."

"Yeah, I think you're right," Brad said. "Let's head back home and get that sleep we need."

CHAPTER SIXTY-FOUR

As Brad drove home, the exhaustion hit again. He'd probably go straight to bed. As he approached his house, he saw a pizza delivery car parked behind the cruiser. *I am kinda hungry, so a couple of pieces of pizza will be great, but then sleep for sure.*

He picked up his portable radio and keyed the mic. "Dispatch, Coulter. I'm off duty at my house."

"Roger, Detective," dispatch said. "Have a good night, sir."

Brad tossed the radio to the passenger seat, tried to organize his thoughts, then he shook his head. This is crazy. *I need to shut my brain off for the night.* He got out of the car and looked for the cops. Lobo barked from the deck. He was probably barking at the cops. They must be doing a walk around. He stumbled up the sidewalk. The tantalizing odor of pizza was strong and his stomach grumbled. Brad willed his feet to move one after the other, then grabbed the handrail and pulled himself up the steps. Lifting his head, he reached for the door handle. *What the hell!*

315

The door was ajar.

He drew his gun, slowly opened the door, and slipped into the house. A pizza box lay open on the floor. Lobo barked non-stop. Brad stopped in the entrance and listened—voices came from upstairs.

Something was wrong. His brain raced through options. He reached for his portable radio—he'd left it in the car. Get to a phone and call for backup. Let Lobo in, he was good backup.

A woman screamed.

Brad kicked off his shoes and crept up the stairs, stepping over the boards that creaked. The voices grew louder as he reached the landing outside the master bedroom. One voice was distinctly male—Wolfe—the other, Maggie.

Gun at his side, he took a quick look inside. Annie, wearing a T-shirt and shorts, was tied to the bed. Tape covered her mouth, her eyes wide with terror. She glanced toward the door and vigorously shook her head.

"I'm gonna enjoy you bitches one at a time."

"The police will be here any minute," Maggie said. "You won't get away with this."

Bastard. What has he done to them?

"The cops are already here. Coulter, why don't you come in and join us?"

"Brad, no—"

A loud slap echoed in the room, then Maggie cried out in pain.

Brad's breath caught in his throat. He steadied his gun and sidestepped into the room. Brad let out a gasp. Maggie and Wolfe were in the far corner of the room. Maggie, wearing a dark-red camisole, was tied to a chair. Blood dripped from her nose and mouth. Her face was red and puffy. Wolfe stood behind her with a hunting knife to her throat.

"Welcome home, pig," Wolfman said. "Set the gun on the floor."

Brad shook his head, gun aimed at Wolfe. "You know it doesn't work that way."

"Have it your way." Wolfe cut the side of Maggie's neck. She screamed. Blood flowed. Then he placed the knife on the other side of her neck.

"Wait." Brad held his gun out in front of him.

"Gun on the floor."

Brad knelt and set the gun down.

"Kick it over to me."

Brad hesitated.

Wolfe pressed the blade into Maggie's flesh. She cried out in pain. Lobo's barking was frantic.

"Okay." Brad kicked the gun toward Wolfe.

Wolfe put the knife over Maggie's throat. "You've got no chances left. My next cut will be back to her spine. Now face the wall and get on the floor."

Brad stared at Maggie. Blood flowed from both sides of her neck and tears streamed. Her eyes pleaded, frightened.

When Brad was on the floor, Wolfe said, "Take out your cuffs, slowly, with one hand. Keep the other hand on your head."

Brad reached behind his back and pulled out the cuffs.

"Good, now put the cuffs on one hand, then put both hands behind your back."

Wolfe picked up Brad's gun, placed it against Brad's head, and knelt. Grabbing the loose cuff, he slapped it on Brad's other wrist and squeezed it tight. Wolfe grabbed Brad by his shirt collar, dragged him over to Maggie, and shoved him against the wall.

"You two can watch the show." Wolfe lit a cigarette. "Annie's first. I've missed her. We didn't spend enough time together. That fuckin' Pickens took her away. I shoulda killed him. We'll make up for lost time tonight. We've got plenty."

Brad struggled against the cuffs. "Leave her alone."

Wolfe sat on the bed next to Annie. "Does this upset you?" He slapped her a few times.

"Wolfe, stop," Brad yelled. "What do you want?"

"I didn't take you for a stupid guy. What do I want? I've got everything I want right here. I suppose it would be better if the prosecutor were here. This works fine for me."

"You don't have to do this," Brad pleaded.

Wolfe turned to Annie. "You're older and your tits have grown." He rubbed his hands over her breasts through her T-shirt. "Worth the wait."

"I'm going to kill you, Wolfe."

"Not gonna happen, pig. The three of you are gonna die, slowly, painfully."

"Fuck you, Wolfe."

"You get a front-row seat while I take my time with Annie. Then you'll know what's gonna happen to your paramedic lady. You're gonna lose your mind."

"You're going to lose your mind when I blow your brains out."

"Time for the party." Wolfe slid up the bed closer to Annie.

"What I don't understand is how you knew I wouldn't be here?" Brad asked.

Wolfe reached across the bed and picked up the portable radio. "Thanks to the dead bitch cop, I have a radio." Wolfe waved the radio. "I appreciate you keeping me informed of your location."

"Were you at the prosecutor's house tonight?"

Wolfman turned to Brad, but kept a hand grasping Annie. "Yup. Earlier today and for the past couple of weeks."

"We got a report that you were there tonight."

"Did you find out where the call came from?"

"What do you mean?" Brad tried to slip out of the cuffs, but they were too tight.

"This was way too easy." Wolfe laughed. "I needed to get you away for a while. I used the payphone a few blocks away, and said Wolfe was outside the prosecutor's house. I watched you fly past. As I got to your house, a kid pulled in delivering a pizza. That was a bonus—distracted the cops. Easy enough to take care of them. Annie opened the door for the pizza delivery, but it was me. And here we are."

"You son of a bitch." Brad struggled against the handcuffs. All he accomplished was ripping his skin. Blood trickled down his wrists.

"Fuck, this gets better every minute—seeing you struggle against your cuffs unable to get free. The sluts are tied up and waiting. For two years all I thought about was the prosecutor, Annie, and the blond cop. I fantasized what I would do when I got out. I had it all worked out, but then you caught me. No way was I going back to prison, I'd never have escaped a second time from maximum security. One of my cellmates had told me he always acted crazy so they'd send him for psych assessment. The judge bought my act and here we are."

Wolfe took a long drag on the cigarette.

"You had cops here and with the prosecutor all the time. You even had cops with the young bitch at the college."

"You were at the college. Annie was right."

"That was a bit of luck. I came here looking for you. Then I saw Annie. Followed her to the college. She looked different, back to blond hair and she'd filled out nicely. I couldn't believe it when I saw both her and the paramedic at your place. That's when my plans changed. Fulfill my fantasy with the prosecutor or take these two. For over two years I'd planned every second with the prosecutor. But you had her too well protected. You were so sure she was the target. So, I still have my fantasy, the same plan, but it will be double the fun."

"Cops will know something is wrong when I don't check in."

"Nice try. You've never checked in by radio after you get home."

"They'll page me and if I don't answer they'll come here to check."

"I'm not stupid! Nobody is gonna come here till the morning. I have all night with you three. Then, I'll go after the prosecutor. I can wait as long as it takes."

CHAPTER SIXTY-FIVE

STEELE AND ZERR SAT IN THE BACK CORNER OF THE RESTAURANT munching French fries. The exhaustion of the past two days was setting in and the food sat heavy in their stomachs.

They ate in silence and listened to their portable radio. Steele had the volume low. Routine calls. Then a frantic voice on the radio yelled, "Officer shot! Sixty-fourth and Deerfoot."

Cops radioed they were responding.

"Should we go?" Zerr asked.

"Nah," Steele said. "Half the city is on the way. Besides, we're too far away and I'm beat."

They listened to the radio. The first cars were unable to find the cop. There was no sign of his cruiser. Dispatch set up a grid search. More cops responded.

"Something's wrong," Steele said.

"What do you mean?" Zerr asked.

"I don't know, it's just my gut. I've got this feeling that something's not right."

"This call? Officer shot?"

"No, well, yeah. It's the call to Blighe's house. It doesn't make any sense. Someone called saying Wolfe had been spotted. The security detail hadn't seen anything. When we got there, we didn't find Wolfe."

"Sure, but we found the car he'd been sitting in. He'd been staking out the house for days if not weeks."

"That's what bugs me," Steele said. "He was in the car sometime today, but no sign of him tonight. It's like we went there for no reason."

"You think we were set up?"

"Maybe not set up, but there must've been some reason for us to be there at that time."

Zerr set his bottle down. "You think Wolfe wanted us there?"

"I'm not sure—well, yeah, I think so."

"Blighe is his target. He threatened her lots of times. He hates her."

"Sure, but he knows we're watching her closely. What if there's a new target?"

"If it's not Blighe, then who?" Zerr asked. "We've gone over the files a hundred, maybe a thousand times. It points to Blighe as the target."

"I don't know, I just can't shake this. Where did the 911 call come from? Who said Wolfe was in the area?"

Zerr shrugged. "That's the info we got from dispatch."

"We need to find out where the call came from." Steele walked out of the restaurant, over to the bar, and flashed his badge. "I need to use your phone."

The bartender set a phone on the bar. Steele dialed. "Dispatch, this is Steele, 114."

"How can I help you, 114," dispatch said.

"Can you check on that last 911 call we responded to. At the prosecutor's house. Give me the address where the call came from."

"Standby, 114."

Steele waited.

"What if the call for a cop shot is false?" Zerr said.

"What?"

"If the call to Blighe's was false, then why not the shooting call. It's like the calls are leading us away from something."

"From what?" Steele asked.

He was interrupted by dispatch. "Detective 114."

"Go ahead," Steele said.

"We have that call coming from a payphone at Eighty-Fifth Street and Forty-Eighth Avenue. The caller didn't give a name."

"What's happening with the call about a shot cop?"

"Must have been a prank. All cops are accounted for."

"Thanks, dispatch," Steele said. "Can you patch me through to Detective Griffin?"

"Standby," dispatch replied.

Steele held his hand over the mouthpiece. "Why would someone report they'd seen Wolfe from miles away? It doesn't make sense."

"That's about four blocks from Coulter's place."

"Oh, shit."

Griffin's voice came on the phone. "Steele, what's up?"

"Call Briscoe and meet us at Coulter's."

"Why?"

"Something isn't right," Steele said. "I think Wolfe is at Coulter's. Get there as fast as you can."

CHAPTER SIXTY-SIX

WOLFE CLIMBED ONTO THE BED NEXT TO ANNIE AND RIPPED THE tape off her mouth. "You and me gonna catch up on old times."

Annie struggled against the restraints and screamed. Wolfe laughed. He grabbed Annie's T-shirt and ripped it off. "That's it. I like it when you fight." Wolfe leaned over Annie and removed her bra, his hands roaming her body.

Brad struggled harder against the handcuffs, but it was no use. The cuffs were too tight, and he wasn't flexible enough to get them around in front of him.

"Hey, Wolfe, you scum sucking maggot. I'm gonna take great pleasure in killing you, you bastard."

Brad put his back hard against the wall, and used his legs to push off, in an attempt to stand. He slid back onto the floor. As Brad tried again, Wolfe looked over and grinned. "Yeah, I don't think that's gonna happen, pig. I'm tired of your whining." Wolfe jumped off the bed and in two strides was beside Brad.

"Your buddy Devlin was stupid. Sitting in a car, window open, eyes closed."

Wolfe punched Brad in the side of the head, driving him onto the floor.

"Just like that. Boom. One pop through the window. Then I dragged his sorry ass out of the car." Wolfe grabbed Brad by the shirt and hauled him upright. Wolfe's knee slammed into Brad's stomach. "Then he doubled over and fell, just like that."

Brad tried to raise onto his knees. He was almost there when Wolfe's boot slammed into Brad's ribs. More kicks followed.

"I could hear ribs cracking. Then I bashed his head into the pavement. I'm not gonna do that to you. I want you clearheaded so you don't miss any of the show."

"I'll ... kill ... you."

Wolfe laughed. "All I see is you struggling on the floor and the little bitch waiting for me. Watch closely to what happens to her because that's what I'm gonna do to the paramedic bitch. Of course, you'll be dead by then. You'll go to your grave knowing what's gonna happen to your woman."

"Leave her alone," Maggie screamed. "If you leave her alone, you can have me."

"Maggie, no," Brad yelled. "No."

Wolfe looked over and grinned. "I'm gonna take you anyway, bitch, doesn't matter which order I do it in."

From far away, Lobo barked, Maggie screamed, and Brad yelled.

"You two shut up," Wolfe said. "And tell that dog to shut up."

Maggie glared at Wolfe and screamed louder.

Wolfe punched Maggie in the head. "Save the screaming for later."

Whenever Maggie screamed, Lobo barked louder.

Wolfe threw Brad into Maggie's makeup table, knocking everything to the floor. Brad lay on his side, gasping for breath. Every breath was agony. He rolled to the wall. His fingers found a bobby pin. He struggled into a sitting position and worked the bobby pin behind his back.

"Hey Wolfe, you fat bastard. I'll bet you're like that other fat biker, LeBeau. He liked the young bikers. You're like him—a dick sucker. You pick on defenseless women to give you power, to feed your ego, because you lack in sexual prowess."

Wolfe laughed. "Watch and learn."

"Wolfe, you dog fucker. When I get these cuffs off, I'm gonna kill you. I'll kill you slowly. You sick bastard."

Wolfe laughed and pointed to Maggie. "You know, pig, I was gonna kill you after I'm done with Annie, but you know what, I think I'm gonna let you live while I rape your bitch over and over, and then kill her slowly. Then I'll send you to hell knowing you were powerless to help her."

"I'll be waiting for you, motherfucker!"

Wolfe climbed onto the bed and pawed Annie's breasts. She screamed as his full weight pressed against her. Wolfe put his hand over her mouth. Annie bit deep. Wolfe jerked his hand free and slapped her. "Scream all you want, bitch. You're gonna take your last breath pretty soon."

The sound of breaking glass came from downstairs. Wolfe didn't notice.

Brad finally got the bobby pin in place, heard the ratchet on the cuff click once, pressing hard against his wrist. Then the cuff slipped free. He drew his legs up while reaching down with his left hand and pulled a gun from his ankle holster.

Wolfe turned and saw Brad's hands were free. Wolfe rolled

off the far side of the bed and grabbed a pistol from the night table as he dropped to the floor. As Wolfe stood, he aimed the pistol at Maggie. Brad kicked out his left leg, knocking Maggie toward the floor. As Brad swung his gun to bring Wolfe into his sights, Wolfe fired twice. Brad felt tearing pain in his leg. Nausea swept through him. He dropped the gun and rolled on his side.

Wolfe was laughing, a sick, maniacal laugh.

Through blurred vision and blinding pain Brad saw Wolfe aim the gun at him, finger on the trigger. Then a black shape flew into the room and knocked Wolfe to the floor.

Lobo's teeth locked on to Wolfe's arm. The pistol clattered on the hardwood. Lobo chewed and swung his head as his teeth dug deeper. Then Lobo dragged the big man across the floor by the arm. Wolfe tried to pull Lobo's jaw off, but Lobo bit deeper.

The air was filled with screams — Wolfe's cries of pain. Maggie and Annie were yelling at the top of their lungs.

Brad's jaw was clenched as his vision cleared. He glanced at Maggie. She seemed okay. He grabbed his gun and swung it toward Wolfe, but Lobo was fighting viciously and was between Brad and Wolfe.

Wolfe rolled to his left and reached out, grabbing his pants. His arm came back and slashed Lobo with a hunting knife. Lobo held tight and bit harder. On the second slash, Lobo released the arm and yelped, falling on his side.

Two shots rang out. Wolfe fell back and slid down the wall leaving a red smear.

CHAPTER SIXTY-SEVEN

Zerr skidded to a stop behind a cruiser, Brad's Firebird, and a pizza delivery car. Steele looked inside the pizza delivery car —a kid lay across the seat, blood seeping from stab wounds to the chest. Steele checked for a pulse—none. He drew his gun and raced to catch up to Zerr at the police cruiser. Steele stared into the car. The driver had his neck slashed from ear-to-ear. The passenger had managed to draw his revolver, but it lay in his open hand, his head twisted into an unnatural position. From the front door they heard screaming and growling. Steele changed the channel on the radio to a secure frequency and keyed his radio. "Dispatch 114 on tactical channel. Two officers down. Code 200 Red, Detective Coulter's house."

"Roger."

They rushed through the open front door. The screaming and growling was coming from upstairs. They followed a trail of bloody pawprints from the entrance up the stairs. The growling turned to yelping, then two gunshots.

Steele stepped into the bedroom first. Lobo lay just inside the room, panting, whimpering, and covered in blood. Behind Lobo, Wolfe was crumpled against the wall, blood flowing from an empty eye socket. Steele kicked Wolfe onto his back—no response. His eyes moved to the bed where Annie lay tied to the bedposts.

Farther to the right Zerr knelt beside Brad and Maggie. There was a lot of blood around Brad. Zerr cut Maggie free.

Steele keyed his radio. "Dispatch. Upper bedroom secure. I need three EMS for gunshot wounds. And backup!"

"Roger 114. Backup on scene."

Boots pounded on the stairs and Briscoe entered the room with two constables.

Steele turned to Briscoe. "We need the rest of the house searched."

Briscoe nodded and sent four cops to clear the house. He pointed to a constable. "Cuff Wolfe and stay with him."

Steele cut Annie's ropes and covered her with a blanket. "Are you hurt?"

"I'm not shot."

Steele nodded in understanding. He called to Zerr. "Charlie, what's the situation?"

"Brad's got a gunshot wound to his leg. The bone's shattered. He's lost a lot of blood. Maggie put a tourniquet on."

Steele knelt next to Lobo. He bled from two large knife wounds and had shards of glass impaled in his body. Lobo's panting was fast and shallow, his whimpers barely audible. His gums were blue.

"Maggie. Lobo is bleeding from knife slashes. What do I do?"

"Put pressure … on the wounds." Maggie's voice was slow and almost a whisper. "Is it bad?"

"Yup."

"Get him to … a vet."

Steele nodded. "Briscoe. You got this scene?"

Briscoe nodded. "What do you have?"

"I need a constable to drive. Lobo's in bad shape. I'm taking him to the animal hospital."

Briscoe nodded. "Go. Go."

Griffin raced into the room as Steele left. "Oh my God." He stepped next to Briscoe.

Briscoe looked back to the corner of the bedroom. Blood covered a large area around Maggie and Brad. Too much blood. "Is Brad still bleeding?"

Zerr shook his head. "No. Why?"

"Maggie," Briscoe called. "Where's the blood coming from?"

Maggie didn't answer.

"Maggie."

Maggie slowly turned to Briscoe. "Huh."

Her face was ashen, eyes droopy.

"Oh, shit," Briscoe said. "Zerr, check Maggie."

As Zerr reached for Maggie, she collapsed on top of Brad.

Zerr pulled her onto her back. She was unconscious. Her red camisole was blood-soaked. Blood covered her legs.

Briscoe shook his head. *Brad's blood?*

Zerr pulled up the garment. Blood oozed out of a bullet wound on her left side.

"Where are the paramedics," Briscoe shouted.

"Right behind you." Dixon knelt beside Zerr.

"Not good," Dixon whispered.

"Thompson, get the spine board up here STAT." Dixon pulled a handful of gauze bandages out of his kit and handed them to Zerr. "Put these on the wound with as much pressure as you can. If the bandages get blood-soaked, apply more bandages. Don't take them off. I'll start an IV while we wait for Thompson."

Zerr put his full weight on the wound. Blood seeped around his knees. "Hey, Dixon, she's still bleeding."

"I should have known. It's through and through." Dixon grabbed another handful of bandages. "You'll have to put pressure on from the back and front."

Zerr nodded. "There's something you need to know."

"What's that?"

"Maggie's pregnant."

"How far along?"

Zerr shrugged. "I don't know? A couple of months? Maybe more."

Dixon nodded and turned his attention to Maggie. He had the IV running by the time Thompson was back with the spine board. Two cops helped slide Maggie onto the spine board and secured her with straps.

"Let's go," Dixon said.

Zerr stood. "Briscoe. The paramedics need an escort to the hospital."

Briscoe nodded and keyed his radio. "Dispatch, 401. I need cruisers for an ambulance escort to the Foothills Hospital. Get two cruisers out front. Block the intersections on Sixteenth Avenue between here and Foothills."

Sharma and Fola pushed into the room. Sharma turned to Briscoe. "Who's next?"

Briscoe nodded to Brad. "Gunshot wound to the upper leg.

He's lost a lot of blood. Maggie put a tourniquet on before she collapsed."

"Maggie what?"

"Not important now," Briscoe said.

Sharma turned to Fola. "Get the leg splint and spine board."

Brad's eyes slowly turned to Sharma.

"Maggie."

"Dixon's got her. She's in good hands."

"What happened to her?"

"I'm not sure. What about you? Briscoe says your leg is broken. What's with the bruises to your face?"

Brad's voice was soft and slow. "Beat up by Wolfe. Forget face. Leg's on fire. Pain races to my brain like an electric shock."

"Okay. I'll get your vitals first then we can decide on some pain relief."

Sharma took a blood pressure. "Borderline. If the pain is that great, we can try a little morphine."

"No. Not until I see Maggie."

"Okay. Let me know if it gets so bad you can't handle it." Sharma placed an oxygen mask over Brad's mouth and nose.

Brad slowly nodded.

Fola was back with the gear. They straightened Brad's leg. He screamed. Once the leg was splinted, they loaded him onto the spine board and carried him to the ambulance.

Briscoe backed out of the room. It was a bloody crime scene. He stood with Griffin in the hall. They stared back into the bedroom where Wolfe lay crumpled on the floor.

"Bastard is finally dead," Briscoe said. "He left a big wake of carnage behind him."

"I saw the ambulance racing away with an escort," Griffin said. "How's Maggie?"

"Not good. She didn't know she was shot. Or she didn't think it was bad. She looked after Brad until she collapsed. She told Steele how to treat Lobo."

"And Brad?"

"Wolfe hung a pretty good beating on him," Briscoe said. "His left leg is shattered."

"Ah, shit. Annie?" Griffin asked.

Briscoe felt red rage up his neck to his face. "Thankfully that bastard Wolfe didn't rape her. She's with Victims Services and on the way to the hospital to get checked anyway."

"I'll stay here," Griffin said. "Go to the hospital. It's a homicide—a justifiable one, but a homicide all the same. Either I'll keep the case or internal affairs will punt me out the door the second they get here. I'll meet you at the hospital later."

Briscoe took one last look into the bedroom and had a sinking feeling.

CHAPTER SIXTY-EIGHT

THE INTRAVENOUS DID ITS JOB AND BRAD'S BLOOD PRESSURE improved. "We'll keep you on oxygen for a while longer," Dixon said. "I can give you something for the pain now."

Brad waved his hand. "After I see Maggie."

At the emergency department Dixon and Thompson wheeled Brad into a trauma room. He was quickly surrounded by emergency staff.

He pushed the oxygen mask aside. "Where's Maggie?"

A nurse he recognized but couldn't remember her name took his hand and leaned close. "She was in the next trauma room." She squeezed his hand tight. "She's critical. They rushed her to the OR just before you arrived."

"Critical? How? She was treating me then she collapsed."

The nurse avoided eye contact for a moment, then looked at Brad. "The bullet hit her spleen. Most of the bleeding was internal. But once her blood pressure dropped, her heart couldn't beat fast enough. Not enough oxygen was getting to her brain, so she collapsed and was unconscious."

"You can live without a spleen, right?"

"Yes."

"But not always?"

The nurse forced a smile. "No sense getting ahead of ourselves."

"She's pregnant."

The nurse nodded. "The paramedics told us. How many weeks?"

"Ten, no, eleven. This is real bad, isn't it?"

"Maggie is with our best trauma surgeons. Now it's your turn. X-rays and then you'll go to surgery, too."

"No, wait. Don't send me to surgery until Maggie is out."

"Brad, I won't mince words. If you don't get to the OR ASAP, they might not be able to save your leg. It won't be easy to repair your femur. After surgery, when you wake up, I'll make sure you know how she's doing."

CHAPTER SIXTY-NINE

THE COFFEE ROOM IN THE EMERGENCY DEPARTMENT WAS CRAMMED with cops and paramedics. Hospital staff had given up trying to take a break there.

The tension was palpable—cops against one wall, paramedics the other. No one spoke. Some sat with their heads back and eyes closed. Others leaned forward, heads low, clasping and unclasping their hands.

When the door opened, every head turned in that direction—false alarms. One hour became two. Some started pacing in the small room. Others left for fresh air outside.

Briscoe, Zerr, and Griffin walked out of the emergency department and leaned against an ambulance. Nothing was said. They drew strength from each other, but it was in short supply. They were numb. The high adrenaline of mere hours ago was followed by an adrenaline low. Just enough to function, no more.

A cruiser, lights flashing, raced up beside them. Steele jumped out. "Any news?"

Briscoe shook his head.

"Neither of them?"

Briscoe shook his head again.

"Where are they?"

"They're both in surgery," Zerr said.

"We should go up there."

"We already tried," Zerr said. "They kicked us out. How's Lobo?"

Steele shrugged. "He's in surgery. He lost a lot of blood. Dogs don't do well with anesthesia. He's touch and go."

Briscoe nodded. Nothing more to say.

CHAPTER SEVENTY

THE INTERNAL AFFAIRS DETECTIVE GLARED AT ANNIE. SHE SAT
defiant, arms across her chest, eyes ablaze. "I don't know which
part you don't understand. I'll only talk to two cops. Coulter or
Steele. I don't know you. I'm not telling you my life story so you
can get *up to date*."

"Are you saying you won't cooperate with this
investigation?"

Annie rolled her eyes. "No."

"If you don't talk to me that's obstruction and you'd go
to jail."

Annie laughed. "That's the lamest threat I've heard. I'll have
to mention your threat to my lawyer."

"Who's your lawyer?"

"Brad Coulter," Annie said. "I'll tell him everything that
happened. I'll even write it down. But only to Brad or Sam. I
trust them. So, we can glare at each other for hours." She
leaned back in her chair and closed her eyes. "I've got

nowhere to go. Or you can get off your ass and find one of those guys."

The internal affairs detective slammed the door as he left.

Annie woke with a start when the door opened. Sam walked in and dropped into a chair. His uniform was blood-soaked. He had blood on his face and in his hair.

"You look like shit," Annie said.

"Thanks."

"Maggie and Brad?"

"Still in surgery."

"Lobo?"

"He's a mess," Sam said. "I need to get back there. I want to be there when he gets out of surgery. But I was ordered by internal affairs to get you to talk." He set a cassette recorder on the table. "They want me to record this."

Annie nodded. "Fine with me."

"Okay," Sam said. "I know the story up to the point where Brad raced away to Blighe's house because Wolfe was spotted there."

"When Brad left, I locked the front door and reset the alarm. Maggie fed Lobo and put him out on the deck. About twenty minutes after Brad left there was a knock at the front door. When I looked through the peephole, all I saw was an arm with a pizza box. Earlier Brad had said he wanted pizza. I figured he'd ordered it before he left, so I shut off the alarm and unlocked the door. We have cops out front all the time so I knew no one would get past them that they didn't think was safe, but something must have happened to them. Maggie was behind me when I opened the door. The delivery guy had his back to us with the pizza in his left hand. When he turned to face us, he pointed a gun and dropped the pizza. It was Wolfe. He was different, shaved head and no beard, but I'll never forget those eyes, dark and empty. He stepped into the house and said, 'Party time.'"

Annie closed her eyes and took a deep breath. She was silent, except for sniffles.

She opened her eyes and wiped away the forming tears.

"He told us to go upstairs. It was weird, like he knew where the bedroom was. He told me to sit on the bed. He told Maggie to put on something sexy. Something she'd wear for Brad. She refused and told him to go to hell. He grabbed her. Maggie punched, kicked and scratched him. She didn't know he likes that, gets him excited. He hit her hard a couple of times. I think she was dizzy. She stopped fighting. Wolfe told her to change clothes. She did, but it was like she was drunk. She could barely stand. When she'd put on a red slip, Wolfe grabbed her and tied her to the chair in the corner of the room."

Tears flowed over her cheeks. Annie sniffled and used her sleeve to wipe her face. "Then he pushed me onto my back and pinned my arms and legs. I could barely breathe with his weight on me. He was angry I didn't fight back. He punched me a few times, tied me to the bed and put tape over my mouth."

"Are you okay to continue?" Steele asked.

Annie nodded.

"What happened next?"

"Nothing."

"What do you mean, nothing?"

"He put a gun on the night table then sat on the edge of the bed with a radio. He had the volume low, but I could hear. It was you guys talking about Wolfe and not finding him. Then Brad said he was going home. Wolfe was practically giggling. He waited for about five or six minutes. Then he heard Brad on the radio saying he was back. Wolfe talked into the radio. I think he said a cop was shot. Whatever it was it got cops excited. Then he stood behind Maggie with a knife at her throat. He warned her that if she said anything he'd shoot Brad and then torture him and make him watch while he raped us."

"Shit."

"Maggie struggled to get away from the knife. That's when Wolfe punched her. She screamed. Then I saw Brad at the bedroom door. I couldn't yell but I shook my head. I wanted him to get away. But Wolfe knew he was there and told Brad to come in. Wolfe made Brad place his gun on the floor and put on his handcuffs. Then Wolfe beat Brad. He kept taunting Wolfe so he wouldn't rape us. Wolfe punched and kicked Brad so hard I thought he was dead. Then Wolfe climbed onto the bed with me. I thought he was going to rape me. I kinda blacked out. Then Maggie was screaming, and I heard two gunshots. Wolfe was standing beside the bed, grinning and pointing the gun. He was going to shoot again, then Lobo attacked him. They fought, Lobo yelped, and then there were two more gunshots. Maggie was still screaming but Lobo only whimpered. Then you and Zerr came in."

There was a knock at the door. Zerr peered in. "The vet wants you back there as fast as you can."

"I gotta go," Sam said. "I'll get Zerr to sit with you. Is that okay?"

Annie nodded.

Sam raced out of the room.

"Is he okay?" Steele asked.

The doctor took a chair in front of Steele and leaned forward. "He lost a tremendous amount of blood. We couldn't get a blood pressure when he arrived. We rushed him to surgery, started IVs. Then we infused blood. He had a lot of wounds. The two worst wounds look like they were slashes from a knife. He was lucky that it missed any major blood vessels, but there's still a lot of bleeding, and his right lung collapsed. He had embedded shards of glass. Where did the glass come from?"

"He jumped through a window," Steele said.

"Wow. Most of the cuts weren't very deep. We got his blood pressure stabilized and removed the glass. We put in a chest tube to help his breathing. He's on a ventilator and sedated."

"Will he make it?" Steele asked.

"I don't know. When he lost all that blood, he wasn't getting much oxygen to his brain. Only time will tell. I don't know what else to say."

Steele stared blankly at the doctor. "Can I see him?"

"He's in recovery. You can see him through the glass, but you can't go in."

Steele followed the doctor down the hall. They stopped in front of a window. Lobo lay on a bed, a tube coming out of his mouth and at least a dozen places where his fur had been shaved.

Oh God. What do I tell Brad?

CHAPTER SEVENTY-ONE

THE FIRST TIME BRAD WOKE UP HE WAS BLINDED BY A BRIGHT LIGHT, then he saw two people. Male and Female. Curtis and Maggie. The light dimmed, then they turned and looked at him. *Curtis was dead. Maggie?*

The next time he awoke he heard voices.

"We repaired the femur. It's more titanium than bone."

The doctor?

"Will he walk okay? Run?"

Steele?

"That's hard to predict. He'll have the cast for six to eight weeks. Then months of rehab. He's got a long road to full recovery. If that's even possible."

"When will he wake up?"

I am awake!

"We'll keep him sedated for another day and see how he's doing tomorrow."

What about Maggie? Annie? Lobo?

He had no idea how much time passed between his short periods of consciousness. He heard people talking. The voices were clear and close. Annie and Sam.

"Brad," Steele said. "Can you hear me?"

Damn it. Yes, I hear you!

In his head, he answered, but he didn't say anything out loud.

"He's still unconscious," Annie said. "Who's going to tell him?"

"They did everything they could in surgery," Steele said.

"It'll devastate him."

"Four years can seem like a lifetime."

Wait, who are you talking about?

They kept talking like they hadn't heard him.

Listen to me, he yelled. *Why can't you hear me?* His brain grew cloudy. *No.*

His eyes popped open and he was blinded by the brightness. When eyes adjusted and he realized he was in a hospital room. He turned his head. Annie sat close to the bed, she smiled and laid her hand on top of his. "Brad, can you hear me?"

"Yes," Brad answered in a raspy voice.

"We've been worried about you," Annie said.

"'Bout time you woke up."

Brad turned to the voice. *Devlin!* "You're okay."

Zerr pushed Devlin's wheelchair closer to the bed.

"A thick skull helps," Devlin replied.

Zerr set a bottle of rum on the table beside the bed. "I owe you that. For when you're feeling better."

Brad grinned when he heard a soft bark. Steele set Lobo on the bed. He crawled up to Brad and smothered his face with slobbery kisses. "I'm glad to see you, too."

Brad glanced around the room, a frown on his face. "Where's Maggie?"

CHAPTER SEVENTY-TWO

Lobo lay beside Brad, head on his lap. Lobo's bandages were gone. He looked like an emaciated, starving wolf with bare areas where his fur had been shaved.

Brad stared ahead, eyes unwavering. He felt empty, like a part of him was missing. And it was. He had long since drained his eyes of tears. He numbly went through the day only to realize hours had passed.

He hated the cast and the crutches. He wanted to run, no, needed to run until he dropped. But he could barely walk, let alone run. Lobo wasn't in any shape to run either.

So, every day they came here and lay on the grass, soaking up the sun. They came when it rained. Others came and went, but he and Lobo stayed. They only left when they were forced to.

"It's time to go."

Lobo jumped to his feet.

Brad turned to Steele and nodded. Steele helped Brad to his feet and handed him the crutches.

Brad took one last look at Maggie's tombstone. "I'll be back tomorrow."

ACKNOWLEDGMENTS

Wow! My third novel in the Brad Coulter Series!

Following the launch of Outlaw^{MC} emails started to come in. I am excited so many people like both Crisis Point and Outlaw^{MC} **AND** let me know.

There were a few themes to those emails.

First, they wanted to know when the next novel would be launched.

Second, if I wasn't working on novel 3, Wolfman is Back, 24/7, why not? They suggested I should change my priorities.

Third, a common complaint. It went something like, "Last night I was reading your novel. I couldn't put it down. I read until well after midnight. I just had to read to the end. Now I'm exhausted at work today."

When a writer gets feedback that readers couldn't put their book down, that's a thrill.

Thank you to those who emailed me to tell me they like my

novels. And thank you for telling your friends about Crisis Point and Outlaw^{MC}.

In March 2019 Wolfman is Back was ready to send to Taija Morgan to edit. But something didn't feel quite right and I wasn't sure what it was. (Spoilers ahead for Wolfman is Back, consider yourselves warned if you haven't finished the book yet!) When I looked back over the series, I realized that life, while chaotic for Brad, was moving along quite well in his personal relationship with Maggie. Early in Wolfman you learned that Maggie and Brad had some wonderful news in their personal life together, and they were making a lot of plans for the future. In fact, the original manuscript had Brad kill Jeter Wolfe with the assistance of Lobo, and the final chapter was Brad deciding he and Maggie needed to get married immediately. Ah, what a nice ending—murder and marriage. But crime thrillers are not about happy endings. Heck, even the original Grimm fairy tales had horrible endings.

There is a writing rule: say _no_ to your protagonist. If they want something, don't let them have it. If they have something, take it away. At every point possible, make the protagonist's life harder.

In April 2019, I was sitting by the pool in Las Vegas running the story through my head and looking at the final chapters of Wolfman is Back. I knew the ending needed to be rewritten but couldn't figure out what that was.

By the last day by the pool, I knew that either Lobo or Maggie had to die. A few readers had threatened me that neither of them could be killed, or my life was in jeopardy.

Lobo was my first dog. Shortly after I finished police training, I was working by myself on a very slow day. I drove to the animal shelter to see what dogs they had. There was this beautiful one-year-old German Shephard. Adopting a pet was easier then and just before the end of my shift I picked up Lobo. Many of the Lobo stories, especially in Crisis Point, are real. He did fetch rocks from the Bow River, and I did mark the rocks to confirm he was getting the same rock each time. After a night shift, I quickly fell asleep. Lobo had been alone all night and wasn't happy that I went straight to bed with no playtime. When I woke up, there was the rubber sole of my boot. He'd eaten the leather and the laces. I couldn't kill Lobo.

Maggie and Brad had become part of my life. Good friends that I wanted the best for and the thought of killing Maggie was devastating.

We boarded the plane for home. As I buckled my seatbelt an idea came. I grabbed a pen and a note pad and started writing. I wrote during take-off, through the three-hour flight, lifted my pen as we touched down in Calgary, and wrote until we stopped at the gate. The final chapters of Wolfman is Back were done. For the last hour of that flight, I cried. The tears flowed in a steady stream as I wrote. The next day, when I typed in the final chapters, the tears flowed again. I have never experienced emotions like that in my writing. The final chapters are almost exactly as I wrote them on the plane. Taija cleaned it up as she always does, but most of that was punctuation and rearranging a few sentences. But the chapters were solid without plot holes.

In Crisis Point, readers said the death of Curtis and the funeral were emotional. I'm sure your emotions got the better of you in the last chapters of Wolfman is Back.

In the next novel, Brad will deal with the devastating events in Wolfman is Back. His world collapsed at the end of Wolfman is Back and the road to recovery will be challenging. Emotionally, he's not ready to be back at work. But he won't have time to wallow in pity as a new threat terrorizes the citizens of Calgary and he is thrown in the middle, as always.

I am very fortunate to have an awesome team supporting me and I want to recognize them for their time and encouragement.

Credits:

Valerie West

Valerie has supported my writing right from the beginning. She understands that when I'm on a writing roll, I might not make it to dinner. I might not make it out of my office for hours and sometimes I will write late into the night. She's always my first Beta Reader and provides just the right amount of critique and encouragement. I'd be so lost without her.

Jonas Saul

A year and a half ago (May 2018) I was speaking at the Creative Ink Festival in Burnaby, B.C. Also speaking at that conference was the New York Times bestselling author of the Sarah Roberts series, Jonas Saul. I attended a panel he was on and some of his comments hit me dead on. After the panel ended, I waited to talk with him. We had a brief discussion, then he was off to another session. He said we'd talk later. From previous experience at conferences, when a big-name speaker says, "We'll talk later," later never comes.

But a couple of hours later there was a tap on my shoulder—it was Jonas. He asked if I had time to talk. What? Did I have time? He didn't want to interrupt what I was doing. I said that was a great time to talk. From that began a friendship and mentorship. Jonas provided direction for my writing, encouragement to keep at it, and pushed (gently) for me to have goals and deadlines. It worked. Wolfman is Back is my second novel released this year. Perhaps there will be three novel releases next year! Thank you, Jonas for mentorship and friendship.

Taija Morgan

One of my biggest challenges wasn't writing, but finding the right editor. In the first seven years I worked my way through several editors. They provided great edits and suggestions, but something wasn't quite clicking. Last year I met Taija. Outlaw^{MC} was in the final editing stage and I had a few chapters I was struggling with, and I needed to write a new first chapter. I asked Taija to look at those chapters and especially the first chapter. When I got the edits back, I knew I had my editor for life! She not only edits but teaches through her comments. The best part is her comments throughout the manuscript. "I love this scene." "I didn't see that coming!" "You had me laughing out loud." Comments like those mean so much to an insecure writer. Thank you, Taija, for your awesome edits, but also for teaching me to be a better writer.

Travis Miles, ProbookCovers

Travis created all the book covers for the Brad Coulter series. His designs are outstanding. Readers frequently comment about the high quality and creativity in his designs. They certainly stand out amidst other novels.

Bill Sturgeon

My good friend Bill Sturgeon was a classmate of mine at the police academy. For reasons neither of us understand, we became friends. After Crisis Point, Bill complained that the novel had needed a brilliant Ident Sergeant. (Bill finished his Calgary Police Services career after more than twelve years in Ident.) So, in Outlaw^{MC} Bill made his first appearance. He assists Brad in Wolfman is Back. Bill is now campaigning for his own series with an Ident Sergeant as the main character. Anything is possible.

Dave Fowles

Dave was another of my police academy classmates. He went well beyond policing, got a law degree and became a Crown Prosecutor in Calgary. Dave reviewed the courtroom scenes and provided great suggestions.

Sheila Clayden - Mom

My mom is my biggest fan (sorry, Susan Sturgeon). My fondest memories were of her reading to me, then teaching me to read. I've had a book or seven in line for reading since I discovered the Hardy Boys. I don't know if it was natural progression, but she had prepared me for writing by sharing her love of reading. She has a copy of the first draft of Crisis Point. She hopes someday it will be worth a lot of money.

Beta Readers

I have a great group of Beta readers that give me early feedback on the plot and characters. Each provide their unique perspective, which collectively gives me the direction I need.

Bill and Susan Sturgeon—Bill, a retired Calgary Police Sergeant, and Susan, retired RCMP, provide feedback on policing. Susan, as well, provides advice on Brad's love life and with each novel threatens me if I do something she doesn't like. Of course, I make sure to add those to the novel. Susan is my second biggest fan and shouts out to everyone she knows (and some she doesn't) that they should buy my novels.

Craig Ilott, as always, pointed out plot errors and out-of-character character responses to situations. I'd be lying if I said his comments didn't make me cry. He'd tell me suck it up and make the changes.

Colleen Peters provides feedback from the reader's point of

view. An avid reader of crime fiction, she understands the genre, knows what she likes, and reads some of the best authors, Lee Child and Michael Connelly. Best of all, she said I fit in with them.

A Final Note to My Readers

I am overwhelmed and touched that you like my novels and how enthusiastic you are in your emails. I even like the pressure you put on me to get the next novel out. At times, I'm obsessed with writing.

On days when the words aren't cooperating, an email from you reminds me why I'm doing this, and I forge on.

Thank you from the bottom of my heart. You are awesome!

ABOUT THE AUTHOR

Dwayne Clayden uses his knowledge and experience as a police officer and paramedic to write crime thrillers.

His first novel, **Crisis Point**, was a finalist for the 2015 Crime Writers of Canada Unhanged Arthur Ellis award.

Outlaw^{MC} is the second in the Brad Coulter series.

Wolfman is Back, the third book in the Brad Coulter Series.

Dwayne's short story, **Hell Hath No Fury**, was published in

AB Negative, an anthology of short stories from Alberta Crime Writers.

His vast experience working with emergency services spans over 40 years and includes work as a police officer, paramedic, tactical paramedic, firefighter, emergency medical services (EMS) chief, educator, and academic chair.

Dwayne is a popular speaker at writing conferences and for writing groups, providing police and medical procedures advice and editing to authors and screenwriters. The co-author of four paramedic textbooks, he has spoken internationally at EMS conferences for the past three decades.

DwayneClayden.com

dwayneclayden@gmail.com